Previous Books in
The Unspoken Series
by Marilyn Grey

Book #1
Where Love Finds You
Ella & Matthew

Book #2
Down from the Clouds
Gavin

Book #3
The Life I Now Live
Heidi & Patrick

Book #4
Heart on a Shoestring
Miranda & Derek

Book #5
Bloom
Sarah

When the City Sleeps

MARILYN GREY

WINSLET PRESS

WINSLET PRESS

When the City Sleeps
Copyright © 2014 by Marilyn Grey

To learn more about Marilyn Grey, visit her Web site:
www.marilyn-grey.com

ISBN-10: 0985723599
ISBN-13: 978-0985723590

This novel is a work of fiction. Names, characters, places, and incidents either are the product of the author's imagination or are used fictitiously. Any resemblance to actual events, locales, organizations, or persons living or dead is entirely coincidental and beyond the intent of either the author or the publisher.

Cover & Interior Design by Think-Cap.com

Printed in the United States of America

First Edition: September 2014
14 12 11 10 9 8 7 6 5 4 3 2 1

To:
Taylor Swift

When I wrote this book I thought of you. The character's have many differences, but I thought of you because when I try to imagine a celebrity who considers the idea of true romance ... I think of you. I believe it's possible to be famous and stay down-to-earth. I believe it's possible to be famous, find your best friend and soul-mate, and live happily ever after. I believe it's hard work, much more difficult than it is for a "regular" person. But it's possible and I believe, Taylor, that one day you'll find the one who won't break your heart. The one who will love you for the little girl inside of you, the one beneath the fame and glamour and songs you write. The one you knows you are more than just a girl with a guitar who empties her heart for the world. You are so much more. And you'll find someone to fill all that you've emptied.

I believe you'll find true love one day. I believe it ...

because you believe

Life is what happens when you're busy
making other plans.
John Lennon

A lot of people in the media, and some everyday
people, really aren't in search of the truth. They're in
search of something worse than that. Money, yeah. I
think the media's the kind of a thing where the truth
doesn't win, because it's no fun. The truth's no fun.
Jack White

The trouble with most of us is that we would rather be
ruined by praise than saved by criticism.
Norman Vincent Peale

I can accept failure, everyone fails at something. But
I can't accept not trying.
Michael Jordan

You miss 100% of the shots you don't take.
Wayne Gretsky

Chapter 1
sawyer

Every Wednesday I requested a table for two, but so far I always sat alone, handing the waiter both menus with an expected sigh. Today I overhead them whispering, wondering if I was being stood up by the same girl every time. I never told them who I was actually waiting for. Figured it would be less interesting that way. But today the young girl took my menu's and said, "The girl over there." She pointed behind her. "She asked if she could sit with you."

I shook my head. "No, thanks."

I didn't look at her. Didn't need to. I saw her come in right after me. Probably wouldn't had noticed her, but she kept smiling at me during lunch. She looked a bit like a freak or a homeless person, but underneath the Yankees hat, frizzy hair, and strange clothing she seemed too pretty to be either.

I looked up and made eye contact with her, then looked down when she stood. Oh great, I thought. Last thing I needed was a whacked out woman in my life.

She sat down in the booth across from me. "Hello."

I nodded and waved to the waitress. When I caught her attention, I mouthed, "Check, please."

"I don't bite," the girl said. "I noticed you wait here for someone every Wednesday, but they never come. Either that's the case or you're too embarrassed to sit here alone, so you pretend like you're waiting for someone."

I took the check from the waitress and shrugged. "Pegged me."

She narrowed her eyes and crossed her arms. "Hm. Good answer."

"Glad I aced your test." I stood and took my copy of the receipt.

"Before you go," she said, standing beside me. "You got change for a hundred? I need four twenties and two tens."

I pulled out my wallet and handed her the cash. She started to hand me the hundred dollar bill, but I saw her name and number inked in red along the edge. Nora.

"Keep it," I said, then walked away, half-regretting the loss of what could've been a friend during one of the loneliest and most confusing times of my life. Of course, I did have Chris.

The city air hit me like a cloud of second-hand smoke. I couldn't stand New York and if it weren't for my brother I would've stop traveling there altogether. I'm not a city guy, especially that city. Too many memories. Not all bad, but mostly not good.

I walked down the street toward my brother's apartment building and saw the strange girl skipping through a crowd on the other side of the street. She turned and waved to me as she rounded the corner. Hands in my pockets, I looked down and reminded myself to pick a different restaurant next week. As much as I didn't want to, I'd be back. Unless he answered the door this time.

I knocked on the door that led to his living room. "Quin, I know you're in there. Come on, Quin. I see your car out front."

I pulled the small mallet from my pocket and banged a tune on the door. He'd recognize it. "Quinton Marshall Reed Junior. Open the door."

I slipped my hands in my pockets and exhaled, wondering why I even bothered. Quin hadn't spoken to me in seven years, but where he lacked loyalty I didn't. I couldn't after what I did to him. I'd come back every Wednesday for the rest of my life, looking like the fool who got stood up every week by some girl when really it was just my brother. Thankfully we fell out of the spotlight years ago, like a one-hit wonder people occasionally resurfaced to say, "What ever happened to...?"

Otherwise I may not had been so keen on The Big Apple. As kids we called it The Big Lemon because we couldn't stand it. Now Quin lived right smack in the middle of it.

Not me.

I hailed a taxi and climbed inside. "Airport, please."

The driver nodded and edged back into the traffic. I stared out the window as people passed in other cars, thinking of the times Quin and I would drive to games and make up stories about people in the cars around us. I watched the people, but they no longer seemed interesting to me. Not without Quin to laugh at the scenarios I'd come up with.

He'd always slap the steering wheel, laughing so hard the car would jerk at red lights, then gather enough air to say, "Where do you come up with these things?"

The taxi pulled into the airport. I handed him double what he asked for and winked. He nodded and thanked me as I turned and looked at the doors to the airport that would take me back to Virginia. I hated flying. Loathed it. Imagined my death every time I boarded a plane. The guys used to call me a pansy. Not sure if I qualify as a pansy or not considering the fact that I played one of the most violent sports in the world—at least you begin to think so after playing it professionally—but pansy or not, I wasn't interested in dying. Which is why Quin had a Stanley Cup and deserved it. And I didn't.

And never would.

The game was his life. For me, it's always been the biggest part of my life, maybe even the deepest, but never the air I breathed. Every hit I took, every slam against those boards, and I'd immediately think of Mom and Dad's grave stones and how I wasn't ready to join them, as much as I missed them.

Something scratched my back when I walked to the doors. I reached behind my neck to fix my tag, but found a paper instead.

Call me ... if you want. Nora. 555-7859.

She had to know who I was. Probably just wanted an autograph or a few thousand dollars. I crumpled the paper and tossed it in the trash can right outside the door. Another reason I hated playing for The Flyers. Ten times harder to find the right woman when you make millions. And I wasn't interested in the wrong ones. Too shy for that anyway. I left the bedroom to my brother. Yet another area he excelled. Although the world believed the opposite. They believed a lot about me that wasn't true.

I paid for my ticket and found a seat. Only an hour wait today. I plugged my ears with headphones and watched videos on my phone. Videos of new players. New faces. I studied their every move. And I loved every second of it.

Chapter 2

nora

It's quite possible to look like you have everything in the world, yet have nothing at all. I know from experience. I'm not looking for pity though. Really, I'm not. It's just that, I don't know, I always felt like there was something more to life. More than passion and dreams and love. I spent so much of my life searching for whatever that *something more* could be, to no avail. I'm sorry. Am I boring you? I'll stop complaining. You probably want to know all about my latest movie, my fancy romance with Spencer, or something else the tabloids are fabricating, and yeah, I'll share some of that with you, but this isn't a story about my fame. It's a story about my heart. I hope you don't mind. I kind of need someone to talk to. Spencer isn't exactly talking material if you know what I mean. I gave my number to some weird guy at a restaurant the other day, not to be flirtatious or anything, only to talk to someone who obviously had no idea who I was. He never called. I figured he wouldn't.

I should've spent my days and nights dreaming of my boyfriend, *Time* magazine's sexiest man alive, but instead I dreamt of some Hollywood romance straight outta the latest Nicholas Sparks novel. Yes, I have read every novel from that man's brain. Can't help it. Guess it's the dreamer in me.

My phone rang. Claire. Again.

I picked up. "Hey, Claire. I know. I'm leaving now."

"Your driver is waiting, Nora," she said. "He's been waiting for twenty minutes and I don't think the producers or Mr. Fallon himself will appreciate your tardiness."

I nodded to Genevieve as she curled the last strand of my hair. She nodded back and pulled my chair out.

"I wasn't lying in bed all day. Genevieve just finished my hair and makeup. I'm heading down now." I looked in the mirror, wondering who I was behind all of the pretending. I never seemed to stop acting even when I walked off the set.

"Be good. Smile. And brush off any comments about Spence."

"Spence?"

"Only good things about him. Maintain your sweet image, kay?"

"Oh ... kay."

***

WELL, MY APPEARANCE ON *THE TONIGHT SHOW* WITH JIMMY Fallon went exactly as planned and was sure to send the paparazzi into a tailspin. Claire probably tried to call me a hundred times, but I turned my phone off. She couldn't have believed that I didn't know.

My driver, Mr. Baxter, winked at me as he dropped me off at my apartment building. I smiled as he shut my door and waited for me to walk through the big glass doors, but when I turned around Claire glared at me with her arms tightly crossed over her chest.

"What is wrong with you?" She rolled her eyes, so maturely.

"Oh, come on, Claire. Like I wouldn't know? Somehow you two were always unavailable at the same time. Your perfume on his pillow? Look"—I waved her off and smiled toward the camera flashes—"I never wanted to stay with a guy like that anyway. I only did it because you told me to for the exposure. Well, now I see you had ulterior motives. And that's fine, really. You can have the jerk."

She shoved her arms to her sides as I walked toward the doors. I shook my head and turned back. She was already gone. Only a sea of flashing lights surrounded me.

I went inside, took the elevator, and finally found myself enveloped by the comfort of my bed and my best friend, Niles. My little Maltese pup. He curled up next to me as I flipped my TV to my Netflix account and streamed Episode 3 of Season 2. My favorite TV show ever. *Fraiser*.

I could already see the tabloids lining the city streets. My face next to

Spencer's with a fake rip down the middle. "It's Over: Hollywood's Favorite Couple."

I wondered if they'd dig up an image of me dealing with springtime allergies and claim I was heartbroken beyond belief. That's what I expected and although I want to say it didn't matter, it did matter a little. I hated that everything around me thrived off of lies. Even the pictures of me on the beach titled "Hot Summer Bod," were photoshopped to make me look smoother, thinner, and overall "enhanced." They used me for their own agenda's, good or bad, whenever it was convenient for them.

My best friend London's name showed up on my phone screen. I answered.

"Wow, Nora. I can't believe you did that. News travels fast in your world. Sheesh. You okay?"

"I'm more than okay," I assured her. "Come on, did anyone really think we had some kind of profound romance?"

"But what does this mean for your career?"

"London, if my career is based off of my relationship with that jerk than I don't want this career. I want to be great, like Julia Roberts or something. I don't want looks or relationships to define my status in this industry. I want to be a good actress because it's what I love. I can't stand this tabloid stuff. It's distracting."

"Well, you—"

"I know."

"Just try to be more low key now. Pull a Joaquin Phoenix and disappear for a while. People might respect you for it. The right people, at least."

"Maybe I will." We enjoyed a comfortable silence for a few minutes, then I finally asked, "Do you think I made a mistake?"

"With what?"

"Following my dream of acting. I'm a celebrity now. It all happened too fast." I paused again. "London, tell me the truth, do you think I want too much out of life?"

"What do you want?"

"I want to be a great actress. I want to win a Golden Globe. And I want to fall in love. True love, you know? Love that never dies. I want to find someone who still holds my hand when we are ninety years old, not out of obligation, but because he wants to."

"There's an exception to every rule, Nora. And you've never failed at being the exception before."

"That helps."

"Get some rest, okay? Come visit soon."

We hung up as *Fraiser* ended and I fell asleep wondering what tomorrow would bring. With Spencer now in my past, what kind of adventure would the beauty of tomorrow hold?

I cuddled up to Niles and drifted into a dream.

hapter 3
s a w y e r

I stared at the family of ducks gliding around my pond, longing for winter to freeze the surface so I could skate again. The local rinks knew me and so did one too many across the country. That was okay sometimes, but I had to be in the mood. Then there was always the option of renting out the rink for myself, but something felt wrong about that.

I lit a blowtorch and held it to the hockey stick blade, applying even pressure until I saw that perfect curve. Many of my old friends, the ones who knew me since way before Dad and Mom died, they always asked me if I missed playing. They wondered if I actually enjoyed being a recluse, as they called it.

I guess in a sense, both. I missed playing, yeah, but it wasn't worth the fame. That ruined it for me. Did I enjoy my isolation here at my house in the middle of nowhere? Yes.

Hockey didn't end for me when I walked off the NHL ice for the last time. It lived inside of me. Probably always will. Every time I made a custom stick for someone, or some kind of furniture made of recycled sticks and pucks, it gave me that same satisfaction of winning a game. Well, maybe not quite that far, but a similar feeling.

If there's one thing I know for sure, it's that I loved being alone ten times more than being chased by cameras.

I sanded the blade down as I soaked some fiberglass cloth in epoxy resin. All the while, wishing I had the nerve to ask the girl I couldn't stop thinking about if she'd like to go out sometime. It's not that I was afraid of being rejected. I'd asked plenty of strangers out in my past and had my fair share of rejection, even amidst fame. I wanted this to be different though. I wanted someone to see through the lies the media said about me and get to know me for who I really was. I wanted one thing in my life, just one thing, to last. Everything I loved died. My parents, my relationship with my brother, my game. Was it too much to ask to have one thing last? Just one?

I guess what I'm saying is I was nervous to find out that the answer to that question might be no.

CHRIS AND I MET UP AT A LOCAL BAR WHERE A BUNCH OF artsy types drank fancy beers. Any kind of normal bar and I'd be noticed, but not *Jared's*. I doubt any of those people even knew that professional hockey players still existed. Perfect for me.

Chris ordered another beer and slapped my arm with the back of his hand. "Just get her number, dude. Want me to?"

I glanced over at her, sitting by the wall with a friend. She ran her hand through her hair and flipped it to one side as she laughed. I have no idea what her friend looked like, but she—the one I couldn't stop looking at—had the most amazing dark hair I'd ever seen. Full and curly and frizzy. I hadn't gotten close enough to see her eye color, but whatever they were, they were incredible. And that smile....

"Look Reed, ask her before I do."

She looked over at me. I didn't look away. Finally, she broke eye contact.

"Maybe in a minute." I focused on my beer.

A long minute of silence passed and Chris finally said, "Seen Quin lately?"

I laughed. "That'll be the day."

"You don't think you'll ever play again?"

"Me? No."

"People said you'd be the Jordan of hockey."

"People also said I was a womanizer and that was never true."

"Well, you did get laid a lot. And then there was—"

"They were practically begging me. I wish I was stronger than that, but I wasn't. Womanizer, though? I'm not even sure I know what that means."

"It means—"

"Shhh..." I stood and faced her as she walked toward me. "Uh, hey."

She smiled and looked down. "Hey."

"Are you free Saturday night? Because if so, I'd like to change that."

She blushed and nodded her head. "I'd like that."

I handed her a business card. "That's my cell. Text me your address. Pick you up at five?"

"Sounds perfect." She brushed my shoulder as she walked by. Her scent lingered as she left the bar. And I couldn't move.

"Nice pickup line." Chris laughed. "Because if so ... I'd like to change that. You sound experienced as a womanizer."

"Blue."

"What?"

"Blue." I stared at the door. "She has blue eyes."

Chapter 4
nora

Well, I guess it was my fault. I really wanted a few snacks for the trip to my friends house in Pennsylvania, but I told myself I wouldn't look at the tabloids in the checkout line. I kept telling myself as I stood inches from them, "Stare straight ahead. Don't glance out of the corner of your eye." I tried to listen to myself, but Dad always said I was too curious for my own good.

I glanced. Then stared. It was even worse than I imagined. My hands shook and I wanted to rip every cover in sight. I thought for sure they'd portray me as some kind of depressed fool. Instead the headlines read, "Heartbreaker" and "She Didn't Deserve Him" and the best one yet … "Back in Rehab."

Back? I'd never been to rehab in my life.

I paid the cashier, bagged my own stuff, and dodged paparazzi as I got in my car and drove away. As much as I loved acting, I was beginning to regret following my dreams, but I couldn't give up. The best things in life take some work, right?

On my drive to Pennsylvania I drowned my thoughts in music until I arrived at Ella and Gavin's house. When I knocked on the door Ella immediately pulled me into a warm hug, at least as much as her huge pregnant belly allowed.

"I'm so sorry to barge in on you guys." I stepped back and tried to smile. "I didn't think Heidi would appreciate me asking Pat and I just needed somewhere to escape for a little before I meet up with London."

"No, please don't feel like you're a burden." She moved aside, making room for me to walk in. "Where are you two heading off to? Did you decide?"

"She wants to go to Paris. I just want to go somewhere far away and quiet."

"Feel free to stay here as long as you like. I made the guest room special for you and you can consider our house your house."

"Thanks, Ella."

"Here." She walked to the steps. "Come on up so I can show you your room."

I followed her upstairs and laughed when she opened the door to my temporary room. "Oh my gosh. You are so, so hilarious."

"Is it too much?"

"Well." I laughed. "Yeah. But in a good way."

She decorated the entire room like my old room when I was about five. "How did you even remember? And Gavin actually let you paint it for me?"

"He painted it." She sat on the bed and rested her hand on her stomach. "And I remember details like that. Gavin calls it my romance brain. I don't know. I just remember little details. I thought you'd like this because you've been having so many issues with people lying about you. Sometimes it's good to remember who you are underneath all of that, who the kid in you is."

I set my bag on the floor and sat beside her. "I haven't told anyone this before, but maybe you're the best person to tell." I pulled my purse onto my lap, stuffed my sunglasses into it, and pulled out my keychain. "When I was maybe five or six I had this best friend in preschool. I can't remember his name, but ... okay, I know this is weird, but growing up I always thought he was my one, you know?" I handed her the locked attached to my keys. "Open this."

"A picture of him when he was a boy?" Her face brightened as she touched the faded image.

"His parents moved for his dad's job or something and we tore this picture of us in half and I gave him the other half on the playground. I childishly believed the picture would magically make us find each other one day. We were only thinking of it in a silly friend way, but I kept that picture in my sock drawer until ninth grade when I moved it to my keychain. Maybe it's dumb of me, but I wonder if he still thinks about me like I think about him. I know we don't even know each other anymore, but I don't know. It's like—"

"Don't feel dumb with me." She smiled and handed me the picture. "Remember, everyone thought I was dumb too. Waiting ten years for a guy I only glanced at across a coffee shop. You'd be surprised at the way some people shun the entire idea, saying it's just too much. Who does that, right? But look at me now. He's the best thing that's ever happened to me and I would've never found him if I didn't believe in things others laugh at. I think this is so sweet, Nora. And I hope you find him."

"Did you ever wonder if you were wasting your life? I mean, did you ever have doubts?"

"Oh, of course. I don't think dreams are big enough if you don't have doubts, and if they aren't big enough then why dream them?"

"Who will even want me after my second round of rehab?" I laughed and flopped back into the bed.

She stood and tapped my knee. "I'm going to find Gavin and Adelaide." She walked to the hallway then turned back. "Oh, and the right one will want you regardless of any flaws or baggage you carry. He'll see through it."

And then she left me to ponder those words. She was right. Or at least I hoped so. I definitely came to the right house to be inspired. Ella reminded me of that quote by someone I read in high school. Something like, oh, I couldn't remember. I'm horrible with details. Anyway, she dreamed big and I admired it. In interviews I always said how acting was my dream and passion and how exhilarating it was to achieve such an enormous goal, but every time I said those words I thought of that picture on my keychain and realized my deepest dream had nothing to do with acting. It had everything to do with finding the kind of love that lasts forever and after all of this junk with the media making me look horrible, I honestly believed it would never happen.

Who in their right mind would date me now? Much less love me....

Chapter 5

sawyer

I wasn't nervous and that worried me. Normally I was nervous before a first date with a girl I really liked, but I didn't feel that way this time. I reclined on my couch watching Fraiser reruns. Seriously brilliant show and my favorite TV series of all time. Downright phenomenal acting and writing, for the most part at least. That David Hyde Pierce cracked me up....

See what I mean. Why was I thinking about Niles and Fraiser when I should've been anticipating my first kiss with her? Come to think of it, I didn't even know her name.

Thirty minutes till show time I flicked the TV off and walked to the door. Gretzky followed me and cocked his head as I twisted the doorknob. I knelt down and rubbed his back. "I'll be back boy. Relax." I closed the door and laughed. Nothing like a Maltese. I'd had a ton of dogs over time, but never connected with one like I did with Gretsky.

• ◄

I KNOW IT'S KIND OF STUPID OF ME, BUT I ACCIDENTALLY deleted her text without saving her number and all I had was my terrible memory to save me. I thought she said 453 Avondale Dr., but I drove down Avondale four times and there was no 453. I kept thinking she'd text again to confirm everything, but of course that would've made it too easy for me. The best things in life are never easy, are they? I thought about that a lot. Thought about the game. The energy and drive that comes when you work together with a bunch of other guys who love the ice as much as you do. Nothing like it. Sports are so much more than tossing balls or pucks around and scoring points. I can't explain it, but there's so much more.

I tapped the steering wheel and said out loud, "Guess there's no hope in finding her house." I shook my head. She'd never believe that I lost her number. If I even saw her again.

I was just about to give up when I saw her standing in the grass with her hand shading her eyes. I pulled in front of her yard and sighed. "I'm so sorry," I said as I walked around my car. "I lost the address and thought it was 453."

She smiled and pointed to her mailbox. "143. Like I love you."

I broke eye contact. "I, uh...."

"No." She laughed. "The numbers. 143. You've never heard that before? The letter I is one letter. Love is four. And you is three."

"Oh." Right. I knew that. I think.

"Shall we?" She nodded to the car. Man, her eyes were ... and those hips....

"It's been a while since I've dated anyone." I opened the door for her and tried not to make it obvious when I looked down her shirt. Green bra. Interesting.

"I know who you are, Sawyer Reed. You've dated plenty."

I closed her door and walked to my side, then sat beside her. "How'd you know?"

"You gave me your business card. Come on, everyone knows Sawyer Reed. Household name who dropped off the face of the planet."

I turned the keys in the ignition. "Maybe I should get my name changed."

"What are you hiding from?"

I looked at her as I hit the gas. "Myself."

"Well, you don't have to hide from me."

"I don't think you told me your name."

"Danny. My friends call me Danny, but my name is Danielle."

I spent the next few minutes debating whether I wanted to be the friend who called her Danny or the one to call her Danielle.

WE HAD A GREAT CONVERSATION OVER APPETIZERS. I TRIED to get over the fact that she knew who I was. So many girls dated me just to get some cash by selling details to the media and it caused me to become reserved. I never knew who actually wanted to know me and who just wanted to get something from me. I wished she didn't know who I was. Not yet at least.

"Did I upset you?" she said, then sipped her water.

"No." I leaned into the table. "Not at all."

Her phone rang. She tried to turn it off, but looked up at me. "Do you mind if I take this? It's my brother and I promised him I'd answer if he called."

I nodded.

"Hey," she said to her phone. "Yeah, I really want to help, but I'm on a date." She waited. "Oh, just some guy." Another pause. "Yes, no, and his name is Mike if you must know." She looked up at me and winked.

I think I smiled back. Maybe I could be myself after all.

She hung up the phone and closed her menu as the waiter approached. I closed mine as well.

"What can I get for you two?" the guy said, ready to write it all down.

"The lemon poppy seed chicken," she said.

"I'll have the same."

Her face lit up. "Really?"

I finally relaxed my shoulders. "Really." I leaned back and looked into those eyes. "Danielle."

LATER THAT NIGHT I COULDN'T SLEEP, SO I WALKED OUT TO the lake and used the grass as my bed. The stars were brighter than normal and the moon made its presence known. I traced the Big Dipper and Orion, then watched the top of the trees move back and forth. Reminded me of a hockey player swaying on the ice. Even the stars reminded me of hockey. I guess the way they glowed seemed like snow. Something wintry about it.

I came outside a lot at night. Mainly for clarity. There's nothing like crickets or toads to clear your mind.

Danielle. She seemed nice. Normal. Couldn't deny that the woman had looks. I don't know, I'm notorious for thinking too much when I shouldn't and not enough when I should, but I didn't like failing. That's why I had such a hard time trying. Everything.

A shooting star, or comet, asteroid, whatever they really are, shot across the sky.

I watched until every trace of it vanished. Gretzky meandered off into the yard. Such a little dog, but not afraid of the dark. He reminded me of my dad in that way. Dad wasn't tall or muscular like Quin. He was 5'10 and skinny, but the man lived for adventure. I always admired that about him.

Clouds scattered across the sky, hiding the stars for a few minutes. I continued to watch, enjoying the silence and even the loneliness. I loved the way the sky made me feel so insignificant, yet part of something big all at the same time.

Danielle crossed my mind again, like a shooting star fading before it had a chance to live. I tried to think about her more, forcing myself to be excited. I finally asked her out. I'd been wanting to for weeks. But I wasn't as excited as I thought I should be. Instead, I was more excited to kick back in my yard and watch the sky. Alone.

Something wasn't right with that.

Chapter 6

n o r a

I s it just me or is there something glorious about staring up at the huge night sky when the city sleeps? I reclined in the grass and watched a shooting star sweep across the sky and by the moon. My mind instantly felt about five clicks better. Sometimes you need to look up to realize the little things down here are just that ... little.

Tomorrow a new dawn would push away the darkness. Same sun, different sunrise. Funny how that works. And I would wake up, smile, and begin the most exciting adventure yet. Perhaps I really would find him and complete the picture. He'd run to me through a sea of faces and, out of breath, we'd hold the picture in our hands and look into each other's eyes. We'd know.

The shooting star had to be a sign. Hey, who knows, I thought to myself, maybe he saw it too. Perhaps we were already together in spirit.

I laughed aloud at the ridiculousness and waited for another shooting star, but ten minutes came and went and nothing happened.

Brushing off the idealism of Ella, I shook my head and walked back toward the house. Yet, brush as I may and brush as I might, I couldn't shake the feeling that somewhere under the night sky the love of my life was tracing the same constellations I just traced.

"CHEESY, RIGHT?" I SAID TO ELLA AS GAVIN SERVED US BAGELS with eggs and homegrown tomatoes.

"It's cheesy alright," Gavin said.

31

Marilyn Grey

"Oh, don't listen to him." Ella handed her daughter Adelaide a half of a bagel. "It's not cheesy. It's romantic."

"No. Come on." Gavin laughed. "Seriously, what are the chances that some guy was watching the stars at 2a.m. at the same exact time?"

"I don't know, Gavin." Ella grinned. "What are the chances?"

He smiled back. "Fair enough."

Ella looked at me. "So what's the plan for today?"

"Not sure. I might go visit Pat and Heidi for a little bit, if she'll allow it. Maybe take a walk through the city, then tomorrow I gotta head back to New York to get my stuff and meet up with London." I took a sip of orange juice. "Surprised you haven't named one of your kids London with your love for all things British."

Gavin laughed as Ella said, "Not yet at least."

I put my plate in the sink and washed it off.

"Oh, don't feel the need to do that." Gavin tapped my shoulder. "I'll get it."

"It's okay. I'm thankful for everything you guys have done. Who redecorates an entire room of their house for a friend to stay a few days? You guys are unreal. At least let me wash my own plate."

"Stay as long as you like," Ella said. "That room is yours until we need it for something else."

I thanked them again and spent a few quiet hours in my room, then finally turned on my phone to 203 missed texts and 41 new voicemails. Most of them from Maury, my manager.

I didn't bother reading or listening to the messages. Instead I called back and got his voicemail. Didn't leave a message. A few minutes later he called back.

"Sorry," I said. "I needed to get away for a little bit. I'm going on vacation with London and when I'm back we can talk about that script."

"You have an interview with—"

"Cancel it."

"That's gonna make you—"

"Cancel it, Maury. That's the last interview I want to do right now and if it makes me look any worse … can I really look any worse?"

"Yes."

I silently weighed my options.

"Nora, in the end I don't give a damn what people think of me and neither should you, but you're a professional. Start acting like it. You've got an important interview. So, instead of backing out and running off, use this as an opportunity to show them who you really are."

I sighed. "I wish it were that easy, but you know as well as I do that they twist my words and cut off my answers. If they want to use me as the latest bullseye of Hollywood, then they will. Nothing I say will be used in the right context."

"Maybe. Maybe not. Either way the professional and adult response would be to go do the interview. After that, your schedule is free until you return."

"So are you filling in for Claire now too?"

"Get back to the city and do what you need to do."

"Yes, Pa."

He laughed as he hung up. I texted London. *Need stay for an interview on Wednesday. Can we leave Thursday morning?*

Sure. Be careful with your words.

Yeah. I'll try.

Truthfully, I was a nervous wreck. Already wiping sweat from my palms. What did I get myself into?

I glanced around the room and so wished I could return to the days of being a little girl. Acting in *Peter Pan* and *Romeo and Juliet*. No stress or gossip magazines. I didn't want to complain though. I knew I was lucky. I loved playing pretend for a living. Just hated constantly having to defend myself to the world.

AFTER SPENDING THE DAY WITH HEIDI AND PATRICK WHO were trying to conceive a second child with no luck yet, I definitely needed to be alone, so I skipped the city walk and drove around country roads until I found a nice place to watch the sunset. It felt so nice and normal to be alone, driving myself somewhere, no demands or flashing lights. I reminded myself that I was still a person. Underneath the glitz and glamour ... I was still Nora Amber Madison, the girl with second toes bigger than first toes and an uncanny ability to eat an entire package of Golden Oreos in one sitting. Not that I'd use that as the description of the deepest part of me, but bear with me as I'm still figuring that out.

The sun kissed the last of the blue sky with dabs of pink and purple lipstick, all smeared and lovely, until it disappeared and made way for the moon.

I wanted to stay until I saw a shooting star, but my thoughts carried me away to dreamless sleep as I lay in a field who knows where. I woke up and checked my phone. Midnight. Wow.

I ignored the missed calls and texts and rolled to my back again, watching the stars glimmer a few more minutes before I headed back to Ella's.

Chapter 7
s a w y e r

I spent the entire night sitting on my brothers steps in the middle of New York City as hundreds of people drove and walked by me, some stopping to ask for a cigarette or a dollar, most ignoring my existence, and only one girl who asked for my autograph, but she thought I was some dude named Josh Duhamel. I just signed his name and laughed to myself as the girl walked away, already taking a picture with her phone.

A young kid without a shirt stood in front of me and shrugged his shoulders. "Nobody live in there?" he said, pointing to Quin's house.

I shrugged my shoulders too as something clicked behind me. I turned and stared at the corner of an index card sticking out of the mail slot. Glancing back to the kid, then the card, I pulled it out and read aloud. "I'll talk when you talk."

I pushed the mail slot open and yelled inside, "You can't do this forever. We need to face this."

Annoyed, I stood and kicked the door, then turned back to the kid. He shrugged.

"You want a few dollars for ice cream or something?"

He raised his eyebrows.

"Here, kid." I handed him a twenty. "Have fun. Treat your friends."

I walked around before calling a cab. Darkness already settled over the city, making it a lot louder and neon-colored. I missed my pond. Winter. The ice.

A little boutique caught my eye, so I went inside to find Danielle a gift. Things were still new and fresh, so I looked at simple shirts instead of fancy stuff like jewelry. Hadn't talked to her for a few days and of course it bothered me that it didn't bother me, but she was cute and funny and sexy.

Not to mention I'd been wanting to date her since I first saw her, but maybe Chris was right. Maybe I'd never be happy with a woman if I didn't stop building them up so much in my head before talking to them. Asking for disappointment I guess.

"Can I help you, sir?" a man said from behind me.

I picked up a size medium of the shirt in front of me and handed it to him. "I'll take this, thanks."

He tried to convince me to buy a few other pricey things, but I politely declined and stood at the register.

"That'll be $126.97. On sale today."

I didn't flinch at the price as I reached for my wallet and handed him my check card.

He swiped and handed it back to me. "Your card expired, sir."

I pulled out the only cash I had left. "Do you have change for this?"

He smiled as he took the $500 bill and handed me my change, followed by a pink and mauve striped bag. I thanked him and left. As I put the change back in my wallet I saw red marker on one of the hundreds. For a second I thought it was that strange girl's number, but it wasn't. That would've been bizarre.

I hailed a cab and took it to Central Park, where I sat on a bench and wondered what to do about my brother. He wanted me to fix what I had broken years ago, but too many years passed. It shouldn't have mattered to him so much. I considered doing what he wanted. Telling the truth to some lucky news reporter. I considered it for an hour, then called Danielle.

I heard her tell someone else in a whisper that I was just some guy, then she asked if she could call me back tomorrow. I agreed and hung up, not wanting to be "some guy," but not wanting to be Sawyer Reed either.

I leaned back with my arms over my head and felt something crunch in my shirt pocket. I pat over the fabric, then pulled out a crumpled, washed $100 bill with faded red ink.

Nora. Either my lack of attention to detail played in her favor or she'd make a great pick-pocketer.

I debated calling for a while. Half of me wanted to talk to a stranger, the other half ... didn't. Eventually midnight rolled around and I figured she wouldn't pick up anyway, which is exactly why I decided to call. I walked to

Bow Bridge, near Central Park. A beautiful, old, ornate bridge that looked even better covered in snow.

When the phone rang instead of going to voicemail I paced the bridge. It stopped ringing, but no one said a word.

"Hello?" I said, clamping my other ear shut.

"Orion, I'm going to call you William Wallace," a barely audible voice whispered. "You kinda look like him."

"Hello?" I said, louder.

Rustling. Buttons pushed. More rustling.

"Hello?" she said.

I laughed. "Hello."

"Who is this?" she said. "I don't recognize the number. You better not be—"

"I'm the weird guy you saw at the restaurant and you're the weird girl who hid your number in my clothes."

A few seconds of silence toured through the phone in between her quiet breaths.

"Hello," she said.

"Hello."

"You called," she whispered.

"Yes."

"Why?"

I waited.

"I mean, why now?"

I paced in the grass. "Bored, I guess."

"Do you have a habit of calling people in the middle of the night when you're bored?"

"It's actually morning." I smiled. "And no. I don't. Do you?"

"No." I could hear her smiling too. "I don't. Just myself."

"Yourself?"

"Well, I stay up a lot at night and think. Kinda talk to myself a little."

"Or Orion."

She laughed. "You heard that?"

"How did you get your number in my pocket?"

"I didn't. I asked the waitress to do it when you handed her your plate.

Thought for sure you'd notice. You must be as oblivious as I am."

"Why me? Or do you have a habit of giving strangers your number?"

"First time since a few years ago. You seemed lonely and I guess ... I guess I am too."

A minute or so of silence went by as I stared at the moon. Definitely one of the more interesting nights of my life, but I kind of liked it.

"Nora?" I disrupted the silence.

"Strange man?"

"It's Sawyer. Why do people think it's only the ones who endure tragedies who need help? We're normal, right? But we need help too." I paused. "Sorry. Don't know where that came from."

"We're not normal. We're our own kind of tragedy. We're all a tragedy somehow."

It took me a few minutes to think of a response, but I lost it when she yelled, "Oh my gosh. No. I'm sorry. Oh my gosh. I didn't know. I'm leaving."

"What are you talking about?"

Something slammed. "Oh my gosh." She laughed. "I pulled over to watch the sunset and I fell asleep until right before you called. Apparently it was someone's private property."

"Oblivious."

"Oblivious to our own demise."

We spent the next few hours talking about everything from favorite colors to philosophies of life. Time snuck by so naturally that I was genuinely shocked when I saw the first signs of the sun making its way back around again.

"It's morning," I said.

"I know," she said. "5:57 to be precise."

"Wow. Well, I guess we should hang up now."

"I guess so. It's been fun, Sawyer. Have a good morning."

"You too. See ya."

"See ya."

I waited a few seconds to see if she'd hang up first, but I could still hear her breathing, so I waited a minute then ended the call. Staring at my phone, I tried to make sense of what happened, but I couldn't. So I stared my phone down until the battery died, then finally decided to hail a cab and make my way home. As much as I tried to ignore it, the thought—or feeling, I couldn't tell—stuck with me. A little on the indescribable side, so I'll just leave you with this.

I couldn't wait to talk to her again.

Chapter 8

nora

My drive back to New York (still refused to call it home) went too fast. Perhaps it was my dreadful interview pulling me into its claws or I suppose it could've been that charming conversation I had with Sawyer. Six hours long and it didn't seem long enough. Spencer and I never talked for that many hours in the entire however many months we lasted together, if together is what you want to call it. With all of my might, I tried to stop thinking about the voice that filled my mind for the first few hours of the day. He needed to stay a friend. That Sawyer. One, I needed to find the guy on my keychain or I'd always wonder "what if." And two, as nice as he was he just wouldn't be able to handle my lifestyle. I barely could.

Which is why I spent my entire morning and afternoon ignoring my impending doom. See, this wasn't just any interview. It was the kind that you walk into knowing the woman sitting across from you is going to ask you difficult questions while that camera stands inches from your face, waiting for you to crack into a million pieces. The kind of interview where you want to smile and nod, never actually answering the questions. While Genevieve curled my hair in long elegant twists, I considered manipulating my interviewer by answering the questions in metaphors, but having already been labeled the crazy girl, I figured it wouldn't be the best idea. After pulling a million ideas out of my head, I decided to do the easiest thing. I'd be myself. The real me. And the world could do whatever they wanted with that.

I SAT ACROSS FROM PENELOPE, MY DREADED INTERVIEWER. She smiled weakly as I made myself comfortable in front of the cameras. I didn't trust her.

She shook my hand and made small talk as the crew busied themselves around us. I focused on her, not them. My hands wanted to tremble, so I folded them in my lap. My foot wanted to shake a mile a minute, so I crossed my legs and placed one foot behind the other, locking them in place.

The lights dimmed. Candles flickered all around us. A crystal chandelier, barely on, sparkled to my left. Genevieve put my hair behind my right shoulder, touched up my makeup, and stepped away. I wanted to reel her back in before this lady sunk her teeth into me.

I swallowed hard and tried to smile as the interview began. Finally. A few minutes of torture and I'd be on my way to Europe.

"Nora, you've had quite an eventful year," she started. "People are beginning to wonder if you are incapable of staying in a relationship. What do you think about this?"

I didn't smile. "You know, I don't think about it. My life doesn't revolve around men. When I think about this last year I think of the great films I've been lucky enough to be a part of and the wonderful people who have taught me so much about the art of acting."

"There are rumors that you dated Spencer Parks purely to get famous, that you intentionally used him to gain exposure. Do you feel like this is a respectable way to gain roles in films?"

"No, I do not, but when you're young and new and people all around you are telling you how to be and act you forget how to be yourself."

"And who are you exactly? People are a bit upset. They call you a fraud and say that not only did you lie to them, but you lied to a man who loved you, just to get famous."

"Spencer didn't love me. Anyway, if my career depends on which guy I'm dating, then yeah, I did something wrong. That's not the kind of actress I want to be."

"Are you acting now?"

A cameraman inched as close to me as possible. "No," I said, scooting away from the lens.

"How do we know?" She narrowed her eyes.

"Perhaps the fact that you don't know is to my advantage." I remained in the same position since the interview started. Clasped and tucked.

"What are you hiding? I get the impression that you are keeping something from us."

"Yes, I am. I'm keeping myself." I uncrossed my legs. "What does my personal life have to do with my acting?"

She leaned in and her notepad crinkled beneath her hands. "Who are you exactly? Many of us are curious."

The camera inched closer again. I stared at the chandelier, then thought of Sawyer. "I guess," I finally said. "I guess I'm my own kind of tragedy. Just like you." I looked right into the camera lens. "Just like all of us."

MAURY CALLED ME ON MY WAY BACK TO MY PLACE, GAVE ME a vocal pat on the back, and told me to prepare myself for multiple reactions. "Some people will love you for that," he said. "And some will hate you."

That's what I expected, but hearing him say it gave me some sort of courage.

London texted me when I got into my house. *Nora so sorry. My dad just found out he has to have an emergency open heart surgery next week. Can we reschedule?*

Of course, of course. How about I come there? It'd be nice to visit home again, my family.

Is this about mystery picture boy?

Nooooooo.

Mmmmhmmmm.

I'll fly out tomorrow. Call ya when I get there.

I fed Niles, cleaned his water bowl, and made myself a gourmet dinner. Ella taught me a few things last time I visited. That girl can cook. My attempt at her baked ziti recipe was nowhere near as good as hers, but good enough. I set my dining room table for one, picked out a red wine, and sat down as Niles rested by my bare feet. The silence bothered me, so I dimmed the lights, set another place at the table, another glass of wine, and played a little light romantic music on my record player. For the next twenty minutes I pretended, with my very best acting, to be on the most romantic date ever with the most charming man in the world. The one who had my picture in his wallet. We talked and laughed and I think I even embarrassed Niles, who stared at me with a cocked head and big eyes.

I cleaned up the mess from dinner and walked onto my balcony. The cloudy night reflected my mood. A slight breeze played with my hair as I leaned against the iron railing.

I wondered if I'd hear from Sawyer again and thought about texting him, but felt weird about it. He already thought I was weird enough, but the conversation would be nice. The company.

I shoved the idea away and grabbed a book from my shelf, took a few candles outside, and opened up to the first page, but I couldn't concentrate, so I watched the lights throughout the city as they sparkled like the stars the sky didn't show tonight. Hotel lights turned on, some off. Midnight slowly approached and the city was still as busy as ever. I missed the quiet of Ella's house. Growing up in Chicago wasn't the most peaceful place either.

My phone rang.

Sawyer.

My heart fluttered and I reprimanded it for doing so.

"Hello," he said.

"You called."

"Yeah, hey, I don't know, you know how when you meet someone of the opposite sex and you play these mind games. Should I call? Should I wait a few days? How many? Well, there's no pressure here, right? I wanted someone to talk to tonight and I guess I don't really care whether it's weird to call the next day or not." He breathed heavily into the phone. "Why are there always so many rules?"

"Something bothering you tonight, Sawyer?"

"Do you have a boyfriend?"

I laughed. "No."

"Is there anyone on your mind?"

"Well, I just got out of a ridiculous relationship, so I'm not running around looking for love or anything, but there's something kinda ... promise you won't laugh?"

"Nope."

I smiled as I leaned against the railing again. "I have this ... I have a ... never mind. Now I feel stupid."

"I have a thing for this girl, but maybe I built it up too much in my head. She's really nice and our conversations are fine. We get along. It's just kind of an odd friendship but we're kind of dating or are we? She doesn't act like it. I think she's still going on dates with other guys. I don't know why this is bothering me so much."

"Do you love her?"

He didn't respond. I waited a few minutes. Gave him some time to think about it while I watched the clouds roll by.

Finally he said, "I don't know if I've ever really loved a girl. How do I tell?"

I smiled. "Are you serious? How old are you?"

A dog barked. "Calm down, buddy."

"What kind of dog do you have?" I said as I rubbed Niles' head.

"Maltese. He gets a little excited about the ducks."

"Ducks?" I sat down again. "I have a Maltese too. I call him Niles."

"I have my own pond. Ducks abound. You have a Maltese named Niles?" He laughed. "This keeps getting stranger."

"What?" I realized I was pacing on the balcony again, so I went inside and sat on my couch.

"Is his name Niles as in Niles Crane? David Hyde Pierce?"

"Don't make fun of me," I joked.

"My all-time favorite show is *Fraiser*."

"Stop." I laughed. "Now you're being mean."

"I'm serious."

"You are?"

"Dead serious."

"Weird."

"Very."

Hours piled up on top of each other again as we talked about our favorite Fraiser episodes, the love story of Niles and Daphne, the time when Niles pretended to do some kind of kickboxing move and knocked Daphne into the table. We laughed and laughed, then drifted into a conversation about acting where I expressed my love for the art and he understood every word I said, without tiring explanations needed. Somehow that naturally drifted into sports, where he passionately explained to me how deep sports can be, depending on the players who make up the team. I can't say I fully knew the feeling, not being a huge sports person, but his passion took me to a place where I could see, taste, and feel every detail he described. And I got it. I understood.

At some point, the sun peeked through my curtains and I didn't remember hanging up the phone. I looked around me, rubbing my eyes. It had fallen beside the couch. Still on. I picked it up and listened. "Sawyer?" Only the sound of his breath, deep asleep. "Goodnight, Sawyer. Or good morning." After a few seconds more, I turned my phone off and fell back asleep as the rest of the city woke up.

⋯⋯⋯⋯⋯⋯⋯⋯⋯⋯⋯⋯⋯⋯⋯⋯⋯⋯⋯

WHEN MY PLANE TOUCHED DOWN IN CHICAGO I TEXTED London. A few minutes later I met her outside the arrivals doors. She jogged to me and hugged me as though she hadn't seen me in years. I hugged back, pressing my cheek to hers, and thanked her for sticking by me through everything. I was never the type to have many girl friends. I didn't have enemies either, for the most part, until now. Really it came down to being raised around a ton of boys. Since eighth grade I referred to London as the sister I never had, eventually she became the sister I always had so much that I introduced her to others as my sister, not my friend.

We drove to Schaumburg, where she now lived, and sang along to 80's music as loud as possible. From Bon Jovi to MaDonna. Sunroof down, summer sun on our faces and her hair glowing orange. I smiled and leaned back into the seat, enjoying every moment of it.

I turned the music down when we parked in front of her house. "So do you think I can find him?"

She slapped my shoulder. "I knew it!"

I opened my door. "That's not why I came here."

"You sure?" She met me in front of the car. "Because I have some news."

"What? No, don't tell me." I walked toward her house and she trailed behind, her keys jingling at her side. I reached the door and turned back to her. "What? Tell me."

She looked around. "You came without flashing lights this time."

"Give it a day or two." I glanced at the door, then back to her. "Are you gonna tell me?"

"I found a clue."

"What? How? You lawyers scare me."

"Come in," she said, unlocking the door. "I'll show you."

Wow. She really changed the place. Funny how she and I both ended up with a lot of money in two totally different ways. After talking about the new decor for a few minutes, she led me to the couch where we sat together.

"Wow, London. Your stuff is fancier than mine."

She shrugged. "I like it." Placing a book in my lap, then another, she smiled and pointed. "Page 32 in this one. Page 41 in this one."

"Yearbooks?"

"I asked the local schools for records of kids who left around that time period. Came up with these two who look similar to your picture. Get it out so we can compare them."

I reached into my purse. "I'm nervous."

"I'm excited." She tapped my knee. "Come on."

I pulled out my keychain and compared the two images. "I guess he could be either of these two, kinda hard to tell." I shoved the books to the couch and sighed. "Who am I kidding? This is ridiculous."

"It is ... but it's fun."

"No. No. I'm done. I'm not doing this."

"I was able to track both of these guys down. Don't have their phone numbers, but I do have their addresses. You may even be able to find them on Facebook."

I looked at his picture again. "What if he doesn't remember me and thinks I'm nuts? Even worse, what if it's not either of those guys but one of them lies because they know who I am?"

"Do you want to try?" She handed me a sheet of paper. "If so, here are the names and addresses."

"I'll think about it." I hid the paper in my purse without looking at it. "I can only imagine what the media would do if they discovered this. Crazy Nora just got crazier. Stalker gone mad."

She stood. "I've got a girls night planned for us tonight. Let's go get comfortable."

"What about your dad?"

"He's fine. Surgery is next week. It's a preventative surgery because of his arteries and the risk of a major heart attack." She walked me to my room which was as nice as many of the fancy hotels Spencer took me to. "Make yourself at home as usual and stop living your life based off of what tabloids will say."

I laughed. "Thanks."

Easier said than done, I thought to myself as she closed the door and called out, "Take a jacuzzi bath and relax. Meet me downstairs in an hour. Comfy jamas required."

Some things never change. She called pajamas "jamas" since we met. Probably since she was three. I liked those endearing child-like qualities in her. As mature and sophisticated as she looked in a courtroom, beneath all of it she was still the little girl I played Barbies with.

I took my bath with plenty of bubbles, remembering the times when London and I took baths together, before it was too weird to do. I tried to read a book, but couldn't focus, so I got into some comfy jamas and met London downstairs. We watched *Letters to Juliet* and talked until midnight, when I began to check my phone incessantly.

"You, uh, you expecting a late night chat?" London stretched and stood.

I shook my head and stood beside her. "What do you want to do tomorrow?"

"Figure out why you just ignored my question."

Chapter 9
sawyer

Unfortunately for me the Internet had one too many videos and articles about that mistake of an interview I did years ago and also unfortunately for me I couldn't convince myself not to watch them again. So I watched, then got agitated with myself, then went back outside to my shop and finished a huge order of custom sticks for a local junior hockey team.

On Wednesday's I always tried to visit my brother, but I skipped this week after what happened last time. Danielle and I spent the night overlooking the Baltimore harbor instead, while cracking open crabs and dipping them in buttery garlic sauce. We had a good time and her looks intoxicated me every time, but it had been a while since I talked to Nora and I found myself distracted with thoughts of her. I'd hammer a crab leg and want to ask her if she liked crabs. Eventually Danielle caught on and touched my hand. I avoided eye contact, but then it hit me. Maybe thoughts of Nora only distracted me because I suspected Danielle was still seeing other guys and didn't want to get too into her. Not that I'd get hurt, it'd take a hell of a lot more to hurt me, but I'd be let down, I guess.

"Sawyer, what's going on?" she said with concern in her tone.

I could've opened up about my brother or my parents or the letter I just got from Coach Jennings. I could've been honest and told her it bothered me that she was still seeing other guys, but ... jerk that I am ... I said, "What's it to you? Don't you have someone you'd rather be screwing right now?"

It wasn't like me. The me I wanted to be. It was Sawyer Reed, hockey star, arrogant self-centered imbecile who hid weaknesses and failures behind manufactured cockiness.

She stared at me, wide-eyed. I shook my head and apologized, surprised that she didn't run off in a blaze of anger.

"Does it bother you that I'm seeing other guys?" she said. "I didn't know what we had was serious or ever would be. You don't have the greatest track record, you know?"

I nodded. "I'm well aware of that, but did anyone ever think for once that the media might just twist things a little bit?"

"Sawyer, never has a hockey player been so in the spotlight as you were and every magazine cover had a different girl around your arm each week."

"What they don't tell you is when the girl around my arm was my best friend's sister, who has felt like nothing more than a baby sister to me. Or the girl I'm hugging is my friends fiancé after their rehearsal dinner where I wished her a great future." I slammed my hand on the table, then mouthed an apology to those around me. "Magazines that make their money off of gossip probably aren't the best source for truth."

She crossed her arms and turned her attention toward the window.

"Haven't you heard the Michael Jackson song, *Tabloid Junkie*?"

She shook her head without looking at me.

"Just because you see it on a TV screen or read it in a magazine, doesn't make it true." I stood. "If you can't see the truth while sitting in front of me then you'll never see it." I flicked two hundreds onto the table and walked away.

When I sat in my car I pulled the letter out of my wallet and unfolded it.

> Sawyer, I know you've been through a lot, but I'm coaching for the Bruins again and I want you. I know you still got what I need to get this group of guys to make it to the top. Just one practice, that's all I'm asking. Two weeks from now. Saturday. You know where.
> —Coach J

I reread the thing fifteen times a day. I couldn't say yes, but couldn't say no either. My age increased every day and you don't get better at sports as you age. You get better in some ways, but the body can only take so many hits before breaking down. If I wanted to play again, now was the time, but the game presented itself with a lot of things I didn't want to deal with. I hated that about it.

Danielle tapped on my car window and asked if she could get in the car. Of course I let her, but we drove to her place in silence. She leaned on the window after getting out and said, "I'm sorry. You're a great guy, but I'm simple. This isn't right for me."

I understood and attempted to smile. She waved, tapped the door-frame, then walked away. I almost told her to stop, but drove away instead.

She thinks she's simple? I thought. *Wonder what she thinks I am.*

AS USUAL, I COULDN'T SLEEP. WASN'T IN THE MOOD FOR movies or TV, didn't feel like going outside, and I've never been one for reading, so I watched the shadows on my bedroom ceiling until the digital clock glowed a neon 12:00. Of course I thought of Nora, wondered what she was doing and if she would want me to call. She never called or texted me. It had been a few days since our last talk and I wasn't sure if my voice would be welcome, so I blinked at her number on my phone screen and waited.

At 12:15 I finally sat up and propped myself up with a ton of pillows, then called. No answer.

Disappointed, I held the phone in my lap and leaned back. Within seconds, I was asleep. The phone rang and woke me up. 12:34.

"Sorry," she said. "I'm at my friends house and kinda needed to escape for privacy."

"Didn't want to tell her that you talk to a stranger every night when the clock chimes twelve?"

"First of all, you're not a stranger." She had a playfulness to her that could've easily made me adore her if I let myself. "Second of all, it's not every night."

"Unfortunately."

She didn't respond for a few seconds, then said, "You called."

"I did." I laughed quietly. "How was your day?"

"It's been relaxing. My sister and I are hanging out in Chicago, well actually Schaumburg. Nothing exciting. You?"

"A little too eventful and not worth talking about." Really I just wanted to close my eyes and listen to her voice. "What made you move to New York?"

She started to say something, but stopped herself and said, "My job. What about your day isn't worth talking about?"

"I don't know, but hearing your voice is already helping."

She fell silent again. I didn't try to fill the gap of conversation either, so I listened to her breathe until she broke the silence with my name. "Sawyer," she said again.

"I'm here."

"You can talk to me. You can trust me."

"Do you feel the same about me?"

"I do," she whispered.

"We don't even know each other."

"At the same time," she paused, "I feel like I've known you forever."

"You first, then I'll answer." I pulled my blanket to my chest, put my headphones in, and leaned back. "What's your biggest fear?"

"Living my entire life without ever knowing who I truly am, because if I spend my life doing everything I've ever wanted on the outside without knowing who I am inside, I might find myself lying there with a minute left of my life and realize, far too late, that I never really lived at all." Her voice trembled. "Your turn."

I processed her words, realizing they were my own. "I don't think I could say it so eloquently, but I feel the same."

"No you do not." She barely laughed, but I still heard it.

"I knew you'd say that."

"I knew you knew I would."

"I really do though. I fear dying without having lived." I thought for a few seconds. "I also fear loving, really loving something or someone, because everything is too easy to lose and I lose everything. Maybe it's sports, the guys, the locker room fights, maybe they've ruined me but I'm also afraid to cry. Afraid to be weak. Afraid to feel pain in my chest. Send a bullet through my heart and I'm fine, just don't take away something I love. Sometimes, because of that, I feel like it's better not to fully love, to just not give myself to anything. Then, when I lose it I won't really lose anything."

All I could think of during the next few minutes of silence was why, why did I say that?

She whispered my name. I didn't respond so I could hear it again. "Sawyer," she said. "Don't take this the wrong way, but it's what I feel ... I love you."

I didn't know what to say. I'd heard those words come from a woman's mouth many times, but never did it sound so real.

"I don't mean 'in love' yet, just love. I hope I didn't scare you, but as friends I want you to know that I love you."

I held onto the word "yet," and after a few seconds, I finally responded, "I love you too, Nora. As friends."

EVERY TIME I TALKED TO NORA, NEVER BEFORE MIDNIGHT of course, we'd talk until we fell asleep. Mostly between four and sunrise. Eventually one of us would wake up and, I don't know about her, but I'd listen to her sleep for a few minutes, then whisper, "Goodnight," before ending the call.

That being said, I needed coffee. Dark, black, no sugar coffee. Chris agreed to meet me at a nearby Starbucks early Saturday morning. After a few nights in a row of late night talks, I was in desperate need of that blacker than black caffeine.

"What the crap?" Chris said when he walked up to me by the entrance. "You look like hell."

"I feel good. Tired, but good."

He pulled the door open and nudged my arm. "Danielle keeping you up at night?"

"Haven't talked to her in a while."

"Someone else?" We stood in line next to the brownies and scones. "Already? Damn, dude."

"It's that weird girl. The one who gave me her number before. We've been talking. We're just friends."

"Right."

"She gets me. I get her. It's weird, but nice and ... you can look at me like that all you want, but it's not like that."

He looked at the cashier. "Earl Grey latte, please. Blackest strongest coffee ya got for my buddy here."

The rest of the morning we talked about this and that but he didn't press the Nora thing. I was surprised and not relieved. I actually wanted to talk about it, about her. By the end of the morning, I parted with Chris and decided I'd call Coach J and say what he wanted to hear. I have no idea why, but that's what I wanted to do. I needed to do something. I kept hearing Mom's voice in my head as though she were still alive. She never pushed me to do something amazing, but she did pressure me to never give up whatever it was I wanted to do, if anything. For her, I wanted to try again. One more time.

"One practice," I said to Coach. "I'm not committing to the team, but one practice I can do. We'll go from there."

Coach J laughed through the phone. "Yes, yes," he said. "You won't regret this."

"I might, but if there's one coach worth the regret it's you. No media yet."

"See ya next Saturday, Reed." He was still laughing when he hung up the phone.

And I already regretted it.

Chapter 10
nora

London and I drove to Chicago. We stayed with her family in the waiting room of the hospital while her dad had surgery. When the nurse told us all went well and he was in recovery, I borrowed London's car to meet my parents for lunch.

When I got out of the car someone stopped me and asked for an autograph, minutes later a crowd formed around me. I tried to push through the crowd, apologizing as I sifted through everyone. Someone groped my butt as I passed and by the time I reached the restaurant door a camera was in my face and a young guy was asking me if I supported gay rights. I took a deep breath and opened the door.

He grabbed my shoulder. "Your manager is gay. Is that right? So you support gay rights and homosexuality. Did you know that's a sin?"

I turned around and noticed a "God Hates Fags" sticker on the camera. Agitated, I stood in the doorway and refused to smile.

"Are you prepared to burn in hell for eternity because you support sin?"

"Look." I shook my head. "I love Maury and I could care less what he does with his personal life. Right, wrong, left or right, it's his life and he has a right to do what he wants. I've got enough of my own issues to deal with. When I'm perfect I'll consider judging everyone else, but it's good to know that perfect people like yourself exist in the world. Very encouraging." I walked inside the restaurant and let the door close behind me. "So much for going unnoticed today." I should've asked the restaurant if I could go through the back entrance. In New York and LA I always had to walk through the greasy kitchen to a secret seating area upstairs or downstairs somewhere, out of sight, where no one would bother me.

My parents waved me over to their table like excited cheerleaders. Slightly embarrassing. They each hugged me for what seemed like an eternity until we sat down and ordered meals. Small talk mixed with more small talk carried us through most of the meal until Dad so characteristically set his fork on his empty plate and folded his hands on the table. Leaning forward, he whispered, "We're worried about you, Nettie." My parents called me Nettie since I was two and unfortunately it stuck.

I shook it off and looked to Mom for an escape.

She looked at her plate. "We just don't want you to get hurt."

"That's part of life though, isn't it?" I smiled. "Mom, when I was learning to ride my bike without training wheels you could barely let go. Dad had to pry your hands off and when I got hurt you were there and you said it wasn't so bad. Boo-boo's happen, but they heal and you ride again." I looked at Dad. "And you chimed in and said that one day I'd learn to ride, but sometimes even then I'd still get hurt. Most important thing is to just keep going."

They both nodded.

"Are you doing what you love?" Mom said. "Is this the path you're happiest riding on?"

"I'm not sure." I thought for a few seconds. "I don't know. I won't know unless I try though. I promise, if this doesn't work out for me in anyway I will leave it all behind."

Mom rubbed her collar bone and refused to look at me.

"What's wrong, Mom?"

She squeezed my hand and said, "Promise me that if you're ever faced with a decision to choose love for acting over love for people, that you'll choose people."

I laughed, wondering why she even considered the idea of me choosing acting over people, but she didn't smile and still seemed genuinely worried. I squeezed her hand back. "Of course. I promise."

WHEN I GOT BACK TO NEW YORK IT WAS LATE. I THOUGHT I'D miss Sawyer's call, if he called. Some nights he did, some he didn't, and there were a few times when I had fallen asleep and didn't wake up when the phone rang. Still, we talked a lot and sometimes I felt like I needed it. Like now.

I crashed on my bed and fell into a half-sleep with Niles on my chest, then woke to my phone vibrating in my hand.

I barely let it ring before picking up. "Sawyer. I've missed you."

"It's only been two days." He laughed. "I had a few long days of work and tried to stay awake, but couldn't." He paused as something clicked in the background. "Are you outside?"

"In bed."

"Good. Me too." Something clicked again. "Close your eyes. This song right here. This is how I feel right now."

An organ played softly, then the lyrics came in and I knew it was Coldplay *Fix You*. I could relate to the song too. "But if you never try, you'll never know just what you're worth." The song faded to its end and I thought I heard him sniff, but dismissed the thought since he said he feared crying. After a minute or so, I still wondered, so finally I asked, "Are you crying?"

"No." Silence again. "My brother's all I have. He's all I have and he can't stand me."

"No he's not." I sat up, wishing I could hug him through the phone. "You have me."

He said nothing.

"What's your favorite movie?" I tried to lighten the mood a little.

"Twelve Angry Men."

"That movie is so well done. So, you like old movies? Do you have a favorite within the last five years?"

"Don't even know if I've seen one. I feel like movies and acting have gone down hill since the world has been deluged in reality shows."

I laughed. "Well, there are some decent actors and actresses out there nowadays. Every now and then a beautiful film comes out." I swallowed the slightest bit of nervousness and continued, "Do you have any celebrity crushes?"

"No way." He laughed. "That's not my style."

"Why not?"

"Just isn't."

"Would you ever date a celebrity?" I almost wished I hadn't asked.

He thought for what seemed like an eternity, then said, "No. That's not the kind of life I want."

"What kind of life do you want?"

"Simple. Real."

"You think just because a woman is famous that she is automatically complicated and fake?"

"Not at all, but the relationship can be. I don't know. It's not going to happen anyway. I'm not one for hypothetical questions that mean nothing."

It did mean something though, and it wasn't hypothetical, but I couldn't tell him that. Early on we made promises that we wouldn't tell each other anything that gave away our identities. It was mainly his idea, but I went along with it because there was something comforting about remaining hidden when everyone knew who you were. It was refreshing and now more than ever I wanted to stick with it, if anything to show him that underneath everything I was simple and real. Maybe one day when the time was right I'd tell him.

Our conversation carried on until 3:14a.m. when he took a while to respond and eventually I realized he was sleeping. I listened for a while, then asked if he was awake. Silence answered back, so I whispered the truth, "I love you, Sawyer. And it scares me because I feel like I'm falling for you, but I'm not what you want so I'm going to try to let you go. I'm going to try to stop myself from falling. I'm going to try ... but I love you. As friends."

A light snore responded.

I smiled, whispered, "Goodnight," and ended the call, hoping the empty feeling washing over me would be gone when I woke up.

I STARED AT THE TWO NAMES AND ADDRESSES ON THE PAPER London gave me and wondered if it was even worth it. I needed someone in the industry, someone who understood and could relate to me in that way.

I texted Ella and London separately, but said the same thing. *I'm not going to look for the boy in the picture. I've decided to let go. Probably too over the top anyway. I'm just going to take it day by day and see what happens. I'm in no rush to fall in love.*

Ella responded first: *If that's the guy for you, it'll happen whether you're looking for him or not. True love will find a way.*

Then London: *Men ... who needs em? Let's go to Paris!*

I texted her back: *Haha ... when can you go?*

London: *I want to be with my family to help until my dad is back on his feet. Maybe first week of October?*

Me: *I'll let you know. I'm reading over a script for a new movie. Not sure what the future holds. Let's see how it goes.*

London: *fancy pants.*

Me: *I'm not the one with marble floors.*

While bantering with her I tore up the addresses of Jordan DePetris and Ivor Lachlan, trashed them, then found my purse on the table by the door and pulled out my keys. I took the picture of the sand-covered little boy and after a few minutes of entertaining romantic fantasies, I kissed it and said, "Here's to the future, the unknown, and discovering both." Then I ripped the picture and tossed it in the trash with the shreds of paper, grabbed a sheet of paper and a pink marker and wrote:

> *Our soulmate is the one who makes life come to life.*
> —Richard Bach

I inhaled deeply and exhaled as I set my keys back down, ready to make the most of the path I had chosen, because really, how do you know what you can do until you try?

Chapter 11
sawyer

The air in the locker room was cool, but I swear you could've choked on the heat in there. Guys stopped talking as soon as I walked in, only looking up every few seconds. Coach J didn't pull me aside to talk. He kept it low key and normal, like I belonged there. My hands trembled as I taped my blade and put on my skates. Some guys avoided looking in my direction, others wouldn't stop staring. I'd nod to them, they'd nod back, and I'd go back to what I was doing, wondering if this was really what I wanted to do.

I focused on a strip of old tape across the room and inhaled. The smell reminded me of school. Lockers lined with posters of girls and hockey players of days gone by took me back to my days with The Flyers. Here I was again, wondering if I made the right decision, but smiling inside as I inhaled again and relished in that musty locker room smell.

Most of these guys were younger than me. Fresh passion and skills ready to take on the ice. One practice, I told myself as a few guys drooled over the cover of a magazine. Part of me wanted to take it from their hands and tell them to focus on the game, but I knew I'd only make enemies. If they didn't have it in them naturally, I probably couldn't beat it into them. Maybe Coach J could though. I figured that was his plan. Sure hoped so.

The ice felt good underneath of me. It'd been a while since I rented out a rink or skated on my pond and it felt so good to be back. There's nothing like it. The sound of my blades scraping lines into smooth, clean ice. The speed. The rush. The fear. The energy. I was there. I was ready to give the game a hundred percent, even if only for one practice.

Coach started us with skating drills. Crossovers, quick feet, puck handling, the norm. I could tell within minutes that most of the guys weren't lacking in skill, speed, or strength, but quite a few of them lacked passion. Coach pushed us hard for a while, acting like a cold-hearted bully. I played along, knowing he had a plan. Seemed like a good one too. One I wanted to be a part of.

Exhausted, the others skated off the ice and headed for the locker room. Coach J followed, well aware of my desire to stay a little longer. He kept the lights on and disappeared around the corner.

I looked around at the empty bleachers and imagined them filled with people. Cheering, excited faces hoping their team would win. I pictured an energetic group of guys eager to win, teamed against another passionate bunch of determined faces ready to take on the world.

I stood in the middle of the ice, pretending a face off against one of the greatest centers of all time, who I undeservedly had the pleasure of shaking hands with. None other than Wayne Gretzky. And there to his right and my left, Gordie Howe. The Gordie Howe.

I looked Gretzky in the eyes, then watched the puck drop between us. Stealing it, I pushed forward and when I found myself surrounded by too many players, I shot the puck to Rod Gilbert and when I was free again he shot it back to me, then, close to the goal I spun it back to him one last time. "And he shoots," I yelled. "For the win. Gilbert does it again."

I slid to a stop, spraying ice against the wall, and looked around again.

Coach J stood on the ice to my right. I glided forward and stopped a few feet from him.

"So you'll do it?" He smiled. "I need you, Reed. This team needs you. Hockey needs you. You know what this team lacks and locked inside that vault of yours you're brimming with it."

I nodded as my heart beat loud and fast in my ears. "I miss it."

"Come on, Reed."

"My brother—"

"Do what you need to do. Media is going to be all over this and you know it. Set the record straight when the time comes. Your brother had his chance. Now it's your turn."

He walked away and clicked the lights off while I remained on the ice, leaned against the wall, and stared at the Boston bleachers I'd soon call home. Life has a funny way of screwing with your plans.

I TOLD CHRIS MY PLANS AT STARBUCKS, BUT I REALLY WANTED to ask Nora what she thought. I couldn't do that without giving away my identity and we made a pact not to do that. At least not yet. I had a feeling we would eventually. Talking to her felt right and even though physically she was a little on the odd side, not really my type, I found myself drawn to her through our conversations, but the last few times I called she didn't pick up and didn't call me back like usual.

I figured maybe she met some guy and had someone new to talk to. It's not like we ever said we were anything more than friends, but I worried a little bit when I didn't hear from her. Not knowing her last name, address, or any of her friends, I wondered if I'd know if she died or was in a bad car accident.

"What's on your mind today?" Chris said. "This decision got you a little upset?"

"No." I stood and tossed my empty cup in the trash can beside us. "Thinking about Nora."

"Phone sex girl?"

"Not like that at all."

He shrugged. "What do you talk about that long? Don't you run out of things to say?"

"Somehow ... no. Haven't talked to her in a while though. Hope she's okay."

"I think her phone would be dead if something happened. You still getting a ring when you call?"

I nodded, half relieved and half confused. Was she ignoring me? Did she find out who I was and get scared off? The media was already hounding me and resurfacing all the old crap about me being a liar, cheater, and whatever else they said. Probably freaked her out.

Chris and I parted ways and made plans to meet up tomorrow before I left for Boston. I'd take Gretzky with me, but left Chris in charge of keeping up the house until the season ended. Thankfully I paid it off a few years back, so renting a place in Boston wouldn't kill me.

When I got home I passed the time by packing necessities and sitting by the pond. I was about to walk back into noise after living in the quiet for so long and I don't think any amount of time could've prepared me for it.

I watched the sun go down, wrestled Gretzky, fed the ducks, went for a summer night jog, then at midnight I called Nora again. No answer. I waited another fifteen minutes and tried again. Still no answer, so I left a message. "Nora, it's Sawyer. I'm worried about you. Give me a call if you can. Hope you're okay."

About five minutes later my phone dinged with a new message. A text from Nora. The first text she ever sent. *So sorry. Been busy, we'll catch up soon.*

For some reason my pulse quickened and my hands heated up. Why would she respond so impersonally? She must've found out about Sawyer Reed, player of women and hockey. I thought she'd know me better.

I called again. No answer. So I called again.

"I told you I'm busy," she said, obviously annoyed.

"My brother is all I have. 'You have me,'" I mocked.

"Stop." She sighed heavily. "I'm still your friend. It's just that ... I'm just busy, okay?"

"Are you crying?" I paced near the edge of the pond. "Nora? What's going on? Are you hurt?"

She didn't respond. Almost felt like she muted the phone. Then finally she said, "Sawyer."

"What? What's wrong?"

"I can't do this anymore. I'm seeing someone and it's not fair to him. I'm still your friend and I always will be, but I can't ... I can't do this."

"Is there something you're not telling me?" Adrenaline fought for a place inside me. "I thought you trusted me."

"Sawyer." I hated that her voice sounded so sweet.

"I need you." I meant it. "Nora, do you understand what I'm saying?" Did I understand myself?

Silence.

"Do you?" I said.

"As friends," she said, then the call ended.

I blinked at the phone a few times, then chucked it across the field. Gretzky looked at me and rubbed his head into my leg. I knelt down and rubbed his head, wondering why I even let her in. It's inevitable, I thought.

I lose every damn thing I love.

Then it hit me like a puck straight to my chest. "I don't know if I love her, Gretz." He settled by my feet. "But if this is love ... it freaking hurts."

Chapter 12

nora

Maury helped me get a good deal for my next movie. The script was unique and the fact that some of my role models were playing lead parts definitely helped. I needed something to keep my mind off of romance and relationships and mostly just Sawyer. I kept telling myself that it was impossible to fall in love without spending physical time looking into someone's eyes and that his frustration with me during our last phone call couldn't have been because he wanted to be with me. He just wanted to talk and I wasn't allowing it. He missed my company. Not me.

Literally day and night for a week straight, I talked to myself inside of my head. Going over our last conversation so many times, wanting to call and apologize, wanting to tell him the truth, but fearing what might happen. Picking up my phone, putting it down. Staring at it from across the room, picking it up, putting it down.

He didn't want to date a celebrity. Unusual as it was, I didn't want to ask him to be someone he wasn't for my sake and at the same time, talking to him would slice me into a million pieces. His voice and the way he fell asleep mid-sentence sometimes. Our colorful conversations from dumb stuff to stuff I'd never told a single person in my life. I missed him, but don't they say love knows when to let go? It was for his benefit. I was letting go because I wanted the best for him.

London and I got off of our plane in Paris and navigated the monstrous airport in silence. I wanted to enjoy our time together, but I was way too distracted. She insisted I tell her what was bothering me, so finally we ordered some fast food in the airport and talked over fries and burgers. I told her everything and at the end she chewed a fry and said, "What sport did he play?"

"I empty my heart onto the table and you ask what sport he plays?"

"Just wondering. Kinda weird that it was his idea not to give away identities. Makes me wonder what he's hiding and there just so happens to be a hockey player named Sawyer who just so happens to be famous for using women and betraying his brother."

"That couldn't be him."

"How do you know?" She bit into another fry while raising her eyebrows. "Look him up. Type Sawyer NHL into Google and see what comes up."

"There isn't a bone in that man's body that would use me."

"If it's the same guy I'm thinking about, then he might be pretty adept at using his b—"

"London!" I pulled out my iPad. "Look, I'll prove it." I typed in "Sawyer NHL" and Sawyer Reed came up. Hockey player for the Philadelphia Flyers. I clicked on the images and scrolled until I saw one without his uniform. My heart sunk as I kept scrolling through images of #23 mixed with the man I saw in that restaurant last summer. Every picture off the ice had some woman wrapped around him. A lot of different ones. Some of them were actresses and musicians I knew. Others I hadn't seen before in my life. All of them were gorgeous. I cringed and closed the iPad.

"I knew it." She crinkled her wrappers into a ball and and pushed them to the corner of her tray. "Try not to think about it, okay? Let's enjoy Paris."

I shook my head. "I don't understand. It's like he's two different people."

"I'm sure he just knows how to play his cards."

"I don't get it."

"What? Don't tell me you were falling for this guy?"

I sipped the last of my soda and looked at her. She had to be wrong. I stood and threw my trash away. "It's just weird, that's all. I mean, unless he knew who I was, all that time he thought he was talking to some weird chick from New York who didn't look like the models he dated before."

"He probably knew it was you."

"Yeah. Just another jerk to add to the list." I lied, but I didn't buy it. Something wasn't lining up and I knew as soon as I got back to the States I needed to see him. In person.

This would be a long vacation.

AS SOON AS I STEPPED OUT OF THE AIRPORT IN NEW YORK cameras were in my face. I smiled and played the part of a confident actress, but all I could think about was Sawyer.

Random people took pictures of me with their phones and of course it started up again as soon as I got to my apartment building. Shoulders back, confident but not arrogant, sweet smile, I reminded myself. When I reached the door a man approached me. "Nora," he said, leaning a camera near me. "Is it true that you cheated on Spencer with Jake Halloway? Are you still seeing him?"

I shook my head. "Where do you people get your information? My life is far more boring than you all like to imagine it." A new doorman helped me inside and introduced himself. "It's a pleasure to meet you," I said. "Don't believe everything you hear. I'll never understand why people are so quick to believe a gossip magazine without even talking to the person their gossiping about."

"No ma'am." He smiled. "I only believe what I see with my own eyes or hear with my own ears."

I smiled and shook his hand again. "You have yourself a wonderful evening, Connor."

"You too, Miss Maddison."

I insisted on carrying my own luggage and tossed it aside as soon as I entered my apartment. Forget midnight. Forget waiting for him to call again. I sat on the edge of my bed and called him. Voicemail picked up. "It's me," I said. "Meet me tomorrow on Bow Bridge near Central Park. Midnight."

I turned my phone off so he wouldn't have the option of canceling, then I took care of Niles and got ready for bed, although I knew I'd never sleep.

SURE ENOUGH, I COULDN'T SLEEP, SO I ROLLED OUT OF BED at eight and ate an apple on my balcony. Niles kept me company after he ate his breakfast, then I took a shower and did my hair and makeup. Subtle and pretty. Nothing over the top. I wanted him to see the real me, not the disguised or dolled up me. Just me. His response would prove if he knew my real identity and if so, we'd have a little chat. If not, well, I was still figuring that out.

The time couldn't have gone by any slower. I ended up taking a nap, watching a movie, and pacing my living room. Tied in knots, my stomach was literally beginning to hurt. Eventually I called London and talked with her until 10p.m. when I freshened my makeup and decided to make my way to Central Park. I knew I needed to be sneaky to avoid any people trying to catch a glimpse of a candid celebrity, so I went to a few nearby places first and meandered about the city until a half hour to midnight. Making sure I had no followers, I walked to Bow Bridge, stood in the middle overlooking the water, and tightened my scarf. Thankfully I wore my favorite crocheted hat, because the temperature dipped and I thought I smelled a hint of snow in the air. Not unusual for October, but certainly not fun either. Autumn never lasts long enough. I buttoned my jacket and waited, hoping he'd show up, but at the same time scared to death. The idea of him being famous in any way made me nervous. As big as my name got within the last year, I still hadn't gotten used to it. Silly as it is, I had my own celebrity role models and the idea of meeting many of them made me feel like a thirteen-year-old standing in front of her favorite boy band member.

I turned my phone on to see if he tried to call, but I didn't see any texts or voicemails. My phone said it was 12:13a.m. and I felt myself wilt like a sunburned rose.

Two minutes later, my phone rang. Sawyer. The wilted rose perked back up as I answered the phone. "You called," I said.

"I did."

The call ended. Confused, I called back, thinking I hit the button somehow, but I heard his phone ring to my right. I turned around and saw him, standing under the street light in the middle of the quiet bridge, hands in his pockets. I tried to move or speak, but could only look at him as he smiled ever so slightly at me. I let go of the bridge and dropped my hands to my sides as a smile warmed my face.

"I'm no artist," he said, still standing too far away from me to clearly make out his features, "but someone should paint this. Right here. You...."

I wondered if my cheeks were as red they felt. "Come here, Sawyer."

"I don't know." He took a step and my pulse ... I think it stopped and accelerated all at the same time. "I don't want to ruin a work of art."

I tried to speak, but I couldn't even move my legs. He took another step and slowly made his way to me. His eyes didn't scan my body, but they seemed to devour my face.

"You ... look different," he said. "I mean, beautiful. You look beautiful, but"—he touched my hair, then twirled the ends between his fingers, keeping his hand there on my shoulder—"different."

I shivered, but I wasn't cold.

"Say something." A laugh barely escaped his lips.

"I..." Shaking my head, I tried again, "You...."

I gave up and wrapped my hands around his neck, pulling my body against his. He gently pressed his face into my neck and smelled my hair. The strength of his hands on my back and the tenderness of his embrace made me wish I could die in that moment, simply to never lose it, but like the edge of a sunset, it was already fading.

I inhaled the sweet masculine scent of his skin, then turned so my back was against his chest. His arms cradled me as I leaned into him and looked at the city lights reflecting on the water. We stayed like that for a long time. No words necessary. After a while, he led me to a bench and never let go of my hand. We held hands as we talked, like normal, like we'd been there a thousand times before. We talked about everything, as usual. He asked me if I planned to pursue acting while in New York and I avoided the question. I didn't want to ruin a perfect night. With my head on his shoulder, I listened to him talk as the dark blue sky turned a little lighter in the east. I wanted the stars to stay a little longer. Never had I so dreaded a sunrise.

"I've gotta get back to Boston," he said eventually. "Can't be late."

"For what?"

"I could tell you, but it would break the rules."

I smiled. "It's okay to be a little rebellious sometimes."

He thought about it for a few seconds, then searched my eyes. "I don't want to ruin a work of art."

"How do you know it will ruin it?"

"Maybe it won't." He stood and pulled me up. "I don't want to lose you, Nora. I thought I already did."

I closed my eyes to keep myself from kissing him, then felt his hand on my neck. Before I had time to imagine his lips on mine, they were there. It was a soft kiss that stayed still, paralyzed by passion.

It just didn't stay still long enough. He stepped back and sweetly said goodbye, but watching him walk away from our first kiss, I couldn't let it be the end. I looked behind me at the rising sun, then turned back as Sawyer halted on the path and looked at me. I ran toward him with a huge smile on my face and jumped into his arms. He held me there as we kissed again and again, but I knew it needed to end. The sun had fully woken and the city was no longer asleep, so I stepped back and said, "Good morning, Sawyer. You should go."

He kissed my cheek. "Good morning, sweet girl. I'll call you."

And less than a minute later my heart was a little less full and the horizon a little too bright.

Chapter 13
s a w y e r

Coach J drove us hard into the season. I forgot what it was like to bond with a team and lose touch with my other friends, but quickly remembered. After that amazing night with Nora I barely had a chance to talk to her. Even when I could call at night, I was always with at least one other person and I don't know, I'm kind of a private person. We didn't text much either. I was never much of a texting guy and just didn't want that kind of relationship with her. So we didn't talk as much, but I thought of her constantly. Also feared she'd turn on the TV and see an interview or something. When I finally broke free from the guys after another near perfect game, I called her from a Los Angeles city bench at exactly midnight and thankfully she picked up. It was finally time to tell her who I was before she found out another way.

"You called," she whispered.

"I did." I smiled. "It's been too long. How was your week?"

"Good. Low key. I need to leave for a work-related thing next Thursday and I was hoping maybe we could see each other again before then?"

"Why do you sound sad?"

"I don't know."

I rubbed my chin and ignored the paparazzi who was obviously taking shots of me from across the street. "There's something I need to tell you."

"Okay...."

"Nora, I'm a hockey player. My brother and I got into the tabloids a few years back, then I did something dumb, pretty much the worst mistake of my life, and he hasn't talked to me since. He had to give up playing because of me and I never felt like going back either. Hated the attention. But I'm playing for Boston now."

She didn't say anything. I stood and walked down the street as she slowly breathed into the phone. Could barely hear her over the passing cars, then finally she sadly whispered, "Does that explain the blonde girl in your hotel room a few nights ago? No wonder you've been too busy to call."

"What?" I stopped walking. "What blonde girl? And you knew? You knew and didn't tell me?" I exhaled. "Why didn't you tell me you knew? How long?"

"I didn't believe it at first. London told me you were trouble, but I didn't believe it." She sniffed. "I should've believed it. I'm just another card in your game."

"No." I raised my voice. "You are so much more to me. Look, I just played a game in LA, but first thing tomorrow I'm flying to you. Meet me at the bridge." She said nothing. "Please."

"Sawyer."

"No. Don't." I closed my eyes. "This is supposed to be the beginning, not the end."

"You only have one heart and it can only break into so many pieces before it's ruined."

"I didn't do it, Nora. I don't even know who you're talking about."

"Maybe she'll know be—"

I looked at my phone as it shut down. No battery left. No charger in sight. I wanted to punch the pole in front of me, but knew it wouldn't do any good, so I sprinted back to the hotel, hoping to dispel some of my frustration, but it didn't work.

When I got back to the room a few of the guys bunking with me were watching TV, so I took a shower and processed everything, wondering if I'd ever win her back. I needed to somehow. She quickly became my best friend, but now she was more than that.

I finished my shower and sat on the edge of one of the beds. "What are you guys watching?"

No one responded.

I tapped Jones. "What's the flick?"

He leaned toward me without taking his eyes off the screen. "That"— he pointed at a beautiful woman—"is the only reason I'm watching."

My lungs refused oxygen for a few seconds. I leaned closer to the television. "Who is that woman?"

"Shut up, Reed." Kurt, best left-winger I've ever played with, said. "Trying to watch a movie here."

I stood, trying to control myself. "What's her name?"

"Nora Maddison." Jones slapped my forearm. "Chill, man."

My lungs had no problem with oxygen now. My chest rapidly expanded and receded. My pulse exploded in my ears. I stuffed a few things in my bag and walked to the door, wondering what the hell I'd say to her when I got to New York. Wondering, also, what the hell to say to myself.

How could one person be everything I wanted and everything I hated at the same time?

The airport was obviously slow, but the next flight to New York wasn't until 8:15a.m. So I plugged my iPhone in, followed by my iPad, and as soon as the iPad powered up I signed on to the airport wifi and sent Nora a simple text. I think it may had been the first I ever sent her. Meet me at the bridge. Noon.

If she showed up I'd consider the possibility of us together, captured and lied about by every magazine in America. If she didn't show, if she didn't know me well enough to not believe the media's lies about me, forget it. Love. It couldn't be love, I thought to myself. It had to be infatuation. That's all. I was lonely and infatuated.

I stared at the iPad, knowing that there are some things you may want to do that you shouldn't do, but I knew myself and I knew I'd look. So I typed her name into Google and waited. I clicked on the images first. Saw a few glamorous shots from award shows or something, a few candid walking down the street pictures, and then about ten million stills of her with some guy who looked like a complete ass who thought he was pretty slick. They didn't even look like they wanted to be together. Whatever happiness existed in those images seemed fake, like a major act.

I clicked back to the Google search, read a few headlines like:

HEARTBREAKER DOESN'T DESERVE SECOND CHANCE
ONCE A CHEATER ALWAYS A CHEATER
SPENCER FINDS LOVE WITH NORA'S AGENT: NORA IN REHAB THIS
SUMMER

Marilyn Grey

I shut the iPad down, closed my eyes, and leaned back. Pictures of past magazine covers with my name on them flashed through my mind one after another. I hated it. More than I can ever begin to express. It practically ruined my life and my brother's life. I could see they were doing their best to make Nora into a villain too. On one hand, I felt sorry for her. I could relate. On the other hand, I already saw the future splashes of lies about us all over those glossy spreads and I didn't think my love for her–sorry, infatuation–was stronger than my hate for that scene.

I'd play one last season out of love for the game, then I'd hide away again. This time forever. That's what I wanted. That's what I'd tell her.

My phone rang. Jones.

"Hey, man," I said. "I have a family emergency. Tell Coach I'll be there for practice Monday. I won't miss anything."

"Oh, good. I thought you were pissed about the joke the guys played on you. I wasn't involved. I swear."

"What joke?"

"You don't know?"

"What joke?"

"Kensington put on your jersey and the guys snapped a picture of him from behind with some stripper going into your hotel room. He blasted on Twitter and the thing blew way out of proportion."

"That's messed up. I don't give a crap about my reputation. That's stained forever. But come on, Jones. We're supposed to be a team here. This stuff is messed up and immature. Coach is gonna be pissed."

"I know. I told them to stop."

I exhaled and shook my head. "Get some rest. It's like 3a.m."

I hung up and stared at the ceiling, longing for the days when hockey was played from the heart by a bunch of guys who knew what it meant to be a brotherhood, a real team who loved everything about the game except the undeserved media praise and criticism.

I MADE IT TO THE BRIDGE WITH FIFTEEN MINUTES LEFT UNTIL noon. For some reason the idea of seeing and talking to Nora in the middle of the day made me cringe. For some reason the entire situation made me cringe. Then just as it began to snow I saw her walking toward me with a red scarf and a white coat, her beauty like something out of a classic piece of art. This was not infatuation. "Shhhh..." I tapped my overworked heart as she slipped her hands into her pockets and stood in front of me, snow-flakes melting in her coffee-colored hair, no cream or sugar.

"You came," I said.

She nodded and softly said, "I did," as her breath visibly drifted to my lips.

I rocked on my heels and started to reach for her face, but hesitated as I fought the magnetic urge to kiss her, to forget the day and get lost in her. Trying to speak, but failing miserably, I hoped she'd say something. Anything. But she only stared into my eyes. When I looked into hers I saw heartache and confusion. Loneliness. I know because it looked like me.

I brushed my fingers against her wrist, then her cheek. "I'm sorry," is all I could say. Her eyes held tears somewhere behind their specks of amber and gold, but she seemed confident in their captivity. "I know," I said. "The guys were watching one of your movies when I got back." She looked down at her feet and sucked in her bottom lip. I touched the edge of her scarf. "Say something," I said. "What are you thinking?"

Her eyes locked with mine, then she turned her head and stared out over the bridge. The edges of the river would soon begin to freeze, then inch their way to the center until the entire surface was skate-worthy.

I zoned back in on her face. Her cheeks and ears and lips. My pulse sped up again and without thinking I pressed my lips against the corner of her mouth, but she turned her face from me. I stayed there against her cheek for a few seconds, then pulled away. The few inches between us felt like five miles.

"Have I lost you?" I said as a camera flashed from behind a tree.

"Did you ever really have me?" she finally said. "I mean, who are we kissing, Sawyer? You don't want this. You don't want me."

"You just said kissing."

She seemed oblivious to the flashing lights. "No I didn't. I said kidding."

"You said kissing."

"Sawyer."

"Sorry." It was getting hard to ignore the looming cameras, so I focused on the snowflakes on her lashes. "I don't want this stuff. It's true. I want a quiet life away from lies and manipulation. That doesn't mean I don't want you, Nora." I forced her to look at me and kept my hand along her jaw. "I want you."

"This is me. Don't you see that?" She motioned toward the excessive flashes. "This is who I am."

"The woman I fell in lo–" I cut myself off, then figured what the hell. "I fell in love with you. Nora Maddison is an actress, but she's not defined only by that. You're so much more than all of this. When I finish this season, I'm done for good. You can be done too. We can be together and you won't regret it." I tugged on her scarf. "I love you, okay? I don't know how and don't ask me why ... I can't figure it out, but I don't think I can stand to think of my life without you."

"But you can't live with me either." Her voice cracked. "You need to accept me as I am if you really love me, Sawyer. Otherwise I'm afraid you still love yourself more than you could ever love me. What are you so afraid of? Some stupid rumors? I've been lied about and it hurts sometimes but I won't let that stop me from being with someone I love."

"But it will. Don't you understand? They'll rip us apart until there's nothing left but some ridiculous money-making magazine article. We're easy targets. Sawyer Reed, hockey playboy. And Nora Maddison, lonely adulteress. We're prime targets. Google our names tonight and you'll see. Probably already twittered or whatever to millions."

She squeezed my hand and started to say something, but stopped. I waited as she untied her scarf and wrapped it around my neck, then untied mine and wrapped it around hers. She opened her lips, but I told her not to say it. Not yet. "If this is the last time I see you," I said. "I want to say goodbye with a kiss."

She kept her lips parted and moved toward me with her eyes closed.

I gently gripped the back of her neck with both hands and savored the feeling of her hair falling on my arms. Then she kissed me, and turned her head to the other side, kissing me some more. My hands gripped tighter as she lit a fire inside of me, then pulled away and blinked at me with longing still glistening on her lips.

I ran my hands down her arms and kissed her hand. "Goodbye, sweet girl." Still confused about why we needed to end it too soon, I called out to her as she turned and walked away, but it only escaped as a barely audible whisper, "I do want you. All of you." Yet I knew, just as she knew, that the logistics were against us. As is, we'd never make it. So I buried my face in her scarf, inhaled the sweetness of heaven, and walked by the flashing lights into the bitter afternoon. Alone.

Chapter 14
n o r a

You know how sometimes life becomes a blur? Or maybe it's just us. We become the blurs, just passing lights on a twilight freeway. Can't make out the make or model, the color, or the faces inside. A blur. Blurring by. That's how I felt in the plane, when it touched down, when I got my hair and makeup done for my first scene, and when I kissed Dan for the first time, in our third scene, on the fourth day of shooting, in front of a bunch of other people, twenty minutes before he asked me out on a date, not in front of a bunch of other people. Thankfully, because I said no. "But I felt a spark between us," he said and I reminded him that we were supposed to. Our characters were falling in love. It was an act, but don't get me get wrong, Dan was as charming as it gets. Sweet smile, pretty eyes, down to earth, and smart too.

I didn't have time to think about why I said no so quickly right after it happened, but I thought about it until I fell asleep and as soon as I woke up because, I don't know, I overanalyze things too much. Plus I knew I should let go of Sawyer, but I couldn't. Then I'd remind myself that for so long I wanted this. I wanted to be in films and grow as an actress. I wanted to work alongside the greats and perhaps one day actually be worthy of it. Did I long for fame, admiration, and money? Not at all. Especially the kind of attention I ended up getting, but I did long to live my dreams and although it wasn't all of my dreams, acting was a part of them and I felt like he should understand that ... if he really loved me. That's another thing. He said he loved me and the look in his eyes when he said it, when he watched me tie my scarf around his neck, it was a look I'd never seen before and I'd never forget. It was difficult to walk away from him, standing there probably waiting for me to run back into his arms like the time before. Only I didn't. I kept walking. I didn't turn around and I was starting to regret it.

I was starting to regret it because my heart wasn't catching up with my mind and I wondered if it ever would. I believed in one person for me. The right person. And I also believed in the right time. So I settled my heart by telling myself that I'd be with him again if he was the right one. When the timing was right, we'd find each other.

After getting my hair and makeup done in my trailer I walked over to Dan's and accepted his request. He smiled, I smiled, and I kept wondering if I was acting, but I shoved that thought away and told him I'd see him on set.

Kat, film director extraordinaire, called me over to her. I walked over wires and tape and stood beside her. She held my shoulder and pointed to the set with the pencil in her other hand. "Yesterday what you did was great, but I want to see less emotion on this"—she twirled the pencil in a circle in front of my face—"and more in this." The pencil motioned to everything below my face.

"So less crying with my face and more sadness with my body?"

"Exactly. Cry through your body first and if it reaches your face don't prevent that."

"Still cry into his arms or no?"

"Use him for comfort, not a crutch, see?"

I nodded and watched Dan walk into the room. We pretended not to notice each other, and I'm glad, because suddenly I wanted to melt like the Wicked Witch.

I walked onto the set as the cameras positioned themselves around us. Kat directed Dan and I into position on the edge of the pretend building ledge as I said goodbye to Nora and allowed my character, Charleigh, to take over.

"I want to get this shot first, okay?" Kat said. "Basically just stare up at him and when I tell you to look down I want you to look below you at what will be the city, then swing your feet and let that nervous energy take over. I'll cut it then and we'll move into the scene where you two are standing there and Charleigh finally lets it all out." I nodded, Dan nodded, and within a few minutes Kat said, "Action," propelling us into the scene.

I stared up at Dan, who was now Ryan. He put his arm around me and pulled my chin to his shoulder. "Look down," Kat said. I stared at the floor, imaging a city, imagining Sawyer's arm around me instead of Ryan's or Dan's, and I swung my feet as I was told. "And cut," Kat said. "Great. Perfect, Nora. You looked contemplative and sad. Exactly how I envisioned it."

I nodded. Dan helped me stand and Kat repositioned us. "Okay." She put his arms around me and stepped back. "Camera is gonna swoop in and then you can start your lines while you're holding each other like that."

I listened to Dan's heartbeat until Kat said, "Action," again and the camera swooped in front of us.

I stepped back and looked up at Ryan, closed my eyes, took a breath, and started my lines. "It's not you," I said, lip quivering. "It's me, Ryan. There's something I haven't told you."

He looked confused.

"I have a daughter." Swallowing my pride, I refused to look at him.

He stepped toward me. "What's her name?" His hand warmed my cheek.

"Emily," I choked up, reminding myself to use my body and not my tears. Not sure if it worked because I kind I lost myself in Charleigh's overwhelming feeling of finally being accepted after a lifetime of disapproval and failure. And I lost myself in Ryan's arms. His comfort. His love for Charleigh even when she came with baggage he didn't necessarily want. He loved her more than that. More than his own desires.

"Cut." Kat walked up to me and smiled. "Amazing, just amazing. Every bit of that felt so real and raw. I could feel your pain mixed with joy. Ryan, your confusion and tenderness was perfect. Great job, guys. Next set everyone. Where's Jessica?"

I stood there with my hands at my sides as everyone shuffled around me.

"You okay?" Dan said with just as much tenderness as Ryan.

"Yeah." I nodded. "Yeah, I'm okay."

HAVE YOU EVER ENDURED A BREAK UP, THEN FELT LIKE YOU

were cheating when you started dating someone else? I tried to focus only on the gorgeous man across from me, sipping his red wine over a delicious Italian meal, but it didn't seem fair to Sawyer. We barely dated, I argued with myself as Dan ordered a refill of his water. It was short-lived and mostly over the phone, that's definitely true, but as Dan and I talked I found myself staring at other couples and wondering if anyone could talk for hours about anything like Sawyer and me.

"We don't have to do this," Dan said. "I know about Spencer and all that."

I laughed. "Who doesn't?"

He shrugged. "I don't want to force this. We can stay friends. Consider this a little outing with a friend instead."

"I'm sorry," I said, picking up my fork. "It's not Spencer. I don't know. I don't know what it is." I paused. "I think too much."

He tried to laugh. "Well, I don't want you to think I'm just another guy trying to win a date with Nora Maddison. I admire you as an actress and you're beautiful of course, but I wanted to know you better. It seems like you have a lot of depth hiding under there."

"No." I smiled, feeling slightly more relaxed. "I'm just a normal girl. Confused, I guess." I paused again, eavesdropped on the couple beside us, then looked back to Dan. "Do you believe that every decision we make in life matters?"

"Absolutely," he said.

"Like every single decision I make will eventually lead me where I'm supposed to be? Being here, right now with you ... is there some deeper purpose in it we can't see?"

"Now you're talking about fate. All choices ultimately leading to the same destiny."

"Yeah." I thought for a second. "Do you believe in fate?"

"No." His eyes brightened as mine probably dimmed. "There's no beauty in that." He smiled at my confusion. "What I mean is that I believe we can make the wrong choices and miss the right things, but the right choices lead us to the right things."

I nodded. "I like that."

"I don't know, but if everything good were handed to us on silver platters I just think they'd lose their value. I don't want that."

"I don't want that either, but it also freaks me out a little."

"That you might miss the right things?"

"Exactly."

"Maybe, but sometimes the wrong things help us find our way back to the right ones."

I smiled and sipped my wine, looking at his face through the liquid. If only he knew what he just said, but he was right. And I wanted nothing more than to call Sawyer as soon as possible, because if there was one thing I knew it was that being with him felt right and being without him felt wrong.

SAWYER DIDN'T PICK UP WHEN I CALLED AT MIDNIGHT, SO I looked up his latest games with the Bruins. All wins except one. People were saying he'd win some kind of cup if he continued playing so well. I smiled for him, knowing from our late night talks that he loved hockey and didn't care about awards or giant cups. I wondered if he'd play again after this or if he really meant what he said, if he really could walk away from something he was so passionate about.

A half hour passed and he didn't call back, so I ordered myself a #23 Reed jersey online and looked up pictures of him. Didn't take long to come across a few of us together, standing on our bridge in the snow. So beautiful and romantic. Of course there were tons of pictures of our kiss. I could almost taste him if I closed my eyes and imagined his lips on mine.

I set my laptop down and pulled his scarf out of my purse. After smelling it, I smiled and wrapped it around my body like a shawl and fell asleep alone, longing for him even in my dreams, until I woke up to rays of sun on my face and a tap on my trailer door. "Ready for makeup, Nora?"

Chapter 15

sawyer

We were on a huge winning streak. Maybe that's why it bummed me out so much when we lost to my hometown's team. Chris took me out to dinner with some of his friends and his new girlfriend to try to get me out of my funk, but I think really he was trying to set me up with his girl's best friend, Melody. He pulled one of those typical awkward introductions where he told me everyone's name, then dwelled a little too long on, "And this ... is Melody." Only thing he was missing was an exaggerated wink. Melody was gorgeous, but nothing like Nora. She had bright green eyes. Nora's were amber, like the sun right before it sets. Her hair was light brown, almost blonde, and Nora's was this deep rich chocolate heaven. I let my mind go back to the last kiss we had when her hair was all over my arms, then I sat down next to Melody—how coincidental that it was the only available seat—and made small talk.

After dinner we decided to go bowling. The girls drove separately and Chris and I drove his car together.

"So, what do you think?" he said. "Pretty hot, right?"

"I was waiting for it." I shook my head. "I told you I don't want a woman right now. Is your brain a sieve?"

He laughed as he shifted into another gear. "Come on. Just for fun. Why does everything have to be so serious with you?"

"You know me, man. I don't like to date around."

"A little fun can't hurt anyone." He looked at me, then back to the road. "Is this about Nora?"

"No," I said quickly. "It's about me."

"Well you need to get over yourself."

"Let it go, Chris. You have no idea."

"I have no idea?" He parked in a spot behind the bowling alley. "You've had paparazzi on your ass for years now because of that stupid shit with your brother and—"

"Alright. Chill, Chris."

"No. This isn't right. I've watched my best friend live in a dumpy state of mind for almost a decade and he refuses to pick himself up and flip the bird to the world and just live his life. Dude, you've been hiding for too long and you're gonna have one hell of a time finding a woman to love your sorry ass self if you keep this up."

"Who said I need a woman?"

"You. What guy sits in his house alone listening to love songs while drinking wine with his dinky little dog?"

"Let's go in." I got out of the car and closed the door maybe a little to hard.

"Who needs to chill now?" He met me in front of the car. "I'm just being honest, man."

I walked toward the building.

"Admit I'm right," he said.

"Shut up already."

"Admit it."

"Let it go."

He opened the door for me. "Ladies first."

I shook my head and walked inside. The girls weren't there yet, so we booked two lanes and bought their tickets. He sat down next to me and untied his shoes as I laced my bowling shoes up.

"You know I'm just looking out for you, right?" he said.

"I know, but sometimes the best way to help your friends is to just be there for them. Preaching doesn't help. I'm gonna make mistakes regardless of your wondrous wisdom."

"Yeah, yeah." He looked up. "There they are. What do you think of Leslie?"

"She seems perfect for you." I looked up as she smiled at him and thought to myself, knowing Chris, they'd be married within a year.

He pulled her into him and kissed the top of her head. Why did everything remind me of Nora?

She tried calling last night, but I was at a late night dinner with the team and couldn't pick up. The more I thought of it though, the more I didn't know if I should pick up as much as I wanted to. I worried I'd fall too fast again and regret it. The media was already going nuts over our kiss on the bridge.

Melody came over to me and I realized the rest of the group wasn't coming. How clever and annoying of my best friend. She sat down a few feet from me on the bench and laced her shoes

"So," she said. "Are you good at bowling?"

I shook my head. "Hockey is my thing."

She smiled nervously. "Oh, that's right. Of course."

"Are you any good?"

She laughed. "Not at all."

"We'll make a good team then."

She blushed and I wondered if I should've said that. Was I flirting without realizing it? Chris said I had a bad habit of that, but I was always just trying to be nice.

Chris and Leslie walked over, joined at the hip.

"Ready to get creamed?" Chris said.

"Sure." I stood. "Then after this you can meet me on the ice."

"Ooh, the tension," Leslie said, sitting down to change her shoes.

I checked my phone. 10:59p.m. I really wanted to be home by midnight to answer the phone if it rang.

"How about we make a bet?" Chris whispered in my ear as the girls talked. "Leslie and I win and you take Melody out again this weekend."

"No way," I said quietly. "You're going to win and I can't do that anyway. You're trying to force something that just ain't happening."

"Is it Nora?"

"Stop saying that."

"It is. I can tell. Why not just call her then?"

"Maybe."

"Man, you're a freaking enigma."

"And you sure know how to get on my nerves tonight."

He laughed. "Okay, you ladies ready?"

I WALKED THROUGH MY DOOR AT 12:34A.M. THE PHONE HADN'T made a sound yet. Gretzky ran up to me like he hadn't seen me in ages. I gave him a good pat on the head and looked around at my place. Same as I had left it, only the fire needed to be lit and the heat cranked up a little. Already November and freezing. Soon the pond would be ready for skating, but I probably wouldn't get a chance to scratch it up this year.

I threw a few logs in the fireplace and did my thing. Within minutes the living room was glowing the color of Nora's eyes.

I stared at the flames for a few minutes, wondering what she was doing and what she called about, then finally walked back to the kitchen to go through my enormous stack of mail. I asked Chris to toss the junk mail, but apparently he forgot. I sifted through the letters of bills and trash, then moved on to the packages. A few packages from Amazon, gifts, and random fan mail sat unopened, but the big one caught my eye. No return address, but the label said it was from California. I sliced open the tape with a kitchen knife and pulled the flaps. A card sat on top of a Taylor Swift record and a wooden record player. Some weird fan, I assumed. I opened the card and scanned to the bottom for the name. It was signed, "Me," so I started at the top.

Dear Sawyer,

I know it's kind of cheesy, but I heard this song yesterday and thought of you. It says everything I want to say to you right now. I miss you, sweet boy. I don't know what to do, but I miss you so much it hurts. I'm here. I'm waiting. I love you. I think of you constantly. Anyway, just listen.

Love, Me

I hooked up the record player and slipped the vinyl out of the package and onto the player. My heart rate picked up again at the thought of her thinking about me. The music began and the lyrics filled the fire lit room. I sat on the couch and listened. Part of the chorus stuck with me. *All I know is we said hello, and your eyes look like coming home. All I know is a simple name. Everything has changed.*

Gretzky fell asleep at my feet by the time the song ended. It was now 1:15a.m. and I wanted to call her immediately, but considered sending a song back to her instead.

Then again, maybe I was going headlong into my emotions again. I reminded myself of the media's claws and how badly I wanted to rip them from my life after this last run. And how she had no intentions of stepping out of the spotlight. If she really wanted to be with me, wouldn't she give it up? It still seemed like she loved her job more than me and I couldn't be with someone like that. Simple. That's all I wanted. A simple woman with simple dreams.

I set the alarm on my phone for 4:30a.m. so I wouldn't miss my flight, then I reclined on the couch and thought of her until I fell asleep to the sound of crackling embers.

AS SOON AS THE PLANE HIT LAND MY PHONE BLEW UP WITH messages. I checked Chris' first. *Dude, you seen this?* He attached a picture of Nora with some guy having a romantic dinner. I cringed and replied, *Don't care.*

Well, Melody is up for a date whenever you are.

I ignored his text and went back to the picture of Nora. She looked absolutely incredible in the low lighting of the restaurant. She also looked happy with the guy. He must've been some kind of actor too. I could just tell.

The flight attendant appeared at the front of the plane, but I didn't hear a word she said. I was glad I didn't call or send something to Nora. Maybe she'd be happier with another famous person. Maybe whatever we had wasn't love anyway. Maybe we were meant to be good friends and if I gave her some time to fall in love with someone we could talk again.

Everyone filed out of the plane as I stayed in my seat thinking about all of the maybe's I mentally listed. Then I added one more to the list for the sake of confusion.

Maybe I couldn't imagine her with anyone else and maybe ... maybe the picture of her with some other dude bothered the hell out of me.

* * *

I SLID TO A STOP ON THE ICE AND LEANED ON MY KNEES, OUT of breath.

"Reed," Coach yelled. "Get over here."

I slid over to him and lifted my face mask. "Coach."

He pulled my jersey and pretended to look inside. "You in there tonight or do I need to drag you out to the bench for tonight's game?"

I nodded, panting. "Got a lot on my mind."

"No excuses, Reed. You know better. Personal life stays off the ice. If you mess this up and show these boy's anything different, I swear I'll take you out of here for good."

"Yes, sir." I flipped my mask back down and skated back to my position. For the next hour I gave Coach my all, but he knew my all today was only half of me. After practice I skipped the shower and shoved my stuff into the locker.

Jones pat me on the back. "What's your secret?"

"Huh?" I shut the locker and turned.

"With women. First Nora freaking Maddison and now Miss Maryland beauty queen."

"Miss Maryland?"

"It's all over the Internet. You and her bowling on a double date. Don't deny it." He jabbed my chest with his elbow. "So what's your secret?"

I slammed my fist into the lockers.

Jones stepped back and shrugged. "Meant it as a compliment."

I walked away. "Never mind, Jones." He would never understand that being a player wasn't a compliment and that the media and its ridiculous stories could ruin my life. It did once. It could again.

I went for a walk as the rest of the team met up at some burger joint.

Eventually I stopped at Subway and got myself some lunch, hoping no photographers would harass me because I was in no mood to be polite. Thankfully, I ate in peace and killed the rest of my time until meeting the guys back at the locker room.

I got ready in silence, ignoring their pranks. Like tying my skates together in seventy knots and the lipstick marks on my locker. After greeting the other team on the ice I skated back to the center and looked up at the screen while my opponent skated toward me.

Then, she waved from the screen. A #23 jersey gracing her curves and a smile on her face. I looked around the audience and spotted her.

Carter, my opponent, sneered at me. "That's about the only thing you're gonna get lucky with tonight."

And before I could look back to her smile, the puck dropped and was swiped by Carter. I sped off as fast as I could, weaving in and out of others and realizing that I was definitely playing for the girl in the stands and there was no way I'd lose this game. I'd win for her and that's exactly what I did, but when the ice cleared after our shut-out, I couldn't find her. The stands were nearly empty and she already disappeared.

I looked everywhere and then gave up and took a shower after everyone had left. I got dressed, walked outside, and saw a figure leaning against my car, but when I got closer I realized it was only Coach.

"You played okay tonight, Reed." He crossed his arms over his chest. "But I'm worried about you."

"I'll do everything I can to help this team make it to finals."

"That's not what I mean."

I nodded.

"You need to make things right with Quin."

I nodded.

Coach clapped his hands together. "Alright, well I'm not gonna act like your father, but if you don't do what you need to do and stop messing around I won't put you on the ice."

"I'm not messing aro—"

"I know, I know." He began walking away, then called back over his shoulder, "Just be a man, boy."

I searched my pockets for my keys and realized I didn't have them.

Couldn't find them in my bag either. I grabbed the car door handle and yanked. Fortunately, it was unlocked, which was unusual for me, and sure enough the keys were in the ignition. I shoved my gear toward the passenger's seat and turned the car on.

Immediately the same Taylor Swift song began playing. At first I thought it was a weird coincidence, but then I noticed that it was a disc playing, not the radio. I scanned the parking lot for Nora, a little weirded out about the stalking thing, but still longing to touch her again. Didn't see her, so I closed my eyes and listened to the song. During the last verse, eyes still closed, I could almost feel her breath on my face.

I opened my eyes and she was leaning over me from the back seat, eyes closed, lips centimeters from mine. If I was dreaming I sure as hell didn't want to wake up. I touched her face and felt myself falling into her again, desiring her in more ways than my mind could understand. Running my fingertips down her neck and across her collarbone, I saw her breathing accelerate. I traced her lips with my thumb, then gave into the extreme urge to taste her again. We kissed passionately for so long we heated the car. Then I pushed the chair back and pulled her onto my lap, where we talked until sunrise. Yes, only talked. Just like old times.

"I need to catch my flight," she said around 6:13.

"Me too." I ran my fingers down her arm and held her hand.

"Sawyer, I've waited to say this." She stopped and looked into my eyes without blinking. "I'm in love with you. I can't stand the idea of being without you."

I looked at our hands. Our fingers linked together. I couldn't stand to be without her either, but the fame … the media … the lies.…

"Do you love me?" she said, moving a strand of hair from her cheek.

I brought my hands to her face and pressed my forehead against hers. "What do you think?"

"Then choose me." She kissed me, then leaned back. "Choose us."

I looked down. "Relationships like this don't last." I tried to look at her, but couldn't. "It won't last. There's too much pressure. Too many lies."

"Don't you believe in love? Don't you believe that it's stronger than any obstacle in its path?"

"If you believe in us so much, then why isn't love more important than making movies?"

She took a deep breath. "That's not fair."

"Why not? You're asking me to give up my desire for a simple life. Let me ask you something." She looked at me, blinking slow and steady. "Do you imagine marrying me? Because I'm not the play for fun kind. I play for keeps and … look, I just want a quiet life with my wife and kids on a nice plot of land with a pond where the paparazzi wouldn't be interested in following me around."

"It sounds like both of us feel the same."

I wiped a tear from her cheek. "I don't understand. What's happening between us? Why does it feel so good and hurt so much at the same time?"

"Because … neither of us are willing to compromise."

"There is no compromise. One movie every few years is no different than one every year."

"I can't do this." She swung her legs over me and stood outside of the car. "I've given you my heart and all I'm asking is for you to want it."

I stood and took her hands, but she fell into my chest. "Nora, there's not a part of me that doesn't want you."

She stepped back. "But I keep telling you, this is me. I am an actress. This is who I am. Why are you so scared of a few cameras and magazines?"

"Why are you so afraid of not being an actress? Is being normal too far below you?"

She bit her bottom lip and shook her head. "This isn't love."

"Then what is it?"

"I don't know." She kissed my cheek. "I'm sorry I tried again. I'll leave you alone now." She turned to walk away, but I grabbed her arm and pulled her back to me. I kissed her again, trying to show her how much I wanted her, but she just looked up at me with dark eyes.

"Why don't we be friends for now?" I said. "I can't lose you completely."

"I can't. I tried dating another guy and all I could think about was you." She crossed her arms over her chest, then dropped them to her sides again. "If you don't want to be with me, really be with me, then you need to let me go and I promise I won't contact you again. It's just that…." Her voice cracked.

I wrapped my arms around her again and finished her sentence, "It's just that I love you." I held her shoulders and pushed her body from mine so I could look into her eyes. "I know I do. You're the most real thing I've felt in a long time."

"This is ridiculous." The volume of her voice went up a few notches. "We're going in circles. I need to go now. Let's take a break for a month and see how we feel on Christmas Eve. No talking until then. Midnight meet me at the bridge."

I reluctantly agreed, then kissed her again before she walked to what I assumed was a rental car. I couldn't help watching her hips as she gracefully glided away from me. The girl had sex appeal no man could deny when she got all dressed up, but I liked seeing her in jeans and boots and a simple sweater. I liked seeing her period. And as she waved from her car I wondered if I could convince myself to be with Nora Maddison and everything that came along with that. Going to awards shows, selling our first born's photographs to *Us Weekly* for way too much money, having private walks on the beach show up on tabloids, constantly being told we are broken up when we aren't or someone's cheating when they haven't.

I'm a hockey player, I thought to myself. *I love hockey. That's it. I'm not cut out for all of this.*

As I turned on my car I switched mental gears and thought of Quin. My next game was in New York and I knew I needed to somehow show him how I really felt about everything we went through. I needed to talk to him face to face before I left. Coach was right. He knew I'd never make it to finals with so much guilt on my hands. Even if Quin didn't forgive me, I still needed to do my part. And I finally would.

hapter 16
n o r a

There were two people I always turned to for relationship advice. I picked them because they were pretty much opposites and often gave different advice so I could see the two extremes and find my own middle place. So I decided to call each one before my evening scenes. I got comfortable in my trailer and started with the most romantic person I'd ever met. Ella picked up after a few rings and we talked about this and that for a few minutes until I finally started my speech.

"So," I said. "I kinda need advice. You probably don't know about Sawyer. I know you don't follow all that gossip stuff, so I'll try to be quick. We met randomly one day and had these late night phone calls for a while. It was so comforting and we have so much in common. Eventually we met up again in person and Ella … it was magical. It was so, so beautiful in so many ways. We literally forgot all of the reasons we might not work and just lived in the moment. I've never felt that way in my life. But things got complicated. We never shared our last names or what we did, but I found out that he was this famous hockey player with a history of gracing as many magazine covers as I do. I kinda went back and forth and then he found out who I was and it hasn't been the same since. When we are together in person it feels so right. For a few hours we ignore the nagging questions and fears we both have and we love each other. I know he loves me and I know I've never felt this way about someone, but he wants me to give up acting. He has this, I don't know, it's like he's anti-fame because of whatever he went through before. I want him to just let it go and he wants me to let go of acting but neither of us will do it. I know your friends Miranda and Derek are getting married soon and they had to overcome a lot of issues, so I figured I'd ask your opinion."

Ella waited a second to make sure I was finished, then said, "Sounds like you guys are alike in another way too."

"What do you mean?"

"Stubborn." She laughed quietly. "With Miranda and Derek it was the opposite. They were a lot different and they've sorta shaped each other. Anyway. Question. Is acting more important than love to you?"

"No, but if it's real love I would think this wouldn't be an issue. I've been wanting this for years and to just leave it...."

"Would you be happier with someone else who understood and supported your career?"

"I ... I don't know."

"Do you want my opinion?"

"Of course. Just go easy on me."

"I remember when Pat first met you. He said that you didn't want to act anymore. You didn't like the attention. Suddenly you made it big and it happened so fast and now you are reveling in it, but maybe your real problem isn't anything to do with Sawyer. Maybe it's that Sawyer reminds you of what you used to be and you're afraid that it's like regressing back to something less than what you are now. Maybe your values have changed."

"Interesting." I replayed her words in my mind. "Okay. I'll think about it. Thank you, Ella. Really."

"I love you, friend. Call anytime."

We hung up and instead of processing her words more, I dialed London.

"When will you learn?" she said.

"Hello to you too."

"Nora, Nora, Nora."

"How'd you know?"

"How does anyone not know?"

"I don't get it. My love life isn't nearly as interesting as they make it seem."

"You're just a good target, that's all."

I sighed. "Things with Sawyer and I aren't like that, London. You gotta believe me. He's not what they make him seem like. I mean, if anything he talks about marriage and the future more than I do. It's like he can't just date for fun and he needs to know it has potential."

"At least that's what he tells you."

"Do you have to be so cynical about love all the time? Just listen to what I'm saying. What we have is absolutely amazing when we're together but the only real problem is that he wants to quit hockey for good after this season and get away from the spotlight. He doesn't want to be with someone right smack in the middle of it." I breathed in loud enough for her to hear. "And that's me."

There was a tap on my trailer door. "Can I come in?" It sounded like Dan.

"One second," I yelled. "Lon, I gotta go. Real quick, what would you do?"

"This might be too advanced for me. I only know how to get my heart broken."

"Please. Anything."

"Be yourself. If he loves you as you are, then he loves you."

I walked to the door and opened it. "I'll call you tomorrow. Love you."

After we hung up Dan asked if I wanted to go for a walk. So we meandered around the trailers to some field behind them. I shivered in the cold and looked up to the cloudy sky.

"Looks like snow," he said.

I nodded. "Almost Christmas."

"Well, let's get through Thanksgiving first."

"Actually I don't celebrate Thanksgiving." He cocked his head and almost smiled. I smiled back. "Yes, I'm serious."

"Why not?" He sat down on a log.

I sat beside him. "Kinda weird to celebrate the massacre of Indians by giving thanks. I think I'd rather be one of the dead Indians than one who celebrates their murders."

He laughed. "Never heard that before, but I guess I see it as a day to be thankful for my family and spending time with those I love."

"Yeah, I know I'm weird. I guess I have trouble celebrating the real origination of a holiday from what consumerism has turned it into." I laughed. "I'm half-kidding. I guess I walk to the beat of my own drum."

He nodded. "Must be hard."

"What?"

"Must be lonely walking to your own drum beat. All alone with no other drummers."

I looked down. "I never thought of it that way."

"It's not bad to be part of something. To be like others and learn to appreciate other beats while contributing your own."

I laughed. "You're something else."

He shrugged. "I've got my own issues."

"Like what?"

"Well ... it's a little ridiculous."

"And I'm not? Come on ... spill it."

He tugged on his coat sleeves and tightened his scarf. "I was engaged before, but I ended it."

"What's so ridiculous about that?"

"I ended it because I can't get this girl out of my head. This is going to sound so dumb, but I met her when I was a kid and then I moved away. She could be married now with kids. She could be nothing like what I imagine, which is possible because I have a wild imagination. Either way, for years I wasn't able to shake this feeling that I'm settling for someone else if I don't end up with her."

I swallowed hard as a wave of nausea crept up inside me.

"I know it's weird." He stood. "I try to move on. When I first saw you I was speechless. I was used to seeing you with all the makeup and everything from your movies, but when I saw you here for the first time you looked natural and real and something about that struck me. I wanted to at least try to get to know you, but"—he laughed—"I realize your heart is with someone else too."

I stood and looked into his eyes, searching for the little boy who stayed in my wallet for so many years. Could it be?

"Nora?" he said shyly.

"Where did you live when you were a kid?" I wrapped my arms around my body.

"Orlando. You?"

I inhaled for what felt like the first time in minutes. "Illinois."

He stepped closer to me.

"I don't think you're crazy." I looked down. "I did the same thing. Waited for this boy I knew as a kid. For a minute I thought maybe...."

"Maybe it was me." He stepped closer again. "Nora." He ran his fingers through my hair ... like Sawyer. "Can I kiss you?"

I kept my eyes from blinking so I could take in the way he looked at me. He wasn't Sawyer. No, he understood me. He was a dreamer like me. Enjoyed the same career. Didn't mind the fame. He was smart and gorgeous and sweet. I continued searching his eyes, as his danced across my face. He leaned closer and held my arms with his hands, heating wherever they touched. I closed my eyes and felt the warmth of his breath on my lips. Closer, closer....

I turned my face and stepped back. "I'm sorry."

"Is it the hockey guy?"

I nodded, holding back tears.

"You love him?"

I turned back to Dan's alluring gaze and forced myself to try. To try my hardest to kiss another man and see ... see if maybe I could be with someone else. If I could really let go of "the hockey guy." Throwing my hands over his shoulders, I pressed myself into his body and kissed him until our noses were no longer cold. He finally pulled away and held my face ... like Sawyer.

"Does that mean you don't love him?" Dan said, still cradling my face.

"I don't know. I thought I did. I thought he did." I looked down again.

He pulled my chin up. "Maybe you did, but maybe now you need someone to help you look up again."

I nodded and he kissed me again. I knew Sawyer and I were on a break. I knew I wasn't cheating, but I felt like I needed to call him immediately and confess what happened.

Dan walked me back to my trailer and kissed my hand as I stood on the step. "I respect you," he said. "If you need to think about what just happened, I understand. Just know that I may never find that little girl from Orlando, but with you I feel like I don't need to."

I squeezed his hand. "Thank you, Dan. I'll see you on set in a little bit."

AFTER A FEW EASY NIGHTTIME SCENES OF LITTLE DIALOGUE, I said goodnight to Dan and walked back to my trailer. It was a little after midnight. I stared at my phone, then brought up Sweet Boy's number on the screen. Call, don't call, call, don't call. After a few draining minutes I finally called. He picked up after one ring, but didn't say a word.

"Sawyer?" I whispered.

"Beautiful," he whispered back.

"Did I wake you?"

"Yes."

"I'm sorry."

"I'm not."

"I know I said Christmas but something happened to me today." My voice shook. "I need to talk to you."

"I'm here, girl."

A tear fell to my hand. I stared at it as a other one ran down my face. "Sawyer."

"What happened? Are you okay?"

"I'm sorry," I cried. "I'm so sorry."

"What's wrong?"

"I kissed another man." Silence responded. Only the subtle sound of rustling made its way through the phone. I didn't expect him to respond, so I explained myself, "He works with me. Today he tried to kiss me, but I couldn't do it. Then something came over me. I've been frustrated with the situation between us and he understands my desire to be an actress. I thought if I kissed him maybe I'd realize I'm not in love with you."

More silence. I couldn't even hear him breathe.

I waited, anticipating closure. A final curtain call to the romance we shared.

He cleared his throat, then said, "You did what?"

"I miss you."

"Stop."

"No, I do."

"Stop playing around with me, okay?" he said. "If you want that life and that guy then stop calling me and telling me you miss me."

"I thought you said we were best friends. I want to talk to you."

"Fine, but then don't whisper that you miss me. Don't say my name like it's not just another dude's name. It kills me." Something slammed and rattled. He brought his voice back to a whisper, "It's killing me."

"I'm sorry." I wanted to hug him. "It's killing me too."

"You kissed him." Something banged against something. Sounded like the phone dropped and he picked it back up. I waited with no words left to say. "You freaking kissed that guy?" he said again.

"Sawyer."

"Stop saying my name like that. This is exactly the kind of bullshit I don't want to deal with for the rest of my life."

"I'm hanging up now."

"Yeah, you would."

"Oh, grow up, would you? I'm not the one making this so difficult. You know what Dan said after we kissed? He told me that maybe I needed someone to help me look up again. This thing we have has gotten depressing, Sawyer. You're the one who—"   "I hope you're happy with your decision."

"This is your decision."

"Goodnight, Nora. For the last time."

He hung up. I shook my head at the phone. Not exactly the response I hoped for. Why didn't he fight for me? Why didn't he tell me he loved me and that I didn't need to kiss another guy to realize what we had? But maybe I did need to let go. Maybe Dan was put into my life to help me do just that.

I stared at the sky outside the trailer window. My body shook inside, but when I held out my hands they were still. I wanted to be happy, like Dan said. I wanted to look up again.

Still ... whether Sawyer was the one for me or not, I did love him and it was real and falling out of love is the worst feeling in the world. Painful and messy.

I lost him, I thought. The curtain closed. "It's over," I whispered.

But it would never really be over. Not with the Grand Canyon of a hole in my heart. I'd always love him. In some way.

I sunk into my bed and pulled the covers over my eyes, then pulled them back down and looked over to the pillow at my right. I imagined his face there, all scruffy and unshaven. His hoodie tucked around his neck as he stared at me like he'd done it a million times before. That half smile and slight squint to his eyes.

Ugh.

What happened to me?

I WOKE UP TO A TAP AT MY DOOR, EXPECTING IT TO BE MAKEUP and hair time, but no one said anything. "Hello?" I said, but still no answer. I rolled out of bed and opened the door. There on the step sat a vase filled with pink and white roses. I picked them up and inhaled their sugary scent, then set them on a table in my trailer and found the card. It read:

Look up. Smile. -Dan

I tried to smile, remembering a few years ago when I broke up with my first love, Greyson who cheated on me. Wondering if I was over him or not, I kissed Pat and although I had no feelings for him, I realized that I also didn't have romantic feelings for Greyson anymore. Not one part of me felt bad kissing another man, but with Dan it wasn't like that. I felt bad and couldn't get over it.

I thought about everything while I had my hair and makeup done for the last scene, and once I finished I arrived on set early to talk to Dan. He got there before too many people showed up, so I pulled him aside to talk in private.

"Thank you for the flowers," I said. "I've thought about everything and I want you to know that I still miss Sawyer. We talked last night and I don't think it's going to work out with him. I really do want to be happy and look up again and I think we could have fun together, but for now I need a friend. If it ever turns into more I figure it will happen naturally, but I really need a friend more than another relationship."

He hugged me as London would. "I can respect that," he said. "Were you and Sawyer actually in a relationship?"

"I don't know. We never said so, but whatever we had almost felt deeper than a relationship."

"Not sure I know what you mean."

"I'm not either." I looked behind me. "We should probably head back."

He started walking back to the set. I waited a few seconds, then followed. *Look up,* I thought. *It's time to look up again.*

Chapter 17

sawyer

Quin's car wasn't in front of his house, so I walked around Manhattan a little, got some lunch at a hot dog stand, and dropped that same lunch all over a beautiful woman's white dress. Ketchup, mustard, and relish. Everywhere.

"Gross." She gasped while staring at her newly dyed dress. "I just bought this yesterday." Her eyes shot up toward me, but not at me. "And it wasn't cheap."

"I am so sorry," I said. "Here." I reached into my pocket and handed her a few hundreds. "Go get yourself a new one."

She looked at the money, then finally made eye contact with me. "It didn't cost that much."

I handed her the cash. "Keep the change. Really, I'm sorry about this."

She shook her head, trying to speak.

"It's fine. I'm serious."

She smiled. "I ... um ... thank you. Can I at least buy you another hot dog?"

I saw a hint of flirtation in her eyes and although somewhat tempting, I declined. She didn't seem to get turned down much, so I tossed a compliment her way to make her feel better, then started back toward Quin's house. As I got closer I saw him going up the ramp to his door and I ran to catch up. "Quin," I yelled. "Hey." Out of breath, I made it to him before he could unlock the door. He tried to ignore me and go inside, but I grabbed his arm. "Quin. You're my brother, not my enemy. We need to talk about this."

He looked around, then motioned for me to come inside. I noticed a wedding ring on his left hand and wondered if he remarried. He wheeled into the living room where tons of photographs of Tiffany still remained. I pretended not to notice them.

"Go ahead and look at her," Quin said. "You didn't seem to mind before."

I sat down on the couch. "It was one night. I was drunk, Quin. I don't remember anything, but she slept around constantly. I tried to tell you before you married her, but you refused to believe me."

"You were jealous." He moved his wheel chair back a few feet and looked at me. "You were always jealous of me."

"You're my big brother and I admired you, but I was never jealous."

He raised his eyebrows.

"Look, man, if you want to believe some smutty woman over your own flesh and blood that's your problem. I can't convince you, but can we at least be brothers again?"

He squeezed the handles of his chair and I watched as his face flushed with blood in slow motion. I inhaled and shook my head, worried that he'd hold his grudge until his dying breath. His face reddened more and finally he erupted. "You ruined my life," he screamed. "You slept with my wife and now look at me. I can't walk. When you lace up those skates, do remember me? Your brother who can't feel his own feet because you shoved him into that wall."

"You swung at me with your stick. What the hell was I supposed to do? I just reacted to your anger."

"My anger?" He shook his head violently. "My anger, he says." He wheeled into the dining room. "Leave now. You've done nothing to fix what you ruined."

I followed him. "You want me to lie, man. To publicly lie for you and damage my own reputation even more. For what? What good would that do any of us? I'm not freaking lying and apologizing for something I didn't do just because you can't deal with life now."

He turned sharply. "Get out of my house."

"I'm not leaving until this is fixed."

"It will never be fixed, Sawyer. You can't make me walk again. You can't bring her back to life."

"I'm sorry, okay?" I got on my knees in front of him. "You're my brother. Forgive me. Please."

He wheeled away again and disappeared into the kitchen. "I said get out of my house."

I stayed there on the floor, wishing I hadn't gotten drunk that night. The only thing I remember is Tiffany hanging on my neck, licking my ear as I shoved her away. Quin had passed out on the couch and after a few more drinks everyone else had left. The next thing I remember is waking up in the middle of the night in my brother's bed to her naked body draped over mine and Quin's fist rocketing toward my face. One stupid mistake and one scandalous woman is all it took to screw up our lives. The media caught ahold of it somehow, spun it around, and asked me in an interview to explain what really happened between Quin and me. I said, "His wife is a slut and came on to me when I was drunk." That's all I said and the tabloids went nuts. Within weeks of being called the "Slutzky of NHL" Tiffany bought white sheets and blankets for their bedroom, white curtains too, then dressed in her wedding gown and shot herself in the head. Quin discovered her body in the red-speckled white room and still managed to win the NHL championship and Stanley Cup, but he wasn't awake to know it. After his winning goal he turned to me with his stick raised and swung. We were going fast when I shoved back and tripped him with my skate. He flung head first into the wall. For the next hour I thought I lost my brother for good, and although he did wake up I never did get him back.

I stood up in his dining room and found him out on his deck. He didn't turn around when I came out.

"She wasn't worth any of this," I said. "And for the record, I wish I had let you knock the life out of me that day so you could've kept yours." He said nothing. Made no movement. I stared at the wheels of his chair, wondering how many Stanley's he would've won. Everyone thought he was going to end up a Hall of Famer. "I'll leave now," I said. "Thanks for letting me in." I walked back inside, down the lonely hall lined with pictures of the woman who started it all, and out the front door.

Everything I touched, I damaged and lost. Nora's sweet smile shot through my mind. I should've never touched her, I thought. She deserved better.

COACH PULLED ME ASIDE BEFORE PRACTICE. I TOLD HIM WHAT happened and he pat my back and said, "You've done what you can."

"When I signed up for this season I wanted to win it for my brother," I said. "But I don't think that's the case anymore."

"You want to win it for yourself now?"

"No." Her smile lit up my mind. "For the best friend I've ever had. The one who knows what a sorry excuse of a man I am, but loves me anyway."

"Aw, shucks," he teased. "Thanks, Reed."

I laughed. "Thanks for everything, Coach."

He slapped my arm. "'You're a good player, Reed. Not the best to ever exist, but you're up there with the greats because you play for love and not goals. You've got heart. That's why I wanted you here."

"I love the game a lot. Always have."

"That's not exactly what I'm talking about."

"What then?"

"I know you're not a basketball fan, but do me a favor and look up Michael Jordan's first MVP acceptance and locker room celebration and you'll know what I'm talking about. Talent can be acquired and surpassed, but that kind of heart is rare and in my mind can turn even an average player into one of the greats. As long as you don't lose it when you become great." He pushed me toward the door. "Check it out sometime. Oh, and you're welcome to come to my house for Thanksgiving this week."

"Eh, I don't celebrate Thanksgiving."

"Oh, come on. You're kidding."

"No. I'm serious. I'm thankful for what I have, but why should we celebrate a bunch of Indians losing their lives? I don't celebrate genocide, slavery, or capitalism."

"Wow, Reed. Weird kid you are."

"You do me a favor and think of their skin burning to ashes as your turkey roasts."

"Okay, okay. Get out there and get ready now."

MOST PEOPLE DON'T KNOW HOCKEY PLAYERS. EVEN WHEN we're famous we're normally not as recognizable on the street as an actor or musician. So I never felt the need to wear a disguise, even when my pictures were all over the papers, but since the pictures with Nora came out I had to start hiding a little.

As I walked down the streets of Boston with two other players, Jones and Kenny, I developed a strategy. I realized that people notice you more when you are trying not to be noticed, so I would do something simple like wear a hat or put my hood over my head, then walk like every other person. Surprisingly, it worked most of the time, but not this time.

Two women walked by, hardly dressed for winter weather, and I immediately heard gasps and whispers. Jones nudged me and Kenny, assuming the women were following all of us, but I could tell by the excited banter behind us that they felt like they spotted a celebrity. After my day with Quin earlier that week, I wanted nothing to do with it, but Jones insisted like a kid in toy store, so I turned around and said, "Hey, girls."

They giggled like first graders.

"I'm gay," I said. "But my friends here would love to spend some time with you."

I shoved Jones and Kenny toward them and laughed inside, imagining the rumors that would be all over the Internet by morning. I smiled and kept walking, alone, like I preferred. After losing my parents, my high school sweetheart, and my brother, I can say this ... being alone came natural to me. It's not that I really liked it, but it came natural. Almost as though it became me.

I knew the different rhythms to my own feet depending on my mood. Tonight I kept my face in Nora's red scarf as I walked to the slow tap of my shoes. I wondered if Quin would ever find joy again, regardless of whether he spoke to me or not. I wanted him to find something, some purpose or dream to run after again.

The air felt more like a snowy December day, but November was still hanging on. I missed my house and the pond. Even Gretzky. Yeah, I loved playing with a team again. With a team, a good one, there's a magic that doesn't exist when playing alone on your pond. But I missed the quiet.

So I decided to walk a little further to Boston Common, where an outdoor skating rink called Frog Pond welcomed me. I didn't have my skates on me, so I rented a pair—always felt like betrayal to do that—and skated slowly, letting people pass me. I remembered when Quin and I used to skate together as kids. The first time I ever put on a pair of skates, Quin showed me how to lace them for optimal comfort and speed. He was always faster and stronger than me. Definitely more talented, but over time he lost the love for it, the pure joy of the game and the ice. It started with Tiffany. She was all about money and status and men. I could never understand why he loved her, but he did, and slowly it ruined him. He got a Stanley Cup, but he didn't even care. It meant nothing to him. The money meant more.

I didn't win any awards and I played against my brother when he won. The press loved it, but I hated it. That game was so hyped up. All about which brother would outshine the other. So anyway, I didn't know how I'd feel winning a Stanley with the Bruins, but I was hoping to find out. I wanted to dedicate it to Nora.

My chin was still covered by her scarf. I'd worn it every day since that night and during games I wrapped it around my torso. Something about it kept me grounded.

A couple skated by, releasing their hands to go around me, then clasping them again a few feet in front of me. My phone beeped. I pulled it out of my pocket.

New text from an unknown number. *Is this Sawyer Reed?*

Who's this? I replied.

It's a friend of Nora's. She's in the hospital and I thought you'd want to know. Mt. Sinai in NY.

I raced off the ice, unlaced my skates, and ran off looking for a taxi. Boston is a nice sized city, but it's not New York. I called a taxi from my cell and kept looking as I ran full speed back to my car, but I ended up climbing into my car before any taxi's came to my rescue. When I pressed the gas pedal I realized my shoes were missing. Lucky for me, I had an old spare in my trunk. Actually a few I had been planning to drop off at Salvation Army for months. My heart refused to stop beating out of my chest even when I arrived at the hospital and parked. What happened to her? Was she in pain? Was it my fault? Did someone hurt her? Why wasn't I there to protect her?

I ran up the steps and into a large entrance. The kind receptionist directed me to the ICU, which I was hoping not to get directed to.

As soon as I burst through the doors a tired-looking woman walked over to me. "That was fast. How'd you find a flight so soon?" She wiped a tear from her cheek. "I'm Nora's best friend. Lo—"

"London. Where is she? Can I see her?"

"Let's sit down first so I can explain things."

"I need to see her, then we can talk. I want to talk to her first."

"Sawyer, she's not awake."

"I'll wait there until she is."

"She's in a coma."

Chapter 18
nora

Everything around me was spinning and falling and I couldn't move. My feet were stuck to the floor and people were shaking me. I was inside of a snow globe, only it was raining styrofoam and ice chips. Every few seconds a young girl I didn't recognize came up and forced me to drink water with tiny pieces of hair in it. I couldn't move, so I drank and my throat itched so bad.

Then I saw London on the other side of the glass. She was life-size and I wasn't. I could barely hear, only soft sounds and warmth on my hand.

"London, can you hear me?" I screamed as loud as possible.

She nodded. "We're going to get you out of here, okay? Don't give up."

I tried to move again, wanting to break the glass and escape, but also realizing I was small enough to fit into London's hand and I couldn't live like that either. So I stood there, watching her as though she lived in another world that I couldn't reach. A world beyond my little snow globe.

I started to cry, but a sharp pain shot through my chest, so I stopped and looked around, taking it all in. London kept speaking, but I could only make out words in waves. Ice chips pelted my body, so I focused on London's mouth as she spoke. Everything looked like it was playing in slow motion. I tried to close my eyes over and over again, but they stayed open.

Another face appeared outside of the snow globe and my forehead warmed. I wanted to move toward the face like a magnetic force was pulling me outside of myself, but I stayed there inside the globe, alone. The face moved closer. Sawyer. It was Sawyer. I tried to bend down and remove my feet from the ground. No movement. I wanted to touch him. I wanted to kiss him, like an uncontrollable need so far beyond desire.

But I couldn't.

I felt a tear drop on my cheek and somehow it disappeared before I could try to wipe it away. Not that I would had been able to anyway.

"I'm not going anywhere," Sawyer said. "I'm right here, sweet girl. I'm right here."

I stared at his lips, then to my right at London's eyes. They remained there, one on each side of me, for a long time. Their faces faded in and out like a painting in the rain. I tried as hard as I could to focus on Sawyer so I wouldn't lose him, but both of them faded more and more until vanishing into tiny dots. When I looked down, I had no feet and the rest of my body was erasing in fragments. I looked back up. The snow globe disappeared along with their faces. It was only me left, a small piece of me, until everything went black.

* * *

I DIDN'T UNDERSTAND ANYTHING AROUND ME, BUT I KEPT squinting to sort through the puzzle pieces on my lap. I could move my hands enough to feel them, but putting the puzzle together seemed impossible.

"Don't give up," a voice said. "I'm here, honey. Please, I love you so much. Keep fighting, okay? We'll get through this. We'll help you. We're all here now."

"Mom?" I said, confused.

No one responded.

I reached for another piece and almost moved it into place with one of its matches, but I didn't have enough strength to make it happen. "I can't do this," I whispered. "Can you hear me? Mom, is that you?"

No response.

My chest tightened and tears welled up in my eyes. "I can't do this. It's too hard."

* * *

MY PHONE BEEPED AND BEEPED AND BEEPED, BUT I COULDN'T find it. I searched all around me every few seconds, wishing someone would just turn the thing off for me, but no one answered.

After a few minutes Ariel from the *Little Mermaid* walked in and turned on a music player. She played my favorite album *Blunderbuss*, then a little John Lennon. I listened, trying to sing along. The music went on for hours. It was so comforting that I didn't want it to end, but right after Son House *Grinnin' on Your Face* ended, the music stopped and the beeping returned.

Beeped and beeped and beeped until finally everything went black again.

Chapter 19
sawyer

It wasn't exactly the way I imagined meeting Nora's parents. Of course, after our last conversation I didn't expect to meet her parents at all, but I never gave up hope. This only intensified my hope.

Machines beeped. Nurses came in and out. Friends and co-workers sent dozens of flowers and cards. London stayed in the room as much as I did and as soon as Nora's parents made it, we both left to give them some space.

"Want to grab something to eat somewhere?" she said, rubbing her eyes.

"And maybe some extremely dark coffee?"

"Definitely. I'm not one for hospital food."

"Me neither." I held the door for her as we entered the parking garage. "But keep in mind I often come with a crew of inconspicuous camera men. Especially now."

She shrugged. "My best friend is Nora Maddison."

"Yeah and she's way cooler than some dumpy hockey player."

"Way cooler." She laughed. "Let's take my car. I got a rental."

"You live in Chicago?"

"Close enough, but not quite." She motioned toward a blue Toyota. "Nora tell you much about me?"

I shook my head. "We kept our identities private for a while. Talked about life and stuff, but never mentioned names until later, but I know some things about you. I'm sure you know too much about me."

She gave me her keys. "You want to drive?"

"Yeah, I can."

"Nora isn't the gossiping type. I don't know everything. Just what

Google told me and that she loves you."

"She does?" I pictured her beautiful face lying in that hospital bed. "I mean, she still does?"

"I don't know. I would think so. I'm not the best when it comes to relationships."

"Why?"

"I don't know. Guys always break up with me." We got into the car. She looked down and played with her fingernails. "Love isn't a magical spell. Not to me, anyway. It's easy to fall in love and think it's real, but you're actually only in love with yourself and your own idea of love. The person you love just becomes a means of fulfilling your love for yourself."

We remained silent until pulling up to the nearest fast food restaurant. Wendy's. I looked at the drive-thru, then London. She nodded, so I continued through the line, bought the food and parked in the back.

"Do you think she'll make it?" London said, sniffing.

"Yes."

"How can you be so sure?"

"She's stubborn as hell. Plus, I'll show you when we get back."

"All this because she ate a cheeseburger."

"E. Coli is serious," I said, staring at my bacon cheeseburger. I wrapped it back up and ate the fries. "She has a bad case, but still plenty of brain activity and they've been able to sustain her kidney's. I think she'll be okay."

"You do realize that she believes you love yourself more than you love her, right?"

"There's not much I love about myself right now, but I love who I am when I'm with her."

"How can you say you love her?" She shifted her position so that she could give me the concerned best friend look. "Do you even know her? You guys have known each other how long now?"

"Okay," I said. "I completely understand your frustration with me. Most of what you know is from Google, and most of it isn't true. I don't use women and never have. No, I'm not a virgin. Yes, I made stupid mistakes while drunk. But I don't use women and I don't sleep around with just anyone."

"Just your brother's wife."

"This is a conversation for Nora and me if she ever wants to."

"You can't explain that one to me?"

"I can, but I won't."

"You're just what I thought you were."

"Or I'm confined to your thoughts and you'll never see me for who I really am because your mind has a different idea it would rather cling to."

She crumbled her wrappers and sipped her iced tea. "Right. I just care about her a lot. She's been with enough jerks already." She sighed. "So have I. Starting to believe good men don't exist."

"Ask me anything about her."

"You sure you're up for the challenge?"

I nodded.

"Favorite color?"

"Yellow."

"Favorite movie?"

"Big Fish."

"Favorite song?"

"Jack White's *Hip (Eponymous) Poor Boy.*" I held up my hand. "I meant deep stuff."

"Like what?"

"I'll tell you and you let me know when I'm wrong. Her biggest fear is giving up and her biggest accomplishment, right now, is learning to cook. She loves acting and considers it her biggest passion, but she doesn't realize that she's actually doing it because she's good at it and gets a lot of critical acclaim, so it validates her worth and she's afraid to let it go. It's the same reason she's a target to the media frenzy. She's insecure and vulnerable. They know that, she doesn't. She loves her parents but has never felt connected to them like she has her best friend who she considers a sister. She's idealistic, but grounded because she's afraid of risks. If she knows she will succeed she will jump, but if there's even the smallest chance of failure, she won't jump and if you push her, she'll rebel and run away." I caught my breath. "She's smart, beautiful, passionate, and everything I could imagine wanting in a woman, but I'm not going to force her to give up what she thinks are her dreams and there's no way I can endure them. There's no way any marriage can."

121

"Who said anything about marriage?"

"I did. When you love someone this much, marriage just kinda pops up as a potential option."

She laughed. "You sound a lot like her."

"How so?"

"Well, for starters, you see an opportunity for failure and won't give something a chance."

"I fail constantly. That doesn't bother me. But I don't like losing things, people mainly. People I love. And yes, I'll avoid it if I can."

"Better to never love at all than to love and lose?"

"Neither."

"Neither?"

"Neither."

⁂

NORA'S PARENTS WEREN'T AROUND WHEN LONDON AND I got back, so I asked London for a few minutes alone with the woman I loved. She didn't respond much to touch or sound, but we noticed a slight twitch of her eyelids when she was spoken to. There was also one or two times when a tear ran down her face. That drove a knife through my chest like you wouldn't believe.

I sat down beside her and leaned into her bed so that my cheek touched hers. I kissed her and whispered in her ear, "Nora, can you hear me?"

Machines beeped and hissed in the background. Even with tubes shoved into her she was beautiful to me. "I know a lot of people think of you as Nora Maddison, every guy's fantasy. Trust me, I hear it in the locker rooms all the time and it pisses me off. I don't care about this stuff. I care about you. Please understand that I love you for who you really are, not all this temporary stuff. I'll wait for you, Nora. Even if you marry someone else, you'll always be my girl." I brought her hand to my lips and kissed her fingers. Her eyes twitched again. I looked out the window across the room as the sun broke through the grey clouds. Would Nora even be home for Christmas? "God, please. I don't ask much, but please help her get better."

A heart balloon caught my eye. I didn't notice it before, but I barely took my eyes off of her so that's understandable I guess. It was tied to a dozen roses. Curiosity always gets the best of me, so I walked to the window and looked for the card. It was small. All it said was: *Look up. Things will get better.*

No name.

"Okay to come in?" London entered the doorway.

I nodded and reached into my pocket. "I have an idea." Navigating my phone, I pulled up Taylor Swift on YouTube and hit play on *Everything Has Changed.* The song started and I watched Nora's response, hoping she'd do something to show me she was there. I know her coma was medically induced and chances were she'd wake up when they wanted her to, but I still worried.

As the lyrics played, Nora remained still.

"Come back and tell me why, I'm feeling like I've missed you all this time. And meet me there tonight and let me know that it's not all in my mind."

I rubbed her hand and she moved her fingers a little. Her parents walked in and came over to the bed. I showed them her fingers and Mrs. Maddison's eyes watered. Then she gasped and pointed at Nora.

She smiled. Nora. It was a subtle smile, but there was no doubt that it was definitely a smile. The song ended and she stopped smiling. I leaned down and whispered to her, "I'll take 'em down for you."

Mr. Maddison tapped my shoulder. "Can we talk in the hall for a minute?"

My stomach knotted. "Sure." I kissed Nora's hand and set it down into Mrs. Maddison's palm, then followed Mr. Maddison into the hallway.

He looked at me with a completely stoic face. "Sawyer, right?"

"Yes, sir."

"What relationship do you have to my daughter?"

"Well, uh, as of now we're just friends." I realized I was blinking way too fast.

"Friends? I find that hard to believe."

"I care about her a lot."

"Hm. Okay." He rubbed his chin and studied me. "We know about your reputation."

"Yes, sir." I exhaled. "I deserve to be spoken about negatively, whether it's true or not, but one thing I refuse to do is try to convince people of the truth. I figure the right people will find that out on their own."

He nodded, rubbing his neck. "She's a challenge. Never seen her commit to something besides acting." He smiled and slapped my shoulder. "I hope you can change that."

"I don't want to change her, sir. I want her to realize what she already has without being coerced."

"We spoke with her doctor a few minutes ago. As of now they haven't detected any issues with brain damage, but they said she may need a kidney transplant soon in order to prevent further complications."

"When will that happen?"

"We don't know. For various health reasons, her mother and I can't donate ours. So they put her on a list." He looked down and kicked the floor. "If it takes too long it could ... it could ... it just wouldn't be good."

"Why don't you spend some time with your family? I need to go make a call."

He agreed and went back into the room. I went straight to the nurses station and waited for them to notice me.

"Um, hi." A young nurse blushed. "Can I help you?"

"Yeah, listen, I'd like to talk with someone about Nora Maddison's condition."

"I'm sorry, but we can only disclose that information to her family."

"I don't know her blood type, but if it's a match with mine I'd like to be considered as a donor."

She smiled, wide-eyed. "I'll be sure to let Dr. Rutherford know."

"Thank you. And please keep this a secret. I don't want anyone, including Nora, to know it's me."

"Of course."

I tapped the desk and walked outside, dialing Coach as soon as I hit pavement. "I'm sorry," I said. "I'm going to miss a few games, maybe even the rest of the season."

"Don't you think she'd want you to play?"

"Maybe, but that's not what I want. I need to be here."

"Reed, we can't lose our best player mid-season."

"I need to do this. I'm sorry, Coach, but I can't."

He breathed into the phone. "If you're gone too long it's not fair to let you back on the ice if we make finals."

"I know."

We hung up and I called Chris and explained my plans.

"If your blood type is compatible with hers," he said. "Let me know and I'll come out there."

"I will. Don't tell your girl, okay? I don't want this getting into the news."

"No problem, man. How are you so confident that you'll have the right blood?"

"Because we have everything in common."

"Everything?"

"A lot. Hey, thanks, Chris. You're like a brother to me."

"Yeah, yeah. Does that mean you'll steal my wife?"

"Not funny."

"Alright, call me when you have news."

HER DAD STARED AT THE CLOCK FROM A CHAIR IN THE corner of the room. London sat beside her mom, talking about pressing charges and stuff. Me ... I stared at her face, memorizing every dip and curve, wishing I could look into those golden eyes again. All of our night-time conversations replayed in my head, like skipping records. I remembered listening to her as she slept, then falling asleep before turning the phone off. Then, I started to sing, out of tune and horribly, "Oh, my love. My darling, I've hungered for your touch...." I finished the song and looked down, hoping I didn't harm anyone's ear drums.

"Thank you," Mrs. Maddison said.

I looked up. "I know I'm not the greatest man in the world, and your daughter deserves that, but I would die for her. Sometimes I feel like I already have." I stood as the room began to cave in on me. I shook my head. "I need some air. I'll be back."

I walked into the hallway and Dr. Rutherford rounded the corner as I reached the steps.

"Mr. Reed, I'm glad I caught you." He shook my hand. "I've been informed of your interest in becoming a donor for Nora. What's your blood type?"

"O."

"Okay, that'll work." He sighed in relief. "We'll need further testing done, however. It's quite extensive, so prepare accordingly. I'll get our living donor nurse coordinator in touch with you for more details, but this isn't a guarantee. We still need to get you checked out and make sure it will be a good match all around, okay?"

"Yes, sir. Can we keep this confidential? I'd like everyone to think of it as an anonymous donor."

"Of course."

CHRIS CAME UP AFTER MY ALL DAY EVALUATION SHOWED POSI-tive as a match, but Nora's kidney's had started to function better according to her medical team, so they decided to hold off and see how it would it go. She wasn't quite at the End Stage Renal Disease level, but close enough that they wanted to put her on a list anyway. I didn't want to wait it out. I wanted to give her my kidney now to save any future issues from happening, but everyone else said to wait. Her doctor was amazed at her improvements and said her kidney's probably wouldn't need dialysis like they thought. At least not yet.

Chris and I finished watching a movie in my hotel room. I hadn't been up for talking much, so he spent a lot of time smiling at his phone.

"Seem pretty enamored with that screen," I said, clearing the thick silence between us.

"I love this girl," he said. "I swear she's the best thing that's ever happened to me."

I moved the curtains back so the sun entered the room, then I stood there wondering why I was annoyed at what he said.

"I think I'm going to do it," he said, still smiling at the screen.

I shook my head. "Predictable."

"I'm asking her on Christmas."

"That's pretty fast, man. Be careful."

"Careful of what?"

I unzipped my backpack and pulled out Nora's scarf, along with the picture I printed out of her sitting in my car. I snapped it during our last time together and of all the glamorous photos taken of her, that simple iPhone image mesmerized me. I sat on the bed and nudged Chris. "Hey, go ahead and call her if you want."

"Nah. Can't. She's at work." He finally set the phone down and tapped his fingers on the nightstand. "You and Nora had sex yet?"

"No."

"You mean to tell me you didn't hit that yet?"

"Hit that?" I laughed. "That should've just pissed me off but I'm too blanked out to worry about it."

"Blanked out? Like depressed? Maybe if you had a little nookie."

"Your maturity level astounds me. There are three words I use to describe sex and 'nookie' and 'hit that' don't make the cut. You know my past. I'm not interested in what a woman can do in the bedroom anymore. And yes, yes, I do like sex and I've been tempted to let it go that far with Nora. I'm not dead, Chris. I just know I'd rather be stimulated up here first." I pointed to my temple, then to my chest. "And here. Any woman can make a man have an orgasm, but how many can create that same level of pleasure in a man's mind and heart? That's her. That's what she is to me."

"Like a mental and emotional orgasm? What does that even feel like?"

"Stimulation, intense excitement that can lead to physical pleasure, but doesn't start there."

"Dude, what? Layman terms, please."

"She makes me think. She challenges me. She changes me. I feel like everything I'm supposed to be has been awakened by her. I can't explain it."

He stopped listening and beamed at his phone again. Watching him text her, the one he thought he loved, I kept thinking no one could love someone like I loved Nora. If only she knew that. I loved her too much to see our relationship become nothing more than another Hollywood divorce.

My phone rang.

"Hey, London," I said. "What's up?"

"They are thinking she might wake up soon. Thought you'd want to know."

Chapter 20

n o r a

London and I finally landed after a long flight. I couldn't stop crying. Occasionally, she looked at me with concern in her eyes and held my hand, but I still couldn't figure out why I was crying.

"What is wrong with me?" I said. "I feel horrible and I don't know why."

"I'd feel horrible too if he did that to me."

"Who?"

"If someone cheated on me and then told the world she was so much better in every way, I think I'd be pretty upset too."

"Oh, I told you I don't care about Spencer. He can keep her."

"No, I'm talking about Sawyer."

I walked toward the exit of the plane and she followed, going on and on about how I need to wake up, take it easy, and not worry about anything. "We're here for you," she kept saying, over and over. I wanted to scream and tell her it wasn't Sawyer, it was Spencer. We kept walking through a large maze of people and I turned to say something to London, but she wasn't there. "London?" I yelled. "London? Where are you?" I turned in circles, scanning the faces. Noises increased. People turned into blurs of color as I continued to spin in circles, faster and faster. "London?"

She appeared beside me. "I'm right here, sweetie. Are you okay?"

I cocked my head at her, started to speak, but couldn't. She grabbed my hand and helped me through the ocean of faces. Never in my life had I seen a busier airport.

"Where did we land?" I said, squeezing her hand.

"Home. You'll be home soon. It'll all be over soon."

Thankfully, we reached the baggage claim in one piece. We stood there, side-by-side, waiting for our bags to come around, but didn't see them. Then I saw him. To my left. He looked perfect. Hair all messy, his hoody hugging his neck like my arms used to. And then she ran to him, jumped into his arms, and they kissed passionately without noticing the people around them. A tear tried to fight its way to my face, but I kept it there in my eyes. She wore my red scarf, the one I gave him that night on the bridge.

London rubbed my cheek, but I pushed her hand away. "We need to leave."

"We can't, sweetie," another voice said from behind me.

"Mom?"

"You're doing great."

"No." I thrashed my head violently, confused and broken. "I can't stay here while he's here. I can't stand to see him like this."

"See who, dear?" Mom said.

"Sawyer," I cried. "Please, please make him go away. Make it all go away."

Sawyer looked at Mom, then me. He moved closer to me and his eyes closed. He reached his hand toward me. I tried to stop him, but didn't have the strength to swat him away.

"Nora," Mom said. "He's been here the entire time waiting for you. He wants to see you."

"No," I screamed. "No. He needs to go."

The people around me shook their heads in agreement. Tons of voices whispered different things to me. I tried to zero in on a few of them, but they all blended together, then began to chant in unison, "He's not the one. Just a cheater, like the rest. He's not the one. Just a cheater, like the rest. He's not the one."

I closed my eyes. "Everyone leave me alone!" I shook my head. "Leave me alone!"

Chapter 21

sawyer

I stared at the nurse's lips as she explained everything to me in the hallway, but I couldn't focus on her words. When she finished, I nodded and said, "Is she going to remember me though? Remember our memories?"

She hugged a stack of folders to her chest. "Hang in there. When patients wake up out of a medically induced coma they are often confused and confusing to others. She probably had some very real dreams while asleep and may even still feel like she's in a dream state of sorts. She was only under for two weeks and her brain is functioning just fine. Try to relax. She'll remember you soon."

I rubbed my hands over my face and tried to believe her, but things weren't in the habit of going well for Sawyer Reed and I was beginning to lose hope. Was I just supposed to leave and not visit her during the rest of her stay? What if she got home and didn't know me?

Chris texted me. *How's it going, S?*

She doesn't want me here. She was screaming and crying and asking for me to leave.

What? Why?

They think she might be delusional I guess ... or not remember me yet.

You want to fly back home with me?

I don't know. I don't know what to do.

Boston?

I don't know.

I'm just about to leave the hotel. You coming back here?

No. I need some time to think. Go ahead back. I'll catch up with you later.

I left the hospital, drove into the city, then took a taxi to Bow Bridge. Snow flakes were stuck to the sides of the bridge and dusted everything with a white glow as I walked up and looked down at the water. It was mostly frozen and collecting snowflakes on top. I pulled out her scarf, which now smelled nothing like her, and watched as white dots covered the red. I thought of my brother walking in on his wife, sprawled out on her white quilt with a puddle of blood around her head, then a childhood memory rushed into view, pushing that horrid picture away.

I must've been about seven years old. Quin and I raced each other on the frozen lake outside of Mom and Dad's house as Mom fed a wild deer in the distance. I stopped mid-race and watched the deer take the food from her hand, like he had so many times before. Mom smiled and brushed her hands on her long coat, then turned to us and smiled. I waved. She waved back.

Quin elbowed me. "Come on. Race ya again."

"I want to do something important when I grow up."

"Yeah, me too. I want to be the best hockey player to ever exist." He nudged me again. "Let's go. One more race. You'll win one of these times … maybe…."

I shook my head. "I want to do something really important. Like Mom just did."

"Mom? All she did was feed that dumb animal."

"That's not how I see it."

The deer grazed its head against Mom's red coat, looking for more food in her pockets. She gave him a small apple, which the deer took happily before running off into the woods, leaving Mom there satisfied and content. It may have been small, and maybe to most people it doesn't mean much, but to me … Mom showed me that even the smallest things can be important. No need to be big and change the entire world. She loved even the wild animals around her that didn't do anything for her. She even treaded lightly on the grass. Once, around my fifth birthday, I asked her why she walked so funny in the grass and she said, "I don't want to hurt the ants. They work so hard all of the time, I'd hate to kill them without reason." She thought about things and people more than herself. I always said I wanted to be like her. I wanted to make a difference even if it meant taking the time to care for wild birds and deer, and I tried, believe me I tried, but I seemed to fail at everything I ever did.

Mom used to say, "Do your best, that's all that matters. If your best is the rest of the world's worst, there's nothing to worry about as long as you are giving it all you've got. Don't spend your life competing with the rest of the world, always trying to be better. Be yourself, son. Be the best you that you can be and I'll always be proud of you."

I walked down to the bridge and made my way to the frozen water. Seemed to be pretty solid, probably about an inch thick or so. I stepped out on the ice where the snow began to gather and knelt down, then wrote, I'm sorry, Mom in the white dust. I leaned back and reclined onto the ice, staring at the cloudy winter sky as snowflakes melted on my face. "I'm sorry, Mom," I said into the air. "If you can hear me, I want you to know that I've always tried my best, but I feel like giving up now."

On what? I asked myself inside. *Life? Relationships?*

"I just want to be alone, Mom. I want to be alone so I don't hurt anyone."

I wished for her warm arms to wrap around me again, like she did all those bedtimes before she died, but the frosty air was the only thing that hugged me.

My phone beeped. A text from London. *She's still really confused. She keeps asking me where we've landed and they gave her ice chips and she thinks they are flavored. Try not to worry, but maybe you should go back to your team. I think it will be fine.*

Is she still saying she doesn't want me there?

She seems afraid of you or something. It doesn't make much sense, but I'll keep talking to her as she comes out of the fog and let you know what happens.

I put my phone back in my pocket and sat up. Go back to the team, she said, as if that were the easiest thing in the world to do. I thought of Mom as my eyes took in the beauty of the winter scene, imagining myself in all the hockey gear, ready to fight for another win. I pictured Coach and all that he'd worked for and I knew I needed to go back to help the Bruins make it all the way. If I couldn't make things right with Nora, maybe I could make it right for my teammates. Maybe, for once, I wouldn't fail at *something*.

AFTER MY FIRST GAME SINCE RETURNING TO PLAY—WHICH we lost—a fresh determination stirred within me. London said that Nora was still adamant about not seeing me and although I couldn't forget her, I tried. I focused on the other guys in black and yellow. I focused on the ice and the plays and my opponents. We lost the first game since I returned, but I upped my passion in our next practice and Coach could see it in my eyes. I guess everyone could. Jones stopped me before I exited the ice and asked what came over me. I smiled and shrugged. "Just want to do the best I can, whatever that is."

"Whatever it is," he said, "it's pretty awesome. Nice work, Reed."

I waved the compliment away. For some reason, it felt like a distraction.

"We just might win this," he said, slapping my helmet. "Keep it up."

He went back into the locker room and I stayed there on the ice until everyone exited. I glanced around at the scuffed up ice. Something about that … I don't know … I always loved the ice after it'd been skated on for so long. It told a story the clean, perfect ice didn't. It had scars and life and mistakes. I held my chin up and inhaled, imagining the seats filled with fans donning our colors, their eager faces waiting to see if we'd pull through and give them something to scream about and I wanted to give them just that.

WE WON THE NEXT GAME. AND THE NEXT GAME. AND THE next one. It'd been almost two months since I last saw Nora, but London kept in touch with me. She was finally going home and she remembered me, but while she was dreaming in her coma she decided that I'm not the right one for her and she wanted nothing to do with me.

I didn't want to push it yet. She needed to recover fully without whatever stress she thought I'd bring her. So I continued to focus on the team, getting so into it that we were on a major winning streak with no signs of losing. The other guys were pumped and happy. Locker room talks grew louder and more pranks were played. It was fun and I told myself I'd enjoy it, no matter how much it killed me that Nora wanted nothing to do with me.

Women are not life, I kept reminding myself, but it didn't take away my thoughts of her. Every night at midnight I'd close my eyes and hear her voice whispering, "You called," wishing it were real, but it never was and the more I immersed myself into the Bruins, the more her voice became a distant memory, like the end of a song fading out to its drawn out end.

The music stopped playing.

Chapter 22

n o r a

As soon as I got home from the hospital I asked Mom and London, who pretty much gave me no choice but to delight in their help while adjusting to being home again, for some time to myself. They busied themselves in the kitchen while I rested in bed and turned to Google for advice. I read everything I could about other people recovering from E. Coli and HUS. Some people got lucky like me and went home with few complications, although I did need therapy, medication, and they'd be watching my kidney's for a while. Others, however, never came home.

After reading for a while I decided to look up stories of people who dream while in a coma. I had these intense, vivid dreams that seemed so real at times.

I scanned the search results and clicked on, *Learning from the Hidden Conscious While Comatose.*

The article came up and I immediately began to read.

> When I woke from my coma I tried to convince my family that I was actually on a cruise for a few months and met a lot of amazing people. They nodded and agreed, knowing it was only dreams, but they were such realistic dreams that I spent the next few weeks asking my wife if a memory I had was real or a dream. But the best part about this is that my mind was trying to teach me while I was asleep and I'm sharing this on my blog so that others who experience this can make sense of it.

As soon as you wake up, record those dreams in as much detail as possible. Then go through each one and try to figure out what your fear or pleasure is in the dream. Maybe you fear losing your job or maybe you find pleasure in something you never knew. Try it out and leave a comment letting me know what you find. And while you're at it, buy my book to read the full story and find out what my dreams taught me.

London tapped on my door. "Brought you some butternut squash soup."

Mom trailed in behind her. I sat up straighter and welcomed the steamy bowl into my hands. London gave me a motherly look.

"What?" I said.

"You really need to talk to Sawyer. Your dreams weren't real and he cares about you a lot. This should be taken seriously coming from me, your trusty cynical friend."

"I don't know. What if my dreams were trying to warn me?"

"Oh, for the love of it all," Mom said. "You've been doing this since you were a child. It's probably my fault."

"Doing what?" I said.

"Your father always tried to push you to accomplish anything you set your mind to and I always stepped in with logic and fear. You've never been good at making decisions and you avoid things you don't excel in. You're living in my fears." She sat on my bed and slumped her shoulders. "Honey, do you love the boy or not?"

I lowered the bowl to my lap and stared at the creamy orange soup. Mom touched my arm and London stood there eager to know my answer.

"Could I have some time to think?" I asked.

"You think too much," London said as Mom sighed.

"I need to think. It helps me feel."

They left the room and I immediately picked up my phone. Weird to be left alone for so long. It felt so normal to sit around with my family and not have a million places to be, but I was definitely ready to get back to work.

I clicked on the Photos tab and went back to the picture I took of Sawyer the last night we spent together. He wasn't looking at the camera in the phone. He was looking at me. And he looked so content and ... entranced. *Yes*, I said inside. *I love him, and why does that scare me so much?*

London entered the room again. "Hey, can I borrow your phone? Mine just died and I have an important business call I need to make."

I smiled and handed it to her. She walked away and returned a few minutes later, set the phone on my bed, and walked back out.

I spent the rest of the night watching TV and around 10p.m. my phone rang and London's name popped up on the screen. I picked up and said, "Why are you calling?"

She didn't answer.

"Hello?" I said.

"That wasn't exactly the greeting I hoped for, but I'll take it I guess."

"What?" I gasped and looked at my phone screen. "Sawyer?"

"Yes...."

"Oh my gosh."

"I'm sorry I called. I know you just got back, but I miss you and London said you wanted me to call."

I couldn't believe I fell for her trick. Changing his name to her name in my phone so I'd pick up, how clever of the lawyer friend.

"I'll hang up if you want," he said.

"Sawyer, stop."

"What?"

"Stop being so nice to me."

He exhaled into the phone. I couldn't tell if he was frustrated or laughing.

"I've spent the last few weeks ignoring you. Be mean to me."

"I don't know what you mean. I don't feel angry with you."

"Why not? I'm angry with you." My voice trembled. "Everything was good. I was dealing with everything so well, then this happens to me and I can't think straight. I don't even know what I'm thinking most of the time. Everything's changed."

"You say that like it's a bad thing now."

I nodded to myself, then shook my head. I felt like two different people having a tug-of-war to see who would speak.

"Nora," he said. "I'm not going to force you to do anything."

"Yes! Yes, Sawyer. Force me. Just force me. Make me have no choice but to be with you. Make it impossible for me to live without you. Force me." I lowered my voice and whispered, "Please."

He didn't say anything, but the sound of him breathing burned like flames in my ears.

"Sawyer," I said. "Say something."

"When I say nothing I mean everything."

"Are you still playing for the Bruins?"

"I'm not doing this, Nora."

"What?"

"This is like a freaking merry-go-round and it's making me sick."

I picked at the loose thread in my blanket. "I'm sorry I can't please you."

"It's not about that. Stop making this about you every time." He paused." Look, I'm not forcing you to do anything. You need to make your own damn decisions. And I'm not playing this game where we ignore reality and pretend to have a normal conversation for a few hours. You need to face reality and stop turning life into a movie. I'm not a puppet in your show. This is real life and you're always trying to ignore it for some cheap fantasy version where no problems exist. That's not noble of you, okay? You're not strong. You're a weak person like the rest of us. You've just learned to excel at avoiding issues. But there are issues. Life has so many freaking issues and if you can't force your own self to face life and make decisions without someone telling you what the hell to do, you're just going to end up another chess piece moved around by others."

"I guess I asked for that."

"I guess you did."

"I want to run away from you right now, but that only proves that you're right. Why am I always running?"

"Same reason we all do."

"Why's that?"

"If you're standing in front of something that can hurt you or embarrass you or steal your happy view of yourself, then the natural reaction is to run from it."

"So we're supposed to face the hungry lion head on even if it could eat our heads off? Just walk right up to pain and say, 'Welcome? How ya doing today?'"

"I'm still figuring this out myself, but when I was a kid my brother was always taunting me to challenge him. He would climb this one huge tree and call me a wimp because I wouldn't even try. My mom saw this one afternoon and pulled me aside. She told me that risking my life for something is never worth it when I'm just trying to prove something to someone else, but that there's always a time when risking everything is the only option."

"When you are doing it for your own happiness?"

"No," he said. "When you're doing it because the thing you love is worth more than your life."

SAWYER'S WORDS STAYED WITH ME THE REST OF THE WEEK. We didn't talk again and I'm sure it was intentional on his part. I replayed those words in my head constantly though, wondering if I loved anything more than my own life. I always thought of myself as strong. I built a wall that kept me from getting hit by anyone and before Sawyer I saw it as a virtue. I was able to focus more and deal with the media better because of my wall. It was a good wall. A healthy wall.

Then he poked a hole in it somehow and I felt like I was peeking through this microscopic hole and saying, "Hmmm ... that looks really beautiful over there, but it's dangerous," so I put some duct-tape over the hole and tried to keep ignoring it.

But since our last conversation, I found myself peeling back the tape and wondering ... wondering a lot of things I never wondered before. He had that effect on me.

Chapter 23

s a w y e r

Quin called me on a Tuesday morning as I was parking my car before practice. Shocked, I stared at the number for a few seconds before answering. I hadn't seen his name on my phone since before the iPhone even existed.

"I found something you have a right to see," he said. "When you get a chance, stop by."

I started to say, "Okay," but he already ended the call. He always liked to have the upper hand and I secretly believe that he found satisfaction in frustrating me.

We played the Rangers again in four days, on their ice, and we had games each night before then. Except one. So I planned to get to NYC the day before the Rangers game and visit then.

I laced up my skates in silence and moved on to taping my stick. Jones sat down and did the same, only silence was unusual for him.

"You alright?" I said.

He laced his skates tighter and faster without looking at me.
I flicked his arm. He grabbed his stick and stomped off. I followed and caught up to him on the ice. "Don't bother," he said. "Some things can't be fixed."

I skated alongside him, although he was clearly trying to lose me. "I'm not trying to fix you, Jones."

He skid to a stop by the goal, spraying ice into the net. I did the same.
"And for the record," I said. "I feel like I'm beyond fixing too."
"It's not like that."
Coach blew the whistle.
"'We'll talk later," I said, and we both skated toward the line with one

143

too many reasons to be distracted.

COACH REALLY GAVE US A TOUGH TIME AT PRACTICE, BUT I noticed that Jones didn't push himself and Coach didn't seem to mind. When Jones and I finally made it to the locker room we were both too exhausted to talk, but I figured I'd open the door back up anyway.

"What's going on?" I said.

He looked around at the guys.

"No one's paying attention." I nodded toward the others. "They're all too busy messing around."

"It's my leg." He pressed his hand into his thigh. "Doc says I'm on the bench for the next few games. Maybe the season."

I stared at his leg, knowing any consolation I'd give wouldn't matter. "Didn't know it was that bad," I said. "I'm sorry, man."

"I know it's not the most important thing in the world, but it was my dream."

"It doesn't matter how important it is to others. It's your dream and that's all that counts. I know how it feels to lose things you love. It's not easy."

He breathed in and rubbed his knees. "Thanks, Reed. Appreciate it."

I KNOCKED ON QUIN'S DOOR, ENJOYING THE BITTER MARCH wind and wondering what he was about to show me. Had to be important if he called me.

Took a few minutes, but he finally opened the door. Didn't say a word as he turned his wheelchair and went toward the living room. I ignored the pictures in the hallway and focused on his arms spinning the wheels. Even if he'd forgive me, I thought, not a day would pass where I didn't wish it was me in that chair instead.

He urged me to sit down, then flopped a book on my lap. A worn leather journal. I looked at him, then the book. He nodded for me to open it. I held my breath, fearing that he had given me his wife's journal, but the first page said: Rosemary Reed. "Where'd you find this?" I said, turning the page.

"I was going through old boxes and it somehow got mixed up with my old yearbooks. I never saw it before. Read the entry." He pointed toward the book. "The one I marked with the bookmark, then you can take it home and read the rest."

I turned to the page and silently read.

Dear Sawyer and Quin,

If you ever read this and I'm gone I want you to know something that has been weighing on me. I watch you two play and it can be so sad sometimes. You two have been best friends since Sawyer's birth. Always inseparable. It's been adorable, but comes with its challenges. I'm worried when I watch you boys.

Quinton, you are always driven by your ego. You're strong and talented, but much too determined to beat down everyone in your efforts to be the best. You push yourself to win a competition, then shove it in someone's face. I've rarely seen you compliment others, but you always give yourself a pat on the back. You don't play anything for the love of it, you play to win and normally do. I've seen you tear down your brother so many times just to feel good about yourself. You don't have to do that, dear. You don't have to spend your life trying to prove that you're amazing. One day you'll fail and be alone because you've climbed to the top of a pyramid with only enough room for yourself. Don't let it get to that point and if you do, learn humility from your brother. He could do without so much of it.

Sawyer, just because you're most often the underdog and the peaceful introspective kid, don't think I'm letting you off the hook. Your humility has become your worst enemy. It's so intense that I wonder if it will be your vice one day, instead of your greatest virtue. It's one thing to believe you are below all men, even when you're not, but it's another thing to be crippled by fear and to no longer try. Sometimes, dear, I think you fear being good at something because you've tasted the bitterness of being the one who comes in last and you don't want to make others feel that way. That's sweet of you and I smile inside when I see you pretending to lose when you race your younger cousins, but if you always let people beat you they may never learn to work hard for something they want. It's okay to win, just win for the right reasons and always encourage those who lose. Oh, and Sawyer, I hope one day you read this. One day when it matters. If so, remember that the bottom of a mountain can be just as lonely as the top.

I hope the two of you can learn to climb together one day. As I'm writing this you are trying to climb the big pine tree out back. Quin is at the top, rejoicing in his victory and taunting Sawyer. And Sawyer is at the bottom, afraid to get hurt and afraid to be sad about it. I'm going to go talk to you two separately now. I hope my words mean something.

Love you boys,
Mom

Quin and I stared at each other in silence. I imagined myself at the bottom and him at the top, but maybe he saw it the other way around now. Maybe Mom was right. Maybe the top of a pyramid felt like it should be the bottom.

"Want a drink?" he said.

"Sure."

"Root beer?" He wheeled backwards as I nodded.

I flipped to the last page of Mom's journal and saw the date. Two days before she died. Then I closed the book and set it in my lap. I wasn't ready to read that yet. Quin came back with two root beers and some chips. He handed me the drink and flopped the bag of chips on the coffee table. I unscrewed the cap and took a sip. He did the same, then set his drink between his legs and said, "I knew you were never jealous of me."

I took another swig of my drink. "Okay...."

"Did you know I was jealous of you?"

I laughed through my nose. "Of what?"

"Read that journal and you'll see."

"Mom didn't favor either one of us. She wasn't like that."

"That's true. But you were so much like her." He wheeled over to a picture of Mom and Dad on an end table. "You always had something I couldn't get no matter how much I fought."

"You have plenty of Mom's qualities too. We're both a mix of Mom and Dad."

"Anyway." He faced me again. "I want you to know that I believe you about Tiff. I need to let go and I want you to know that I don't blame you."

"But you should, Quin. It was my fault. After that first drunken mistake she kept trying to seduce me, jumping on my lap and stuff and snapping her bra. You weren't talking to me so she just kept showing up at my place. I turned her down so many times and finally she came to me wearing nothing but a little coat, threatening to kill herself if I didn't make love to her. I told her I never loved her and I regretted having sex with her and she smiled and walked away." I imagined her face that day, the last day I saw her. "I didn't realize she...."

"It wasn't your fault." He paused and bit the inside of his cheek. "You and Mom loved people. I didn't know how to love her so she kept looking for someone else. Of course she'd go after my brother."

147

"Either way, the woman was messed up in her head before you married her. Some people can have a savior stare them right in the face and still choose to give up. We couldn't save her. She didn't want to be saved."

He tried to speak, but coughed instead.

"I really am sorry, Quin." I scooted to the edge of the couch. "For everything."

"You haven't changed at all." He laughed. "Still apologizing all the time, aren't you?"

I shrugged.

"I think ... I ... I'm ... Listen, I'm sorry." He looked down at his legs as his body started to shake. "I'm sorry, Sawyer."

I stood and touched his shoulder. He shook for a few minutes, hunched over and crying without tears. I stayed there and held his shoulder until his body calmed down. Head still bowed, he reached for my hand and squeezed it, then looked up at me with clenched teeth. "I hate you," he whispered.

I loosened my grip on his shoulder.

"I hate you!" He thrust his body forward and flopped off of the wheelchair. His legs landed in awkward twists as he reached for the carpet and tried to rip it out of the floor. In frantic, strong motions he yanked and yanked at the floor, then his hair, then the floor again.

"Quin, what are—"

He grunted and yelled like a man dying a slow death. I stood in place and swallowed hard. He punched the ground over and over while screaming as loud as his lungs allowed, each muscle in his arm flexing as he pulled back and plummeted toward the floor again. My brother was the strong one, the one who never cried, the one who lost a beautiful girl and moved on to the next, the one who broke his leg so bad the bone was visible and just said, "Ouch," the one who lost our parent's and went on a date the next night. Now ... he looked like Nicholason in *The Shining*.

His screams turned to howls. His arms flexed with less intensity as he bit the carpet and shook his head like an animal. My eyes burned with the scourge of everything I destroyed, of everything I ... crippled. Quin flipped to his back and stared at the ceiling in a trance, saying, "I'm already dead," in a hoarse voice.

I waited for the right time, but when that seemed non-existent I sat on the couch near his head and said, "How can someone be dead if they never really lived?" He didn't seem to hear me. "Get up, Quin."

He continued to stare.

"Get up, Quin," I said louder.

He stared. Not even a blink.

I leaned to the ground and slipped my arms around his back and chest. He shook his body, resisting my efforts. I gripped harder and pulled with more strength, scrunching my face as I pulled him up with all the power I had. He knocked his head around, tried to punch me, and sunk his teeth into my arm. I forced him to stand with me as blood dripped down my wrist and his chest.

"Remember what it's like to stand?" I said, panting. "Good. Because the only thing different between this and sitting in your chair is the view." I eased him on to the wheelchair. "You didn't live when you had legs. You did a lot of stuff, but you didn't live. Now that you're here, what the hell do you expect?" I shook my head as his chest rose and fell rapidly above his clenched fists. "As far as I'm concerned, the wheelchair only provides a physical sign of the way you've always lived. So sit here and whine about your problems or get the hell out of the chair and live for once. Do you even know what that means?"

His knuckles turned white and his eyes narrowed. "The last thing I need is advice from the little brother who couldn't climb a tree."

"I climb plenty of trees. I just choose which ones are worth it and I'm afraid that's something we've rarely agreed on."

"What is life, huh? For an orphan with no legs and a dead wife? Tell me that, Dr. Sawyer. What is life if you can't walk on a beach or skate on a pond? What is it, huh? If you can't drive a car or walk down the street or have sex? I sit here in this damn"—he whacked the wheels—"chair and watch life walk by me. They all just walk by."

"I'm sorry."

"Stop apologizing." He reached for the chips and popped the bag open, completely ignorant of the blood on his shirt and carpet. "So since you've decided to come here and be all wise, tell me the meaning of life."

"I don't know."

"Exactly." He crunched a chip. "No one knows."

"Maybe it's just to live."

"Breathing isn't enough for me."

"Mom lived. And she barely left the house."

"Mom loved. There's a difference." He tossed the bag to the table and watched it spill over.

I imagined the deer brushing against Mom as she smiled, and the times she insisted on catching the mice in our house so we could release them back in the fields. The way she laughed when I looked out the window on the first snow day of the year. Sun barely had time to rise and she was the first one building a snowman. The way she kissed Dad when he got home from work and never complained when he watched too much TV. All of those times we couldn't pay the bills and lost electric and she made hot summer nights without lights and air conditioning seem like magical adventures on pirate ships.

"I don't know," I said, staring at the chip-covered floor. "Is there a difference?"

Chapter 24

nora

Dressed in one of my weird disguises, I took a long walk through Manhattan. Life felt normal again, except it had been over three weeks since I last talked to Sawyer. April arrived with the promise of new starts and warm weather, but no Sawyer on my caller ID. I followed his games and it looked like the Bruins would make it to the playoffs. Meanwhile, I debated whether or not I should go to the premiere of my last movie. Maury insisted I go and not give the media more grounds for gossip, but they'd gossip anyway. Spencer would be there with my lovely ex-agent and I had no date. I could only imagine Sawyer showing up with me. That'd be the day.

I stopped at a food stand and ordered two hot dogs. One with ketchup, mustard, and relish. The other with tons of nacho cheese. When I turned around I tripped over the curb. My hot dogs soared through the air in slow motion and landed all over a girl standing in line with her boyfriend. She flailed and screamed as though someone shot her as her boyfriend reached for napkins. I apologized and ran down the street in the opposite direction, slowing down once I rounded the corner. Gasping for breath, I leaned my back against the wall of a corner mart and looked up past the monstrous buildings to the cloudless blue sky. I thought of my last conversation with Sawyer, of my strange need to run from everything that felt uncomfortable in some way.

The blue sky reminded me of his eyes.

I ran back and found the couple on a bench not far from the food stand. They looked up when I stood in front of them. First, I took my Yankees hat off and my baggy jacket. Then, I pulled my messy teased hair into a bun and smiled.

They glanced at each other, then back to me.

"Hi," I said, reaching out my hand. "My name is Nora." I shook both of their hands as they nodded. "I'm really sorry about your dress. I'm so clumsy and I didn't want someone to recognize me and blow my disguise. Now I feel ridiculous."

They nodded in unison.

"Here's a bit of money. Maybe you can buy something nice to replace that."

More nods.

"Oh ... my ... gosh!" a voice said behind me. "Nora Maddison? No way!"

I turned. A young wide-eyed girl stood in front of me with one hand over her mouth and the other hand clutching her bright green phone. I smiled and looked around, still a little unsettled with the entire situation.

"Um ... wow ... oh my gosh ... can I get a picture with you?"

I laughed. "What's your name?"

"It's, um, Debbie. I'm just a huge fan. Like really huge."

Others started to notice and double look as they passed. I put my arm around her as she snapped the picture, then five more. She put the phone down and looked at me, searching for something to say.

"I'm no different than you," I said. "I'm just an actress, that's all."

She smiled. "Thank you so much for this. It seriously made my day."

I hugged her and held it for a few seconds.

She walked away as she typed on her phone. I turned back to the couple on the bench, but they were already gone so I walked back home and called Dan, left a voicemail, then reheated some leftover fettuccine while listening to a vinyl record of Jack White's *Lazaretto*. During *Entitlement* my phone rang.

"Sorry," Dan said. "I was meeting with a director. How are you?"

"I'm good." I put my bowl in the sink. "How've you been?"

"Long week. Ready for some good news."

"Well...." I let a few seconds of silence linger.

He laughed.

"Well ... I was wondering if you'd go with me to the premiere for *Yesterday's Dream*."

"Only if it's a date."

"Things are still weird with Sawyer. I don't know."

"The hockey player?" He laughed again. "If he's willing to let you go he's not worth hanging on for. You deserve better. You know that, right?"

"Funny you say that. I was just listening to a Jack White song and at the very end he says we don't deserve a single thing. No one does."

"Yeah, maybe, but do you really want to spend the rest of your life waiting for him to choose you?"

"It's not like that. I think he wants me to choose him."

"Seems like you already have."

"He wants me to give up my career for a simple life." I stepped on my balcony and looked up at the moon. "I'm not sure I can do that."

"Okay, I'll go with you to the premiere. I'd be stupid to decline the offer. Just tell me this ... if you hadn't met Sawyer would you and I be together?"

I blushed and smiled, shaking my head. "I don't play hypothetical."

"That wasn't a no."

"It wasn't."

"Well, miss, have a good night. I'll see you soon. What color dress?"

"Emerald."

THE BRUINS WON THE EASTERN CONFERENCE AND WERE OF-ficially going to the Stanley Cup Finals. Genevieve did my hair and makeup while I watched recaps and interviews on TV. So many interviews with Sawyer. He seemed different, but I couldn't place it.

"How does this look?" Genevieve said. "You like it?"

I glanced at the mirror. "Looks perfect, Genevieve. Thank you."

"You're an easy one to please." She smiled. "Or are you just distracted with someone on that TV?"

"Both." I laughed. "Makeup time? I'm thinking red lipstick as usual. Something natural with the eyes."

She nodded with a bobby pin between her teeth. I turned back to the TV as a reporter asked Sawyer how things were going with his brother.

"I'm here to play hockey. What I do on the ice has nothing to do with my personal life."

"Are you currently dating Nora Maddison?"

He smiled as another player slapped his shoulder, then he looked back to the reporter. "Any questions about hockey?"

"Will you come back next year?"

"No." Confidence oozed from his voice. "I love it here and these guys are great. Coach is the best in the NHL. But I miss my quiet yard."

Camera fizzled out and two guys at a desk popped up, discussing predictions for Stanley Cup winners and making fun of Sawyer. Apparently his answers didn't settle well with them.

I turned the TV off and closed my eyes. Genevieve finished my makeup in silence. She never talked much no matter how much I pried.

"Must be fun doing hair and makeup for a living, huh?" I opened my eyes and admired her work.

She nodded.

"Is there anything else you would do if you could do anything?" I stood from the chair and shook my head a little to make sure the hair stayed in place.

"I love what I do," she said quietly. "But I've always wanted to be a doctor."

"Really? You should do it."

"Oh, it's too late. Too much school."

"Do you ever feel like you're missing out on your dreams?"

"Not at all," she said. "I'm just happy to wake up every day."

"Just to wake up? What about goals and passion and dreams?"

She smiled sweetly. "I have those."

"What are they?"

"My goal right now is to get home in time to make dinner for my boyfriend. My passion ... I guess right now I'd say sewing. Dreams, well they aren't crazy or anything. Right now I dream of learning to bake better." She crossed her arms and smiled. "What about you?"

"No, no. Nothing about me."

"It's okay. I'd love to know."

I looked at the clock. "I better get going. Let's continue this next time."

OUR LIMO DRIVER RAN ABOUT FIVE RED LIGHTS AND SWERVED corners so fast that I nearly fell on top of Dan each time. We laughed, but it was the strangest thing ever. "Say something." I nudged Dan. "Is he drunk?"

He laughed and pulled me into him. "I'll save you."

"Gee, thanks." I smiled, remembering what it felt like to be surrounded by a man. "Oh, thank God we're here."

I searched the red carpet for Spencer, hoping to avoid him. So far so good.

Dan looked at me instead of opening the door, then leaned in closer as though he were going to kiss me. I tilted my head slightly away from him and he took my hand, kissed it, and opened the door. Camera flashes immediately bombarded us. I smiled and pretended to be oh so happy to be there. Really I couldn't wait for it to be over, but I guess I wouldn't be able to avoid Spencer forever.

Dan offered me his arm as we walked the stairs. Fans yelled out to us as we shook a few hands along the way. I glanced ahead and spotted Spencer grinning his way through an interview. He had his arm around a new girl and his agent stood behind him. A few other cast and crew members mingled near the entrance.

Dan and I stopped near a few journalist's and they immediately asked me, "Are the rumors true? Are you and Dan dating?"

I tried to politely decline, but Dan stepped in and said, "I find it an absolute honor to be in this woman's life."

"Are you still friends with Sawyer Reed?" another one said.

I nodded, slightly agitated by Dan's interruption. "I'll always be friends with Sawyer," I said. "At least I hope so."

"What was it like making this movie as a new actress working with big names?" another said.

"It was a wonderful experience. I'm very grateful."

"You seem to have a knack for dating men you work with," another said.

I smiled and nodded as Dan took my hand and led me away. It sickened me when they asked personal questions. Made me more nervous than an audition.

I caught Spencer looking at me. I looked at Dan to avoid his gaze, but I could see his figure moving toward us anyway.

"Great," I said under my breath.

"Watch this," Dan said, then he pressed his hand into my back and pulled me into him. When his lips landed on mine I tried to pull back, but he held the back of my neck so the kiss lasted longer than I would've allowed.

"Looks like you get around," Spencer said as Dan removed his hand from my neck.

I faked a smile and shook Spencer's hand, then walked around him. Dan followed close behind, but I now regretted asking him to come. As soon as we entered the theatre I grabbed his arm and whispered, "What do you think you're doing? This is not the way to make me want to be with you."

"Just trying to make him jealous, that's all. Trying to help."

"This isn't helping. Now Sawyer will never call."

"Give it up, Nora. He's not right for you. He doesn't understand or want this life. I do." He moved as close as possible to my face, then brushed his lips against my ear and whispered, "I want ... you."

Unwanted shivers climbed down my neck and arms. I turned away from him and kept walking, feeling naive and stupid and confused. I glanced at Dan as he walked beside me. He was gorgeous and smart and confident and ... he wanted me. Sawyer was gorgeous and smart, but not confident and he only wanted parts of me. Not all of me.

I watched Dan's feet as we walked into the screening. He touched my back as he held the door for me. It was nice to be fought for, but the magic was missing. The chemistry. I still missed Sawyer.

Dan and I sat down. I leaned over the arm of the chair and whispered, "I can't get over him, but I know I can't be with him."

He kissed my cheek. "Let me help you get over him. It's not fair to him either. To keep going back and forth, getting his hopes up, then choosing this path again. You want to be an actress? So be one. I love that you know what you want and don't settle for anything less." He placed his hand on my knee. "Be yourself."

"Dan, I really like you and all, but what I had with Sawyer was so ... the chemistry was unexplainable."

The lights shut off. He grazed my ear again and said, "Give me a chance to sweep you off your feet. Just one chance. The hockey player will be there if you change your mind."

He offered me his hand. I stared at it for a few seconds, then looked at him. He motioned for me to take it. I waited, looking into his eyes until his charm won me over. I linked my fingers with his. He squeezed tighter and kissed my fingers. I smiled and looked at the screen, wondering why I felt butterflies with every guy who kissed me. Shouldn't those only be reserved for the one? Maybe what I had with Sawyer wasn't so special at all. Maybe I was a sad excuse of a girlfriend. Maybe I was an attention hungry woman who fed off of relationships for some kind of fulfillment and used men to feel less alone.

Maybe ... I really needed a glass of wine. Without delay.

Chapter 25
sawyer

As I knocked on Quin's door I thought about life and how it resembled a ladder. Do you ever feel that way? Like life is one big uphill climb and there are always more people and circumstances tripping us and trying to pull us back down the ladder, while very, very few people ever stop to give us a hand up. "Fend for yourselves," seems more like the motto of the world. Survival of the fittest doesn't exactly leave room for encouragement.

I noticed an envelope taped to the side of Quin's door. My name was written on it. I opened it up and read the short note:

I knew she was going to do it. I didn't stop her. Sometimes being at the bottom of the tree is better. That's what I'm going to do now. Goodbye, Sawyer. I hope you find the right tree to bark up.

Huh? I rubbed my head and reread the note. What? I continued to bang on the door, then called 911. Images of his body surrounded by blood slid through my mind, one after another. Cops arrived within minutes and entered the house. I waited outside to hear the inevitable.

An officer stepped outside. I held my breath and lowered my chin, trying my best to maintain eye contact.

The officer shrugged. "He's not here. We searched everywhere. You sure he—"

"I'm sorry," I said. "Maybe I overreacted. I'm sorry to have wasted your time."

He called the other guys and they were gone within minutes. I sat on the steps and took a deep breath, then hid my face in my hands and shook my head. Did normal people have normal relationships? And if so, what made me so abnormal?

PLAYOFFS STARTED. WE FOUGHT HARD AND WON THE FIRST game. Right before the second game Jones came up to me in the locker room with tears in his eyes.   "Doc said to stay on the bench?" I said as I taped my stick.

He nodded. "I need this, Reed. I need to play."

"Don't make it your life." I tapped my stick on the ground and leaned on it. "Be passionate about it, but don't make it your life."

A few guys walked by and slapped a magazine on my lap, then rubbed my head and kept walking. My blood pressure spiked as I saw the cover. Nora. Completely naked in a provocative pose. Barely any imagination needed.

"Damn," Jones said. "Let me see that."

I slapped his hand away and flipped to the article. Pictures of her and that same dude from before were plastered all over the place. Them kissing at a premiere. Them holding hands in NYC while she wore my freaking scarf as an accessory.

I tried to ignore the images and read the article, skimming over music tastes and personal interests, until I found what I wanted to find. The interviewer asked her about me. Her response, "It just didn't work out." Then she was asked about the other dude, some celebrity guy named Dan. She said, "Yes. We are dating." Then, as my body temperature escalated, I started to read what she loved about him, but gave up a quarter through it and tossed the magazine into the trash.

"Those guys ain't gonna wanna mess with you tonight," Jones said as I slammed my locker.

"I don't play with my anger. I play with my heart."

"Thought you wanted to win this for her?"

"No," I said. "No. Not anymore. I'm winning this for my mother."

I grabbed my stick and headed toward the hall where the rest of the guys were pumping each other up. As I rounded the corner I exhaled, releasing my frustration and replacing it with love. Love for the game, for the guys, for the ice, and most importantly ... for the woman who taught me how to live. I needed to do one thing right before I died. One thing she'd be proud of.

WE WON THE NEXT FEW GAMES AND HAD ONE MORE TO WIN before we were officially the Eastern Conference winners. Practice was longer and harder, but none of us were drained. We were excited. I saw Coach transform a group of strangers with attitudes into a team that genuinely loved each other. Some of the guys even smiled more than when we started. Coach breathed life into them, gave them goals and the hope to attain them. I'd miss it. I'd miss them. But I was ready to win and go home. I was more than ready to go home.

During the last game we almost lost. Came down to the last ten seconds when our left winger swiped the puck and shot it through a small crack between the goalies head and the net, sending us into over time. Within minutes, we were huddled together on the ice claiming our victory as the other team walked back to the bench. Coach watched, calm and pleased, from behind the wall. I nodded to him. He nodded back. And so we were going to play for The Cup.

"For you, Mom," I whispered amidst the cheers. "For you."

DURING THE NATIONAL ANTHEM OF THE BIG GAME THE screen revealed Nora and her boyfriend sitting in the stands. I pretended not to see her and convinced myself to not let my frustration ruin the night. Then the screen showed Quin, sitting in the stands with a serious face. I almost fell over as I tripped up the rest of the anthem, realizing my hands were shaking worse than a cocoon in a thunderstorm.

The referee whistled us to our places. I stood in the center and the game began. Face off was horrible. I lost the puck to my opponent and fell when I turned around, then took forever to get up as I imagined Nora's boyfriend whispering, "What a joke."

By the time I skated across the ice we were already down a point. Coach shot me a look. I ignored him and skated back to the center. This time I lost the puck again, but quickly recovered and retained it, passing it to Lenny, who passed it back to me, then to Perry for the goal. The puck ricocheted off the goal and fumbled back to the ice. He missed. I sped in and whacked it before their goalie had a chance to, but he blocked it and shot it back to his team.

The screen kept showing Nora and it annoyed me that she was there, but what agitated me even more is that she cheered for me and wore my number. While sitting with that jerk. I needed to stop looking at the damn screen.

I couldn't focus. The entire first half was a disaster. Coach reamed us out in the locker room, specifically focusing on my mistakes. I kept my head down until he made me look at him. "Is it the girl?" he said in front of the guys. "You're going to get this far and lose because of an insolent, cold-hearted girl?"

"Don't talk about her like that," I said, head down again.

"Face up, Reed," Coach said. "This"—he pointed around the room at all the young faces—"what you've got here is better than the girl in those stands."

"She's always been and always will be more important to me than…" I looked around, knowing I'd quell their spirits if I said what I really wanted to say. "She'll always be first."

Coach threw his notebook at me and raised his voice. Everyone jumped, including me. "Then get out."

I shook my head. "I'll play better."

"No. You'll leave. Right now." He stood in front of me and yanked my jersey, forcing me to stand. "Get off my team, Reed."

"I said I'll play better."

"Play better next time. For some other team."

"Coach." I glanced at Jones, who just stared at me with unreadable eyes.

"Go." He shoved my back, then turned back to the team. "Morris, you take his place. Now get out there. All of you. And win this thing."

"Coach," I said again, but he was already rounding the corner.

Jones waited for me to say something, but I couldn't. I sat back down, ignoring the earthquake inside of me. He scooted across the bench until his leg touched mine.

"Don't let it be your life," he said. "Be passionate, but don't let it become your life."

"Yeah." My chest throbbed. I looked up at the ceiling and closed my eyes. "I'm sorry, Mom."

I failed at everything. At every single thing I did. And it never changed.

"I'm at the bottom of the ladder," I said to Jones. "Everything and everyone wants me to be at the bottom. Life doesn't let me climb."

He stood and put his hand in front of my face. "You've helped me up, Reed. Now let me help you up."

I stared at his outstretched arm, then gripped his hand and stood. We faced each other for a few silent seconds, then changed our clothes, grabbed our stuff, and walked out, leaving our dreams of the Stanley Cup behind us as we journeyed toward a completely unknown future ahead of us.

I wanted to wake up from the nightmare.

"Wait a second," I said to Jones. "Quin was here. I need to see him before he disappears again."

Jones stopped and turned back toward the locker room. "You want me to go out and look for him?"

I nodded. "Thanks."

He walked toward the bench and came back within a few seconds. "Don't see him there anymore."

"Figures," I said. "Let's go."

Chapter 26

nora

London continued to lecture me about the magazine article I did. And of course the pictures. I curled up on my couch as the air conditioner hummed in the background. Every few seconds I'd take the phone away from my ear, then bring it back. "You gonna do this all day?" I said.

"I can't believe you don't care," she said. "What happened to the Nora I grew up with?"

"I'm still Nora. Do you know how to exaggerate or what?"

"You're not the Nora I know."

"What? Because they convinced me to do that cover picture? I didn't want to, but they kept pushing and pushing. I just felt weird, okay? Like a prude or something."

"Well, prude or not, the entire article and all of the pictures made me lose respect for you. I'm watching my best friend go from a free-spirited beautiful person to a self-absorbed princess who only has time to pamper her own dreams."

"That's not fair, London. What are you talking about?"

"Do you even know what Sawyer did for you? Do you even know how much he loved you and probably still does? And you threw it all away for a life of emptiness with a guy who obviously just wants to have Nora Maddison, the trophy wife." She paused, sucked in air, and breathed her frustration into the phone. "I'm surprised he hasn't proposed yet."

I thought about our date the other night. The random stop in a jewelry store, where he asked my ring size as nonchalantly as possible. I didn't think about it until she said that.

"He didn't propose, right?" she said.

"No."

"Would you marry him if he asked?"

"I don't know. Why are you overreacting? I took a few pictures for a magazine and I'm dating someone who happens to care about me and loves this industry. He understands me. He gets me like Sawyer didn't. He wants me, London. Do you know what it's like to date a bunch of guys all throughout your life and feel like no one ever cared enough to like you—all of you? They all just stopped calling or disappeared. Sawyer included. He may think he loves me or whatever, but he doesn't understand me like Dan does. He didn't care enough to call. What was I supposed to do? Wait around waiting for him to decide that he wanted me?"

"Is Dan brainwashing you? You ever think maybe he's a little biased?"

"Who's side are you on anyway?"

"I'd always choose the doormat's side over the person who walks all over it."

"Please. This is getting ridiculous."

"I love you enough to be honest with you and all I'm saying is I don't see you heading down a good path. Keep going if you want, but it's not going to end up well. You'll lose everything good for you and end up miserable. There's a difference between a man who's okay for you and a man who's actually good for you, really good for you."

I listened to her rant for a few more minutes, then finally told her I needed to go. Dan was picking me up in a few minutes for a quick date before he had to leave for his next film. I still hadn't chosen a new movie to do and kind of needed the break. My personal life was overwhelming me, I guess.

I tried not to think of London's words as I stood in front of the mirror. I checked my reflection. A self-absorbed princess. I didn't feel self-absorbed. I didn't feel beautiful either, but I did still think of myself as free-spirited, fun, and happy. Sad and miserable seemed impossible. I had nothing to be sad about. Confused, sometimes, but sad?

I fixed a few loose strands of hair, then left the mirror, gave Niles a kiss, and walked down to the front of the building. Dan stood outside the doors holding a violet rose. He chose a different color each time we saw each other. I stepped out, smiled at him as camera's flashed around us, and took the rose. We kissed for a few seconds, gave the flashes a good show, then got into the car. The driver accelerated.

"So," I said. "Where are we going tonight?"

"It's a secret."

"Oh, how mysterious of you."

He reached for my hand, then pulled me toward him and kissed me again.

"I love you," he said, centimeters from my lips. "I love everything about you."

"You do?" I teased, avoiding the response he wanted to hear from my lips.

"You're perfect."

"No one's perfect."

"You are." He leaned back and stared into my eyes.

I wanted to tell him I loved him, but it was happening so fast. Everything in my life moved at the speed of light. My heart was dizzy and my mind couldn't keep up. Dan put his arm around me and pulled me into his chest. I thought of Sawyer. That night on the bench. The many late night talks while the city slept. Dan and I didn't talk like that. Not yet at least.

You have to let go of Sawyer, I told myself. *He let you go, now let him go. Move on. Move on. Move on.*

"You okay?" Dan said, kissing my head as the driver parked.

"Just been tired lately." I perked up and looked out the window. "Where are we?"

"It's your favorite bridge." He opened the door and gave me his hand.

"No ... I can't go here right now." I inched back into the car. "I can't."

"Come on, beautiful." He leaned against the doorframe. "I want to show you something."

I slowly moved toward the edge of the seat, looked around, and scooted back inside. "I can't."

"Please," he said.

"No." Tiny needles pricked the backs of my eyes. "Dan, I can't. Seriously."

He sighed and got back into the car. "Okay," he said. "I'll just show you here." He pulled a jewelry box out of his pocket and set it on the seat between us. "I brought you here because I know you have memories of Sawyer here. I know part of you still hopes that maybe he'll come and profess his love to you, but he's not coming back, Nora. He gave you up. And I'm here to tell you that I'll never let you go. For the rest of my life I will love you, every part of you. I'll dream of you at night when I'm sleeping and kiss you first thing when I wake up. You're everything I ever wanted in a woman. You are perfect and I love you. I want to spend the rest of my life with you, but..." He opened the box. "I'm not stupid enough to propose yet."

The diamond earrings sparkled in the black velvet slots. "Dan ... I ...."

"I don't want to rush things." He took the earrings from the box and held my hand. "But I do want you to know that I'm serious. That I love you." He placed the diamonds into my palm. "That I'll be here for you no matter what you choose to do in this life."

"I ... Dan ... I'm sorry." I covered my eyes with my hand and tried to bite back the cry that desperately wanted to escape my lips, but it came anyway. *Everything changed. Everything changed*, I kept telling myself. Why did it happen so fast? Tears covered my hand. Dan wiped the wetness from my face and kissed my forehead.

"Let me love you, Nora."

"I don't know what love is." My hand fell to my lap. The earrings shimmered in the streetlight. "I don't know anything anymore."

"It doesn't have to be painful. Love doesn't have to hurt." He pulled my head into his chest and rubbed my arm. "It doesn't have to be difficult."

This isn't right. That's all I kept saying inside of myself, but I couldn't pry my head from his body. He made it so hard to decline the love he offered. He made everything so easy, yet so complicated. I wanted to run again. As far as possible. But I kissed him back when his lips touched mine and I thought of Sawyer's words. "Just a chess piece getting moved around by others."

I stared at the diamonds. "Dan ... I don't think this...."

"Shhh..." He kissed my cheek. "Love never gives up."

I attempted to smile.

"That's my girl," he said, kissing the corner of my mouth. "Let me see that gorgeous smile of yours."

I laughed. "Oh, stop."

"There you go." He kissed me, passionately, while holding my hands in his lap. "I'm gonna make you the happiest woman alive."

IT DIDN'T TAKE LONG FOR THE TABLOIDS TO GO CRAZY. eople were speculating the wedding date and saying I was pregnant. Photoshopped pictures of me with a larger stomach were all over the internet. Maury yelled at me, telling me I needed to focus on my career and stop being such a target for the media, and London and Mom left about a thousand voicemails on my phone. Or at least it seemed like it.

Thankfully Dan went to Europe for his film. I needed the space. I needed to take the darn earrings out of my ears, leave them on my nightstand, and call Sawyer. One last time.

I waited until midnight, for the sake of old times, put on a vinyl of Passenger, got comfortable on the couch, and swayed back and forth as I called him.

"We're sorry, but this number has been disconnected and is no longer in service...."

I double-checked and dialed again. Same message.

I texted London. *You awake?*

She responded a few minutes later. Unfortunately, yes. Huge case I'm working on. You finally decided to call me back?

Do you have Sawyer's new number or his email?

Oh no ... not this again Nora. You're engaged!

I'm not engaged. I need to talk to him one last time. I need to make sure....

Make sure what? You made your choice a long time ago. He'd be stupid to take you back now.

Thanks Lon... great friend you are. Way to make me feel like crap.

You dug this grave, not me.

Dan loves me!!! He loves me!

You keep saying that, but do you love him?

I stared at the text, started typing, erased, typed again, the finally said, *Love confuses me now. I don't know anymore. I don't believe in soul-mates anymore,*

London. Neither should you. Look at Sense and Sensibility. Ella always talks about this. You could say Willoughby was her soul-mate, but it didn't happen and she ended up with the guy that cared for her the most. I always hated that ending. I did. But here I am and I get it now. I see the romance in letting someone in when they love you, whether you feel all oogly googly over them or not. I'm happy Sawyer and I had our time together, but it's over now. He changed his number, he probably hates me.

He doesn't hate you.

How do you know? Are you guys buddies now?

I'm not texting about this. Call me tomorrow, if your princess self has time.

You are so rude right now. What happened to MY friend, London? The one who didn't believe in soul-mates either?

Call me.

I tossed my phone to the other side of the couch. Niles rustled beside me. I pulled him toward my chest and nuzzled into his neck. "What am I gonna do, boy?" I whispered to him. "I don't want to be self-absorbed." I replayed recent memories, the last two years, my experience in the industry and everything going uphill so fast. I was trying my hardest to stay normal. I really was. "Am I different now?" I said to Niles. "Am I worse?"

He whimpered and curled up beside me again. I stared into space as *Golden Leaves* by Passenger made me think of Sawyer. Not my media-designated fiancé. *What's left to do when we've lost all hope and what's left to break when our hearts are broken?* The lyrics spilled out of Michael David Rosenberg as though he were channeling them from my own heart. I listened as I stared at the ceiling, wondering how to make sense of a life that no longer made sense. An hour passed, the record ended, and as though it were timed perfectly … my phone rang.

Chapter 27

sawyer

I don't know why I dialed her number. London convinced me that it would be different this time, but I had my doubts. Merry-Go-Round Nora wasn't my favorite ride and after everything with The Bruins and Quin, I just wanted to be left alone to my quiet life at home, but I couldn't leave myself alone when I knew she called. I tried to stop myself for an hour or so, but I needed to hear what she wanted to say.

It was 1:09 a.m. when I called and I didn't expect her to pick up.

"You there?" I said when the phone stopped ringing.

She sniffed. "You called."

"I did."

"Sawyer, I'm sorry. I'm so, so sorry." She sobbed so bad I could barely understand her words. "I'm sorry for everything. I hate this. I'm so confused."

I listened, longing to hold her and tell her it was okay, to forgive her and kiss her and feel her back against my hands. To make her mine. But I knew better. She flip-flopped all the time, so I kept my heart calm and waited.

She cried a little, then continued, "I can't stop thinking about you."

Man, I missed her voice. Not a day passed when I didn't think of her. "You're in what appears to be a serious relationship with another man."

Silence answered back, followed by a few soft cries and crackling sounds.

"Do you love him?" I said, hoping she'd say what I wanted to hear. Hoping she'd leave him and tell me she was mine.

"I don't know," she said.

"Your dad talked to me at the hospital. He made it seem like you have issues with commitment. Later London told me you've never been without someone for long. Always short relationships, one guy to the next. I'll bet my entire savings that you'll be with another guy within a few months. Why are you doing it, Nora?"

"Is that how you see me?"

"Yes, because that's how you are." I shook my head as though she could see me. "At least right now."

"I called to give you one more chance, but here we go arguing again. You know what Dan told me? He said love doesn't have to be painful. He promised to make me happy."

"Then marry him already." I stood and paced the floor. "What the hell are you waiting for?"

"Goodbye, Sawyer."

"Thanks for the mature response."

"Why is every conversation about how much I need to improve? You have issues too."

"I'm working on them."

"I'm hanging up now."

"Okay."

"Okay," she whispered.

"Okay," I said again, waiting for her to hang up, but she never did. I listened to her breathe like old times. Twenty minutes later I whispered her name a few times, but she didn't respond. So … I unloaded. "Nora, I do love you. You may not think my love is like Dan's and London told me all about that 'fight for me' nonsense. I am fighting though. I lost my dream of winning the Stanley because I couldn't stand seeing you with that guy and Coach saw how distracted I was. I guess he wanted to make a point and show the guys how serious the game was and I get that, but I lost it all in an instant. A year of hard work. Gone. Just like that. I'm losing you now because I love you too much to see you change for the worse. I've seen this industry turn people into demons. It scares me. I can't be involved with it and I can't watch someone I love become ruined with my support. I will always love you. And the second you show up at my door, I'm yours. Goodnight, sweet girl."

I waited, listening to the humming of a fan in her room mixed with her breathing. A few minutes later, my eyes fought for sleep, so I hung up the phone and thought of Quin. We always had our problems, but money and fame changed him within the blink of an eye. I love the arts, don't get me wrong, but so few people have their heads on straight enough to maintain a truly down-to-earth attitude in any Hollywood-soaked industry. My brother wasn't one of them and I saw it chew him from the outside in. He always wanted more and better and obviously married someone with the same values—or lack there of. It's not that I hated movies and thought acting was wrong, I just hated what it became for some people and I didn't see Nora as someone strong enough to keep her head above water.

But I did love her, okay? I don't care what anyone says, I loved her.

A FEW WEEKS TRICKLED BY IN MY SIMPLE LITTLE LIFE. I cleaned up the yard, picked some fresh grown cucumbers and heirloom tomatoes, swam laps in the pond, and got my business in full swing again.

I thought of Nora constantly. When I went to the grocery store I swore I heard her laugh. In Friday's rush hour traffic I flicked on the local college radio station and heard Jack White, obviously thought of her singing along on the phone. Couples smiling at each other while stopped at red lights reminded me of our long talk in my car before everything started to fall apart. Everything reminded me of her. Constantly. But what really got me was the couple at Starbucks. Both had rings on their left hand ring fingers. She was obviously pregnant and pissed off. They weren't smiling at each other, that's for sure. I pretended not to listen, but they were right behind me and even their whispers were clear to me.

"I do so much for you," the man said. "Go to work so you can spend it all on clothes and shoes, the dishes, taking care of Carter when I get home. How can you say I don't fight for you?"

"You don't get it," she said. "What happened to the romantic man I married?"

"Life isn't all roses, darling." Ouch. Wrong words buddy.

"I don't want roses, Adam. I want you to desire me again. Is that so much to ask? Two kids later and video games are more fascinating than your wife."

"Why can't you play them with me instead of complaining all the time?"

"Why can't you treat me like your wife instead of treating me like one of your little friends?"

"First time we've had a babysitter in months and this is how you want to spend it?"

"I just want you to fight a little, I guess." She sighed deeply. "Whatever, Adam. I'll take your scraps."

"This Hollywood idea of romance has you all messed up, Jane." He scooted his chair back so hard it screeched. "I provide for you. Isn't that appreciated? Isn't it romantic when I go out of my way to bring a dozen roses home from work?"

"I told you I don't want roses." She stood, bumping my chair with hers. "I want my husband to choose me. Simple, Adam. Not extravagant. I want to feel loved again."

"What about how I want to feel?"

She walked toward the doors and outside. He tossed their trash in the cans and followed. I watched as they walked to the car in silence. I knew that silence. Yet not long ago I knew another kind of silence. A natural, comfortable silence where she breathed into the phone and I listened.

We became a bickering married couple. Unhappy and focused on our own wants and needs, without sacrificing for the other. What kind of love was that?

I didn't want to be that.

I threw my cup away and got into my car. I looked at the clock. Still had fifteen minutes until I was supposed to meet with Chris.

Surprisingly, he hadn't proposed to his woman yet, but when he finally asked me to help him look for a ring I wasn't the least bit shocked.

We met at a local jewelry store and I pretended to like stuff he picked out, but none of it caught my eye. Too gaudy and common. Too heavy for Nora's small hands.

"Don't tell me you're thinking about her again," Chris said as a clerk handed him a ring.

"I did for a second."

"Dude, you're just as bad as she is."

I tapped the glass. "I know."

"You need to give Melody a chance. She's a good woman. Mature, nice, hot." He handed the ring to the girl behind the desk and pointed to another one. "Could I see that one, please?"

She pulled it out of the display and handed it to him. He slipped it on his pinky, cocked his head, then gave it back to the girl. "Could you try this on for me?" he said to her. "I need to see it on a woman's hand."

She did as he said, then looked at me. "Are you Sawyer Reed?"

I nodded, wishing she hadn't asked.

"You were talking about Nora Maddison?" She seemed unaffected by the fame factor. "I'm sorry if I'm saying too much, but I'm with Chris. She's not wife material."

"Yeah." I appreciated her honesty. "Just hard to tell your heart to stop beating."

"That's the one," Chris said. "I'll take it."

"You sure?" the girl said.

"Absolutely. She'll love it. She's a size 6." He twirled the ring in his fingers again. "What's the next step?"

"Let me get the papers and see if we have a size 6 around." She disappeared into the back.

Chris turned to me. "I'm asking her on Saturday. Nothing big. Just waiting for the right time."

"I'm happy for you, man."

His eyes brightened while he looked at the ring. "You know you're my best man, right?"

I nodded. "And you're mine."

"If you ever get married."

"Thanks, Chris."

He shrugged. "Melody will be the maid-of-honor, I bet."

"Give the Melody thing a break already."

"Only letting y—"

"I'm going to be with Nora." I stood and shoved my hands into my pockets. "I don't care what she does for a living anymore."

"You sure about this? I mean—"

"I've been thinking about it the last few days. I'm sure."

175

"You're going to propose?"

"No. Just going to tell her how I feel."

"But she's with that other guy."

"She doesn't love him."

"Then why'd she date him?"

"Fear."

"Of what?"

"Saying no."

THE REST OF THE DAY TICKED BY SO SLOW I WONDERED IF MY clocks were broken. I tried not to think about what I'd say when I called her. Wanted it to be real, not rehearsed, but either way I felt about as nervous as a guy proposing. In a sense, I was.

And I also feared the life I tried my best to avoid, but as the great Wayne Gretzky said, "You miss 100% of the shots you don't take." I walked outside to the pond and imagined the ice. I didn't play hockey like I played life. Hockey was easy because I didn't fear physical pain or losing games. Life, on the other hand, hurts worse when it hurts. And you fail harder when you fail. I thought of Jack White's song Would You Fight for My Love? and let the lyrics skate through my mind.

I checked the time on my phone and decided I didn't want to wait until midnight. I wanted to hear her voice now. I needed her and yes, I wanted to fight for her love. "Mom," I said as the phone rang. "This is the one thing I won't fail. I'm gonna do anything for her. I promise."

"Sawyer?" So good to hear her voice again.

"Don't sound so surprised." I smiled, my stomach jam-packed with excitement.

"No ... it's just that ... I mean...."

"I know. I didn't want to wait until midnight though."

"Okay...."

"I need to talk to you."

"I did it because you said I wouldn't. You have no right to be upset. This is the life we've both chosen."

"What are you talking about?" My smile vanished. "You did what?"

"Don't pretend you don't know." She sounded tired. "I don't—"

"Please tell me you did not marry that guy." I paced along the pond, in a much different way than I did the first time we talked.

"You don't know?"

"Dammit, Nora." I kicked dirt into the pond. "Are you crazy?"

"What? What was I supposed to do?"

I inhaled, wondering if it were possible to breathe enough oxygen to calm myself down. I pumped my fist and squeezed the phone.

"I gotta go, Sawyer," she whispered. "He doesn't want me to talk to you anymore."

"I can't...." I yanked on my hair to ease the tension in my chest.

"It's too late." She sniffed. "Please try to forget me."

"Never." I raised my voice. "Do you hear me? I'll never forget you."

"Goodbye, Sawyer."

"I love you," I said. "I'm in love with you, Nora, and I don't mean as friends."

But she was already gone. I sunk to the ground and held my chest. Gretzky wagged his tail and huddled up to me. I looked up as a ton of balloons floated toward the clouds. A cemetery sat adjacent to my land and over the last few years I noticed a trend with people releasing balloons for funerals. Always reminded me of Mom. Those nights as kids when we camped outside at night after Dad died. Mom helped us write letters to him and we sent them into the sky inside balloons. She said he'd get them and I never believed it, but there was something liberating about it. Like releasing the cap of a shaken soda can and getting out whatever is begging to come out.

The balloons calmed me down a little as they disappeared into crumbs and I decided to write Mom a letter. Didn't have a balloon, but the letter would be fine.

I went back inside and sat down at my kitchen table with a pen and spiral notebook. Gretzky warmed my feet as I dated the letter and stared at the paper. "Mom," I said. "I'm not giving up this time."

I addressed the letter to someone else instead.

My Nora,

I'm not the best with love letters, poems or songs. Don't mind my grammer and spelling, but for me this is about so much more than eloquint words and perfectly placed periods and commas. You've already shown me that you can look beneath flaws and imperfections to see the goodness in me so hopefully you can in my meezly attempt at a love letter.

I guess you're married now...and I won't be sending this anytime soon but I will be saving it because I believe one day you will be mine. Everything goes wrong for me and it seems like it always has, everything gets messed up and here I am feeling alone at the bottom. For a little it felt nice to have someone sit at the bottom of the tree with me.... I worry that everything is going well for you and maybe you believe you're at the top but I know your right here with me at the bottom. I don't think we'll ever get to the top without each other. I need you....

I know your the one thing in my life that has been right. I'm not saying perfect because I know we have our issues, you and me both, but it's right even when it's wrong. I can't explain it....

I'm starting to see that there are some things in life I can control and others I can't. Those things I can't control like death and random bad circumstanses, I just need to learn to handle better instead of avoiding but I see now that what we had is lost not because of you. Just me. It's all me and I'm sorry. I know I say sorry a lot but I mean it.

One day even if it's when we are 90 I hope we will talk again. Like we used to. Till then I'll wait for you. I didn't die for you when I had the chance, so I'm doing it now.

Till we meet again,
That hockey player

Chapter 28

nora

London and I set the boxes down in the living room. She panted and leaned on her knees. "As much money as the two of you have combined, can you please explain why you didn't hire someone to move this stuff for you?" she said as she stood back up. "I mean, Dan is like Brad Pitt level celebrity and you're climbing up quick."

"I don't want to be like that." I noticed a vase of daisies on the dining room table and read the note. "I don't need servants, no matter how much money I have."

"And what exactly do you consider your personal hair stylist?" She walked over to me and held the note up. "My darling Nora, thinking of you every second of the day." She set it back into the flowers. "How cute. When's he gonna propose? Or is moving in with him enough?"

I tried to smile.

London slapped her hips. "Okay. What's next?"

"You don't have to be so cheery, you know. It's obvious that you're pretending."

"Me?" She pressed her hand against her chest. "Hey, I'm not hiding the fact that I think you missed out on a good guy, but maybe this is better for you. Not to mention ... now that Sawyer is single...."

"Don't even think about it."

She laughed. "I wouldn't do that, but a guy like that won't be single forever."

"I just want him to be happy."

"Are you?"

"I have nothing to complain about."

She nodded and walked back to the living room, pivoted in a circle, and moved closer to the fireplace mantle.

"I'll be redecorating a bit," I said. "He's letting me do whatever I want."

She picked up a photo on the mantle and held it close. "Who's this?"

"His ex-girlfriend. They are still really good friends, like brother and sister."

"She lived here too?" She put the picture down and looked at the next one. "Did they have sex?"

I shrugged.

"I'm going to assume so, and if that's the case … you're okay with her pictures hanging around?"

I ignored her and walked outside to get the last box from the porch. I brought it inside and set it down with the rest. "Let's get this stuff unpacked."

"You're ignoring my question."

I nodded. "Dan loves me. He's romantic and charming. I trust him."

She crossed her arms and stood in front of me, trying to examine the feelings behind my eyes, but she wouldn't see them. I put on a mask the day Dan asked me to move in and now I needed to play the part. All throughout my life people told me I lived too much from my heart, not my mind. Well, here I was, trying to be mature, trying to do what I *thought* was best, instead of what I *felt* was best. Trying to let go of the Hollywood romance for the realistic one. Dan was good for me. He was a good partner in a business I was still learning so much about.

As London and I unpacked, my body wanted to give up. I fought with my lungs, trying to give them oxygen, but it didn't seem like enough. I leaned into the wall and inhaled as much as possible.

London put her hand on my back and moved my hair from my face. "You need to take a break?"

I shook my head and inhaled again. "I feel really tired."

"You don't look so good." She placed the back of her hand against my forehead. "Are you okay?"

"I've felt tired lately, irritable, but I don't think I'm sick." I tried to walk away from the wall, but everything started to spin and the sudden urge to throw up tightened my stomach. "Maybe I am."

"When's the last time you went to the doctor, Nora? I'm worried about you."

"It's nothing, Mom." I fell into the couch. "Maybe I need a nap."

She pressed her index fingers into her lips, like a steeple. "Take a nap. I'll put some of your clothes away while you rest. Let me know if you need anything."

"Thanks." My eyes were already heavy. "Wake me up in an hour."

I FELT A MILLION TIMES WORSE WHEN I WOKE UP AND LONDON insisted that I go to the ER. I called Dan and left a message on his phone. He probably wouldn't get it for a few hours since he was across the globe. Took a while to get back to a room and when they finally ran the tests I started to feel a little better. "See," I said to London. "I was probably just tired from lack of sleep."

"Hope so," she said as someone walked in.

We both turned as the nurse or doctor, couldn't tell, looked over a few papers and said, "Looks like your kidney's are having some trouble, Ms. Maddison. We need to get you into the hospital for further evaluation."

"What do you mean?" I said. "Are they failing?"

"Your doctor is going to have to make the ultimate call, but I'd say you are either going to need dialysis or a transplant. I'm sure they prepared you for this when you were released from the hospital."

I nodded. "I'd like to go back to the hospital I was at."

About two hours later I was hooked up to machines again and staring at the ceiling. London called my parents, although I asked her not to. "It's not a big deal," I kept saying, hoping it were true, but a few hours later Dr. Rutherford confirmed that I'd definitely need a kidney transplant as soon as possible.

"You have significantly reduced urine output again," he explained. "Your blood pressure is also quite elevated. You've got a low glomerular filtration rate and a slight case of proteinuria, which is what we are concerned about as it's most likely heading toward End Stage Renal Disease. Seems progressive right now and although dialysis may hold you over for a bit, I think we're going to need a transplant sooner than later to err on the safe side."

"So, what do I do now?"

"We're running a dialysis here in a few minutes and we'll keep you monitored. I think you should stay here for a few days, but after that you are free to leave and come back for dialysis treatments until we find you a donor."

"How long will that take?"

"It depends. You are considered a priority right now, but you've got type O blood and it's most difficult to find a donor for this. Do you know what type of blood your boyfriend has? Perhaps he would be willing to donate. It's always best to find someone you know. Quicker that way." He pat my knee and smiled. "It'll be okay. We'll get you taken care of."

I nodded as he exited and spoke with a nurse in the hall.

"I'll be right back," London said. "Gotta go to the bathroom."

I listened to my heart rate and watched the green lines on the monitor. Back again, I thought, trying not to complain. Dan was probably enjoying some European beach with his costars. I wondered when he'd call me back and if he would be able to come and see me before I had surgery. Probably not. I wouldn't even ask him about the blood type thing. It would only make him feel bad that he couldn't do it.

A nurse walked in and checked the machines, then began to speak to me as she did something to my arm. I nodded, but I was already somewhere else. On a beach with Dan where everything was golden and warm.

Chapter 29
s a w y e r

London explained everything and I didn't think twice. I jumped on a plane to New York and met with Dr. Rutherford.

"Are you sure?" he asked for the seventh time.

"I wanted to do this before so it didn't come to this, so yes, let's do it," I said. "Just do it now before she even leaves the hospital."

"And this is anonymous, correct?"

"Yes, please. I'm not sure how much her husband would appreciate it and I really don't want the world to know."

"Husband?" He coughed.

I nodded. "Yes…."

"Okay." A weak smile turned up one side of his face. He furrowed his brow, then explained to me the next steps. I called Chris and told him I'd have surgery tomorrow. He was bringing Leslie as soon as possible and I couldn't had been more thankful for him. Where Quin and I lacked true brotherhood, Chris more than made up for it, proving to me that blood didn't matter as much as faithfulness.

I met with the anesthesiologist and a nurse practitioner in the hospital's PREP center. They gave me detailed information on how to prepare for surgery tomorrow. No food or drinks after midnight. I had some lab work done again and they explained the recovery process. A social worker also met with me for a half hour to talk about the emotional aspect, which didn't concern me.

That night, I tried to sleep in a nearby hotel, but couldn't. Kept imagining her in the hospital and wishing I were by her side, but she had Dan now. I'm sure he was holding her hand and kissing her eyelids while she slept, enjoying the prize he won. It irritated me so much I wanted to walk in there and physically remove him from her life, but I never forced her in the past and definitely didn't want to now. She'd come back to me if she wanted. At least I'd get to be a part of her now. Really be a part of her every day of her life with my own flesh and blood working together with hers.

He couldn't say that.

An image of their bodies joining in the shadows taunted me, so I turned on the TV. My hands shook and my veins throbbed. I paced the room a few times, took a steaming hot shower, and tried to sleep again.

Thoughts continued distracting me until finally my brain gave up and surrendered to sleep. A few hours later, I woke up and went back to the hospital. Once I got settled in the pre-op room, I wondered if anyone would do the same thing for me if I needed a kidney. Parents were gone. Brother disappeared, sold his house, and hadn't contacted me again since the last time I saw him. Chris … Chris was probably the only real family I had.

The idea of Melody was starting to sound more appealing by the minute.

A patient escort wheeled me out of the pre-op room, down a hall, through some doors, then down a stark white hall with bright windows. I focused on the tiles in the ceiling, trying to dispel any feelings of nervousness. Something creepy about an operating room. They wheeled me inside and I saw the surgical instruments on the table across the room, where several scrubbed people hovered and handed each other things. The anesthesiologist quickly showed up and stuck me with a needle to start the IV, then asked me to count backwards from 50. When I got to 47 the ceiling tiles blurred a little. And then a little more.

43 and … a black room. That's the last thing I remember.

Chapter 30
nora

Dr. Rutherford told me they found a living donor who matched all of my criteria, so we scheduled it and before I had time to think I was lying down in a pre-op room with London holding my hand. My parents hadn't even gotten there yet. Those are the moments where being a celebrity made no difference. I was a normal person, in a difficult situation, experiencing normal people things. Something about it humbled me and made me realize that no matter how big we get on the outside, we're always small inside. I was a girl in need of a kidney to survive and I wanted my parents and my best friend to hold my hand through it all. It felt good to remember how small I was.

We still hadn't heard from Dan, so I gave him one more call before it was time to go into the operating room. Surprisingly, he picked up and I explained what was going on and asked if he could come out to see me.

"I'm sorry, Nora. You know I gotta stay and finish this up," he said. "But I'm there with you in spirit. Always, okay?"

"Yeah." A single tear fell. "Okay."

"Don't be upset. I would be there if I could, it's just the nature of this business."

"I know. It's not your fault." I wondered if he'd show up if it were my last few days on earth.

"I love you, Nora." He whispered to someone in the background. "I gotta go. Director's calling me. Be safe and call me when you're in recovery."

"I will." I hung up with him and looked at London, who pretended not to notice the awkward stifled conversation I just had with ... my boyfriend. Still weird to say that.

"You okay?" London said, putting her phone down to make eye contact with me.

"I'm fine. Can't wait till all of this is behind me."

"Me too." She exhaled. "Been an intense ride. Your life is truly like a movie."

"Hopefully it has a happy ending."

"Well, depends what you consider happy. Romeo and Juliet seemed to have a happy ending to some people, although that's not exactly my ideal fairy tale ending."

I laughed. "Me neither."

"What's yours?"

I thought for a few minutes, but she interrupted me. "Remember what you said before?" She paused. "I want to be a great actress. I want to win a Golden Globe. And I want to fall in love. True love. Love that never dies. I want to find someone who still holds my hand when we are 90 years old, not out of obligation, but because he wants to." She paused again. "Still feel that way?"

"I don't care about acting anymore. Or awards. I've already fallen in love and it will never die, so I don't know. What's my ideal happy ending? Probably to get to my last moment on earth and know that I truly lived."

"Wow."

"What?"

"Different for you."

"Yeah, life happens."

A nurse came in and asked me to remove my clothing and put on a fancy hospital gown. London stood to leave, but I held her arm and made her sit back down. The nurse left as I changed, then came back in and started an IV in my arm and explained to me the precautions and side effects that could occur. I signed a few papers and smiled at London every few minutes, thankful that she was with me. "Not exactly Paris, huh?" I said to her.

She squeezed my hand and leaned down to hug me. "I'll be waiting."

The nurse wheeled me through an extremely bright hallway with white walls all around. She talked the entire time about apple pies and random weird things. I guess she was trying to comfort me, but something about it made me more skittish. Once we entered the operating room, I realized I hadn't breathed for a few seconds and took a deep breath. The only other time I had been in an operating room was when I was knocked out and completely unaware of it. This wasn't enjoyable, I can tell you that. They helped me onto the table and I rested my head on the pillow. As the anesthesiologist explained what he was doing I pretended to listen, but all I could think about was the tube that was about to be down my throat and the ventilator next to me that was going to keep me alive. Everything creeped me out and I couldn't wait to be asleep. A few minutes later, the world grew hazy and I blacked out.

I WOKE UP IN MY RECOVERY ROOM WHILE A NURSE CHECKED on me. She spoke softly and kindly, but I was still too groggy to understand what she said, so I nodded and looked around for my parents or London, but instead I saw Sawyer sitting next to me. My eyes were still heavy and I faded in and out of sleep, wondering if I was dreaming about him beside me and hoping I wouldn't wake up. If I could hold on to him for a few more minutes….

"I could die like this," I said to him.

"You have a lot of life ahead of you," he said. "You're not going to die."

"I mean with you."

Then I blacked out again and entered a crazy dream about roller coasters and *The Nutcracker*, when I awoke he was gone and London was sitting by my bed reading a book.

"Rise and shine," she said. "You've been in and out for the last half hour. Finally up for good now?"

"I had the weirdest dreams."

"Like what this time?"

"I dreamt Sawyer was sitting in here, not you. Then I dreamt I was on a roller coaster that shot up toward the stars and suddenly I fell back down and was performing in *The Nutcracker*."

She laughed. "Well, part of it was true at least."

"Sawyer was here?" My throat hurt from the ventilator tube. "Are there ice chips around?"

"Hit that button and the nurse will answer."

"Sawyer really was here?"

Her eyes closed as she nodded her head.

"Why do you seem upset about it?"

"No reason." She handed me the remote to call the nurse. "Here."

"What time is it?"

"Around 10p.m."

I almost pressed the button for the nurse, but she walked in.

"Just need to check your bladder," she whispered. "Do you need anything?"

"Maybe some ice chips."

"Sure. You'll have IV fluids for a while, until you are able to receive food and regular fluids. I'll be coming in throughout the night to check your bladder and drain the urine. We want to measure and evaluate it to make sure the new kidney is functioning as it should." She checked my blood pressure, then continued, "You'll also be receiving anti-rejection medications, which we'll be monitoring as well. Take it easy tonight and we'll talk more in the morning." She checked a few more things, drained my urine, took a blood sample, and asked, "What was it you wanted again?"

"Just ice chips."

"Any movies or anything? I can bring you the list."

I looked at London. She shrugged.

"No, thanks," I said. "The ice will be great, thanks." I turned back to London once the nurse left. "So, why was Sawyer here?"

"He cares about you, Nora. Why else would he be here?"

"Don't be so snappy."

"Just feel bad for him."

"Yeah," I said, pressing the button to make my bed a tilt up. "Me too."

Chapter 31

sawyer

The morning after my surgery I woke up feeling disoriented as hell. They made me walk around the night before, only hours after my surgery. Don't know why, but that really exhausted me. I slept like a baby all night and woke up, rubbing my eyes as London, Chris, and Leslie talked at a small table across the room. I kept my eyes closed and listened to their conversation.

"I don't know," London said. "She acts happy and Dan does a lot of sweet things for her. It's hard to tell."

"Why would she marry him if she loved Sawyer?" Leslie asked.

"Because she wants attention and Sawyer wasn't giving her what she wanted," Chris chimed in. I tried not to laugh. Typical Chris.

"She didn't marry him, guys," London said. "Sawyer called while Dan was with her and he asked Nora to get him to go away for good. She felt pressured, so she just said whatever he told her to say. She moved in with him, but that's it."

Silence. My heart may had stopped beating for a few seconds, then filled with more life than it had when it stopped.

"I just think Dan says and does all the right things," London continued. "And she felt like it was the right thing to do. Sawyer wasn't budging. He wanted something from her she couldn't give, so she confided in Dan and he sort of filled a void she had, I guess." She sighed. "Nora's always dated a lot of people. She's kind of sporadic and I'm surprised she actually committed to moving in with someone, honestly."

"I think she did it just to piss Sawyer off," Chris said.

"No," London said. "She wouldn't do that to him."

"My ass she wouldn't."

"Chris!" Leslie said. "Be nice. Sheesh."

"She did it"—I coughed—"because he's *People* magazines sexiest man alive and I'm just a washed up hockey player who slept with his brothers wife and then paralyzed him."

Everyone turned. I smiled. London and Leslie tried to smile back, but Chris refused. I turned my face from them and moved my legs off the side of the bed. London rushed to my side and put her arm around my back.

"How do you feel?" she said, helping me stand.

"Is Nora recovering well?" I took a step toward the bathroom, thankful to be catheter-free. London didn't respond. I turned back to Leslie and Chris. Their sad eyes belonged in a chick flick or something. "What?" I said. "Why's everyone staring at me like that?"

"Why'd you do it, Sawyer?" Chris walked toward me with droopy shoulders. "I'm tired of seeing my best friend like this."

Leslie stayed at the table and London scooted toward Chris, as though she were taking sides.

"You're practically her sister," I said to London. "How can you not support me? She could die without this surgery."

"It's not that. It's just…" She rubbed her hands together and shifted her balance to one leg. "I love Nora a lot, but she makes decisions and changes them in an instant. I worry she'll never grow up. Most of the time she is more concerned with what people will think instead of following her heart." She wiped a tear from her nose. "It's hard seeing your best friend ruin her life and not taking advice to make it better. She's gotta make her own mistakes." She glanced at Chris through wet lashes. "I know how it feels to be the one who is stuck watching your best friend go down the tubes knowing your words have no meaning in her life."

"I'll win her back," I said. "You don't understand what we have."

"Sawyer." London dried her cheek with her sleeve. "In the beginning I was so cautious about you. Nora always said I was love's greatest cynic, but I guess when you've been alone for as long as I have and hurt by the one man you did actually let in, you can get a little skeptical about all this romance stuff. But … seeing this … you … the way you love has changed me. I believe in love now because I've seen it up close and personal." She wiped her cheek again. "I just wish Nora loved you as much as you love her, that's all."

"I know her," I said. "You might know the way she thinks or feels, but I know the way her soul experiences life. I know because I'm the other half of her. Incomplete without her and one day she'll realize it and come back." I looked at all of them, welling up with an urge to make them all leave. *Since when does a person need to defend love?* "You don't have to believe me."

Chris shook his head. "This is getting old, man. Since when is loving some girl worth your own demise?"

I slammed the rail of the bed, looked at Chris, then Leslie, and back to Chris. "If you don't know"—I looked back to Leslie—"then you haven't truly loved."

"Whatever, man."

"No." My hands shook as I shoved my finger in his face, then lowered it. "Sorry." I looked down. "No. I'm not actually. For once I'm not sorry. I'm sick of this. If you love somebody you'll jump in front of a moving train to save their life and everyone will call you a hero. But here I am ... giving her everything I've got even if it breaks me and all you people think is that I'm some kind of victim. I'm jumping in front of the damn train though, whether anyone likes it or not. What kind of pathetic love only dies physically for the one it loves? That's easy." I walked toward the bathroom. "A victim is a person who unwillingly suffers. I'm choosing to do whatever it takes and I'm not a victim. Stop pitying me."

I closed the bathroom door louder than I needed to and stared in the mirror for a few seconds, washed my face with freezing cold water, then leaned against the wall, thinking.

Maybe they irritated me so much because I needed their support. Someone's support. Even just one person, a stranger. Because somewhere under my heart's determination, my mind wanted to give up and run off like my brother.

I thought of Bruce Wayne in *The Dark Knight Rises*. When all hope was lost and he was at the bottom, the only way out was to push through the pain and fight for it. Maybe it was love for his people that fostered his determination. Or maybe it was his anger toward Bane. Either way, he needed that one person at the bottom, that one person to say, "Get up. You can do this." Otherwise, who knows ... he could've rotted at the bottom without ever finding the will to try.

I pictured Mom's smile at the bottom of the tree as I swung my legs around the first branch. "You can do it," she said. "Now try the next branch."

Shaking, I reached above me and gripped the calloused wood. My feet refused to move.

"Falling might hurt for a few minutes, but giving up will hurt for a lifetime," she said. "Come on, son. Fear giving up more than you fear falling. You can do this."

I smiled inside as I pictured Mom's glassy eyes from my perch at the top of the tree. She waved and beamed and I've never felt that way since.

I looked back in the bathroom mirror and saw that same boy in my eyes. She believed in me and if she were still alive she'd tell me to climb. She was, after all those years in Stony Hill Cemetery, still the most alive person I knew.

"You can do this," I whispered to myself. "Because giving up hurts worse than failing."

Chapter 32

n o r a

I don't know why I always insisted on reading rumors about myself, but this time it started with people saying nasty things to me on my Twitter and Facebook accounts. It got so bad that I needed to delete them from my phone and iPad so I didn't get tempted to see what people were saying. I was trying to figure out what they were going on about by typing my name into Google, but Dan called and asked me why Sawyer was visiting me at the hospital.

"He's not," I said. "How are you? How's the movie coming along?"

"Don't play games. I've seen pictures of him coming in the same day you were admitted and leaving in different clothes a different day. Everyone's talking about it. I'm not stupid."

"Is this what everyone is going on about? Don't tell me you believe the rumors. I don't know if he's here or not. I haven't seen him. My parents are here and London. That's it."

"You know I'd be there if I could. I'm not some loser who has nothing better to do."

"I know you would, Dan. I never said anything about that."

"If I find out you've been seeing him I'll make sure you both regret it."

"What?" My palms heated up within seconds. "Are you threatening me? What kind of trust is that?"

"I didn't mean it like that. Calm down. I love you, that's all."

"You threatened me, Dan. Love doesn't threaten. Love let's go even when it hurts, if that's what the other person wants."

"Are you telling me you want me to let go?" He grunted like an odd animal. "That's not in my nature. When I win a prize I don't lose it."

"Dan. You're freaking out over nothing. You remember all those nice talks we used to have? Gone. Now all you can talk about is how much you don't trust me and Sawyer, Sawyer, Sawyer." I inhaled and exhaled loud enough for it to sound like wind in the phone. "I let him go, okay? I let him go. I. Let. Him. Go."

"Have you?"

"Have you let go of your ex who is still sitting on our fireplace at our home?"

"She's one of my best friends, Nora. Like a sister to me. You can't pull that card."

"I can pull whatever card I want to. You convince me to move in with you, then run off to Europe to do a film while I move my stuff into a house I've never seen before with pictures of some girl still hanging up all over the place. This is so messed up. And here I am, trying to make the best of my mistakes and you're treating me like I'm some kind of slut. I don't cheat on people. I never have. I never will. That," I said sternly, "is against my nature. No matter how unhappy I could possibly be in a relationship, faithfulness overrides it all."

"Are you saying you're unhappy? That I'm a mistake?"

"I'm saying this is all confusing to me and you're not doing a very good job at making me feel welcome in my decisions. You talk about all this love, love, love, but I don't see it."

"I'm sorry," he whispered. "You're right. I'm sorry."

"Okay."

"Do you love me?"

"Sure."

"Say it."

"I ... love you, Dan."

"I love you, Nora. I'll be home as soon as I can. Take down whichever pictures you want to take down."

"No."

"What?"

"That's your job if you want to do it." I thought of Sawyer. "I'm not forcing you to do anything."

"Fine. I'll do it when I get home. To our home. I love you."

We hung up and I refused to look at London. I could imagine her perplexed and intrigued gaze waiting for me to explain myself, so I closed my eyes and hoped she'd respect the silence I wanted to entertain.

"Nora, you have to be kidding me." Short-lived silence.

I exhaled as a nurse walked in. Perfect timing. She checked my vitals and all that fun stuff, made sure I was producing good urine. I looked at her when she checked the bag.

"Looks good," she said. "Better than most cases I've seen."

I nodded. "Thank you."

"Do you need anything?"

"No, thanks. I'll let you know."

She tapped a few keys on the computer by my bed, then walked out.

London, of course, didn't waste time. "That conversation was … interesting."

"Can we please talk about something else?" I shifted in my bed, then pushed the button to move the bed into a better sitting position. "Please."

"Well, gee, let me think. The weather? Or TV? Which superficial topic would you enjoy most?"

I rubbed my face. "London."

"Why are you staying with him? It's obvious you don't really want to be with him, Nora. Maybe he's a nice guy … on the surface, I guess, but is he the man you want to be married to? Is this how you want to spend the rest of your life?"

"Two problems. One, Sawyer doesn't want to be with me anymore. I've ruined it. Two, I don't want to deal with the media's stupidity if I leave Dan right now. He's so loved by everyone. Not to mention the lovely fact that everyone thinks I'm unfaithful and crazy. What would I prove if I left him? Apparently there's rumors of Sawyer being here at the hospital and me having an affair while recovering from surgery. I can only imagine the stuff that will be said if I leave Dan. He's been a loved celebrity for the last decade. I'm the new girl everyone wants to hate. It'll be the end of me."

"I don't know, Nora. This sounds awful and if I were you I wouldn't care what those people say."

"Easy for you to say." I sighed. "Dan is wonderful. He does everything for me and he is really, really sweet."

"Sweet?"

"Most of the time."

"It's so fake." She stood and paced beside my bed. "You want to know something?"

She stopped beside me and put her hands on the rail. "When Sawyer called you that last time … he was going to tell you he didn't care what you did for a living, he wanted to be with you and fight for your love." She tapped the rail. "But you said you were married."

I looked at the moving images on the TV screen, but they looked like blurry strokes of chalk in the rain. My eyes stung and I tried my hardest to keep the dam from erupting, but a few drops escaped and before I knew it I was shaking on the bed. London leaned in, wrapped her arms around me, and said nothing. She didn't need to. What could she say?

She could say that, but she didn't need to. I already knew. And she knew I knew.

I soaked her shoulder with my tears, then pulled back and dried my face with the sheets. My lungs wanted to give up and my heart was pounding so fast I didn't think my body could keep up. I shook my head, dried new tears, and stared at London.

"He gave you his kidney," she said, holding my hand. "He told me that if he couldn't be with you that he wanted to at least be part of you and be able to die with you. He had planned to give it to you since the first hospitalization, but since you didn't need it at the time they waited. I called him when you came in here again and he was here within hours."

I shook my head. "Please, stop."

She nodded as a tear, then another, traveled down her own face and landed in the wetness my own tears left on her sweater. "I believe in love now," she said.

I covered my mouth to hide the trembling.

She squeezed my hand, then stood and walked to the door. "He's right down the hall, in case you're wondering."

She left the room and the warm tan walls darkened as the sun hid behind the clouds. My chest jerked, trying to shove more pain out of my body in heaves and tears, but I inhaled as much as I could, exhaled, and closed my eyes to keep it inside. Lips pursed tight, I willed my eyes to stay dry. I thought of happy times, but every one involved his face. So I opened my eyes, but they were wet as can be. I almost closed them again, but his clouded face stared at me from the open doorway and I couldn't look away.

He stepped forward and became a fuzzy puddle of color. I tried to shake the tears away. All of it away. But I messed up. I messed up so bad and I didn't deserve anything he did for me. I didn't deserve to see him, standing there in a blurry heap of color, with glistening streaks on his own face.

I didn't deserve love.

Chapter 33

s a w y e r

Her shoulders drooped as her body crumpled into itself on the bed. I stepped forward. She held up her hand like a stop sign and sobbed into the other. I took another step as my own eyes betrayed me. Seeing her in pain was so much worse than any pain I experienced.

"London said you wanted to see me," I whispered. "I asked the nurses for some privacy." I closed the door. "What happened?"

The stop sign fell to her lap. She clasped both hands together and stared up at me, chin down and covered with tears. I took another step and held my hands up as though I were approaching someone with a gun. She looked down and rubbed her fingers, sniffing away the last of her cries. My breathing couldn't figure out if it wanted to be deep and slow or fast and sporadic. I wanted to hold her as my body filled with this unexplainable warmth at the sight of her, but I feared what she'd say if I tried. So I took another step as a sudden pang shot through my side where her new kidney used to live. I flinched and held the edge of her bed. She reached over and heated my arm with her gentle touch. I stared at her fingers, long and beautiful, traveling to her soft hands and olive-toned arms. I let my eyes follow the path to her shoulder, then her collarbone as it rose and fell above her chest. I started to follow the path downward toward the curves hidden by white sheets, but went up instead. To her quivering chin and bottom lip as it parted from the other. She caught me staring at her lips and drew them into her mouth, then released them. My body, if it was in pain, couldn't feel it anymore. I pressed my thumb into her cheek and smeared the tear between my skin and hers. Our eyes met and a sudden dose of electricity shot through my veins. Her golden eyes were shaded by the storm inside of her. She was at the bottom. I knew the feeling. She needed someone to believe in her, but all I could think about was her lips luring me in every second.

I looked down. Her hand was now on mine. Without thought, my body fell toward hers. I put one arm over her head and touched my lips to her temple. My shirt hung from my chest and draped over her face. I could feel her quick, short breaths through the fabric as she tilted her chin up.

She's with someone else, I said inside. *This isn't right.*

But wrong as it was, it felt right. Every fiber of my being felt right as my lips moved down her cheek and to her lips. I waited there to see if she'd stop me, but ... before I could stop myself my lips were one with hers, tasting her tears as she tasted mine.

She pulled back and shook her head. "I'm…" she whispered. "I believe in faithfulness … I believed."

I leaned my face into my arm above her head and whispered, "I'm not sorry."

She grabbed my shoulders and pulled me into her. We stayed like that for a few minutes until she serenely pushed my body from hers and gazed so far into my eyes I thought she'd get stuck in there. I wished she would.

"I'm sorry, Sawyer. I don't deserve your love or"—she broke eye contact—"even Dan's. As if I wasn't already horrible enough, I just did the one thing I swore I'd never do." She covered her eyes for a second, then peered up at me. "I'm a cheater now. The world was right all along."

"No." I stood. "It's my fault. I shouldn't ha—"

"I kissed you back." She took my hand. "And I wanted to."

"We belong together," I pleaded. "Whatever I did, I'm sorry. Leave him. Please, just leave and come back to me. I'll fight every day for the rest of my life."

She let go of my hand. "Sawyer … I…."

"We belong together."

She held the stop sign back up. "You're making this so hard."

"It's hard because you're telling the one person you are meant to be with, the one who makes you complete, to go away. I'm not making it hard. It just is."

"I need to tell Dan what happened. If he leaves me, that's his choice, but I can't start a war. Not right now."

"It doesn't have to be a war."

She closed her eyes. "You need to leave before I kiss you again."

"Kinda hard to leave knowing that." I smiled for the first time in weeks.

"Sawyer." She held back a laugh. "You need to go now."

I nodded, looking down. "Okay," I said. "If that's what you want."

"You'll always be with me." She touched her chest near her ribs. "You're more of a part of me than anyone else."

"She told you?"

She nodded. "Thank you."

"I'd give you the other one too."

"I hope you find someone who deserves you, Sawyer."

"I'm not looking for that. No one deserves anything. I'm just looking for someone who is willing to forgive me and someone I can't help but forgive."

Someone tapped the doorframe. London forced a smile. "Can I come in?"

"I'm heading out." I hugged her on my way to the hall, then turned back and waved to Nora. She looked down and leaned back into the bed. I managed to walk away as a nurse walked in, then immediately saw her parents walking up the hall. Mrs. Maddison's eyes were glassy. She stopped in front of me and opened her arms for a hug. I walked into her embrace and pat her back.

"She'll be okay," I said.

She pulled back and shook my chin. "It's not her I'm worried about."

I shrugged. Mr. Maddison reached out his hand and I shook it. He pulled me into a quick hug and said, "Thank you for taking care of my little girl, son." He pulled his wife into him. "If you ever need anything, let us know."

I nodded, thanked them, and kept walking.

"Son."

I turned back to Mr. Maddison.

"Hey, let me give you a lift to the airport."

"Oh, I'm fine. Really. I was just getting a cab. I'm not leaving the state until I know she's okay."

He caught up with me. "I'll walk you outside." We walked in silence until we reached the sidewalk. "How do you feel?" he said, stuffing his hands into his pockets.

"I've got some good pain meds. I'll be fine. Some hockey injuries hurt worse."

"No, son. I mean, how do you feel?" He looked around, as uncomfortable with the situation as me. "I know your parents died a long time ago and London told us about your brother. I know they can't be replaced, but I mean it when I call you son."

I opened my mouth to speak, but had nothing.

He squeezed my shoulder, tapped my chest, nodded, and walked back inside, leaving me alone in the thick summer air. But I didn't feel alone this time. He gave me the best gift I'd received in a long time. Something normal people took for granted. He gave me the gift of family. Of feeling, even for just a few minutes, like I had a father to lean on during one of the roughest times of my life.

I wondered if I'd ever call him Dad.

A taxi pulled up and splashed my pants with nasty gutter water. I shook it off and opened the door.

"Wait!" London grabbed my arm as she panted for air. "Can we talk?"

I looked at the car, then back to her. "Where?"

"Hey, buddy," the driver said. "Coming or what?"

I waved him off and shut the door. London stared up at me, rubbed the side of her neck, and cleared her throat. "Sawyer, I know this is crazy, but after everything I just need to be honest. These last few months I've tried to fight this, but seeing you there, the way you left her room ... I want you to be happy."

"I'll be fine," I said. "I'm not going to pretend to be happy, but I'll be fine."

"No." She rubbed her neck again, looking at her feet. "What I'm trying to say is...."

"I understand, really."

"Sawyer ... I think I love you." The corners of her mouth twitched as the words repeated in my mind. She rocked on her heels and tilted her head back, then looked at me again. Her eyes were bright and hopeful and

I hated to be the one to dash those dreams.

"You don't love me," I said. "You love the way I love Nora, but you don't actually love me." Her eyes glazed over. I touched her cheek. "London, you're gorgeous and smart and loyal. Someone will steal you away from this world and make you feel the way I feel when I look at the woman I love, but that man isn't me."

She ran her hand through her hair and let it fall over her eyes. I moved it and put it behind her ear. "I'm your brother. I'm here for you, okay? But my heart belongs to her."

She smiled and nodded. "I don't know what came over me."

"People do their best to not let passion begin. It's dead before it has a chance to start."

"Hey, that's...."

"Jack White. You're being passionate. It's good. I admire that. It's just misplaced, that's all."

"You're a good man, Sawyer." A fool"—she laughed—"but a good man."

"Yeah, enough of that." I hailed another cab. "Get back in there and take care of my girl. She needs you."

GRETZKY WAS HAPPY TO SEE ME, WAGGING HIS TAIL AND rubbing against my leg as I skimmed through the mail. Nothing worth opening except one large envelope near the bottom. From Quin. I tore the edge off and pulled out an 8x10 photo of the tree we climbed as kids. Little Quin waved from the top, hanging off like a pirate on a ship. I turned the picture over. A small note said: *I'm done. Your turn. -Q*

I flipped the envelope back over. No return address.

I set the picture on the dining room table and smiled. His bottom was my top, and my bottom was his top. I hoped by "done" he meant that he was going to let himself fall to the bottom and finally be content with losing sometimes. For me, I needed to be okay with winning. And for once I wanted something enough to win it.

I would stop at nothing to get her back.

Chapter 34

nora

I was finally released to go back home, to Dan's home that I was supposed to call our home, but truthfully it felt like his home. London, Mom, and Dad helped me get settled inside and I noticed Dad looking at those pictures on the mantle. It always bothered me when he made those inquisitive faces, but never asked the question behind his eyes. *Just ask already*, I wanted to say, but he never did. Mom would ask privately later. That's her way.

"That Sawyer sure is a sweet boy," Mom said, rubbing lemon juice into my bleeding heart.

I shot a glance toward London, who told me in the hospital that she professed her love to Sawyer, only to be turned down because he loved me. You'd think maybe I'd be upset about that, but what right did I have really? She explained that maybe it was misplaced passion or something, that she loved the way he loved me, the dedication he had to making it right, and wanted that for herself.

Flowers sat on the dining room table again. I picked up the note to make sure it was from Dan, then set it back into the flowers. Dad brought the last of my bags inside and Mom busied herself in the kitchen with London, banging pots and talking about how enormous the house was and wondering why single people needed so many unused rooms. Famous or not, I wondered the same.

Dad put his arm around me. "You hanging in there?"

I sighed. "I guess."

"Been a tough year."

"Kinda." I smelled the flowers. "But a lot of people wouldn't understand that. I've released two movies, made more money than I can handle, dated some of the world's most coveted men, and survived a crazy infection thanks to a man who loves me more than I love him." I looked back to Dad. "Some people would be annoyed if I complained about a tough year."

"They probably would," he said. "But I knew as soon as you started this acting thing that you wouldn't have an easy life. Money and fame don't make life easy. If it did you wouldn't see so may celebrities committing suicide or dying from drug overdoses. You're in this world now and you need to learn to play well if you want to survive." He pat my head as though I were five. "You'll figure it out."

"I'm not so sure I want to stay here, Dad," I said. "Every decision I make is plastered in papers and online. I miss privacy. I miss going to a restaurant through the front doors and eating peacefully without random people snapping pictures with their phones. I miss dating a guy, breaking up, and not being called a whore because of it. I miss truth and honesty and being myself without worrying about what some stupid article is going to say about me." I picked a petal from the flowers. "Sawyer was right."

"Hate to say this … but you asked for it."

"I know, I know. The inevitable 'I told you so' is dying to come out of your mouth."

He laughed, then pressed his hands into my cheeks. "You are my daughter. I want the best for you and I want you to listen to what I'm about to tell you." He dropped his hands and I gave him my full attention. "Sometimes the best for you is the most painful thing in the world. Sometimes it's not. Sometimes it's both at the same time." He lowered his chin and leaned his face toward mine. "Do you understand what I'm saying?" I nodded and he continued, "I don't care if you win awards. I don't care who you date or marry. I don't care if you have kids or not and I don't care how you raise them. The only thing I care about is that you figure out who you are and everything you do from now on comes from your own desires." He shook his head. "I don't mean to be careless or selfish. I mean, do your research, take your time, figure things out, and make decisions that you feel good about. If everyone else thinks you've made the wrong decisions, don't defend yourself, don't feel sorry for yourself. Why would you?"

I nodded and wrapped my arms around his neck. "Thanks, Dad."

His palm held the back of my head. "If you want to ride a bike and everyone thinks it's too dangerous, get yourself on that bike. And if you fall … get back up and don't give up." He pulled away and smiled. "You'll be okay. I know you will."

Mom and London stared at us from the other side of the table.

"Good advice, Dad." London smiled. "So, Nora … does this mean you're getting a divorce?" She winked.

I inhaled and held my breath, shaking my head.

AFTER EVERYONE LEFT, I SET MY RECORD PLAYER'S NEEDLE over a beautiful vinyl of The Beatles and sat down with water and strawberries. Niles begged to come on the couch with me, so I pulled him up and let him relax by my feet. I allowed my mind to rest too. Didn't think of one important thing at all. Just sat there and listened to the guitars and drums and lyrics. After *Don't Let Me Down*, I looked through my box of records and found John Lennon *Instant Karma*. I put it on and bobbed my head as it started.

Niles stared at me, perched on the couch, his tail wagging as I started twirling around the living room. The lyrics resonated with me so much more than ever before, like they were made for me. *Laughing in the face of love. What on earth are you trying to do? It's up to you, yeah you.* I continued dancing around the living room, regardless of my pain from the surgery, using my empty wine glass as a microphone as I leaned over Niles and sang to him. *Better get yourself together darlin'.* He cocked his head as I spun back around and sang my heart out with a huge smile on my face. *Who in the hell do you think you are? A super star? Well, right you are.* Tears dropped from my lashes, landing in my smile. *We all shine on, like the moon and the stars and the sun. Yeah, we all shine on.…*

I spent the next hour singing my lungs to sleep by belting out fun songs from the 60's and by the end of it when I finished the Grass Roots *Let's Live for Today* I wanted to do just that. I wanted to live for today … or whatever was left of it. I picked up my phone and checked the time. 11:54p.m, which meant 4:54p.m. where Dan was working on his movie.

I dialed his number and waited for the voicemail, but instead the phone crackled and rustled, then went silent. I hung up, waited a few seconds, then stared at Sawyer's number instead.

My phone rang. Dan.

"Hey," I said.

"Beautiful," he said. "How are you? Everything okay? It's late here. Or early. Dark."

"Dan." I bit my lip, then took a big long breath. "Dan, I have something to tell you."

Silence responded.

"Are you still there?"

"I'm here." He paused. "Go on."

"You were right about me."

"You saw him?"

"He kissed me."

"And you told him to leave? That you're done?"

"I let him kiss me, Dan."

He grunted and coughed. "That's okay. It won't happen again."

"Dan."

"I'll be home soon. I know you're just lonely. I promise, we'll get through this." He coughed again. "Listen, I need to get some rest. Let's talk tomorrow. And not about this, okay? It's in the past, just take his number out of your phone. Don't talk to him anymore. Don't let your friends tell him what you're doing. We'll get through it."

"Dan...."

"Tomorrow. We'll talk more. I love you."

We hung up quickly and I brought Sawyer's number back up on my phone.

Judge me all you want, but I didn't delete it.

I called it. And I didn't think twice.

Chapter 35

sawyer

Some people listen to happy music when they're feeling down. According to them, it cheers them up and lifts them out of the funk. Unfortunately, that's not the case for people like me. See, people like me need to dwell in the emotion, whatever it is. Positive, negative, doesn't matter what it is ... I need to dwell in it. I need to feel it. So I put on the record I bought when I got home and listened to Rufus Wainwright sing one of my favorite songs. *Hallelujah.* Maybe it's inspirational to you like it is to Chris, but for me ... it's deep and moving in an emotional way that suits me when I'm feeling like crap.

The song played and ended, then I repeated it. Poor Gretzky probably thought his best friend lost his mind. I stared at him as the song continued and I wondered if my determination would win the day this time. The needle got to the end of the record again and I let it sizzle and pop for a few seconds, then my phone rang.

I glanced at the clock. Midnight.

Her name lit the screen, then it went black. I shot off the couch and ran to my room for the charger, but it wasn't in its usual spot. I checked my computer for the USB charger. Nothing. Finally I ran outside and found the charger on the passenger's seat of my car, conveniently locked with the keys inside. Why did I have to be so stupid?

I glanced at the keys, then to my house. A hanger would work, but what would be the point in all that? I stepped back and lunged into the window with my elbow, shattering the glass into the seat and my arm. I unlocked the door, grabbed my keys, and realized it was the wrong phone charger. It was my old one with the broken wire.

Great. I yanked it up and walked to my house, chucking the broken charger in the trash on my way inside. Gretzky did his business in the yard, then followed me. I closed the door and threw my phone on the couch, then sat beside it, wishing I had a house phone. Then I remembered that I left the charger in the shop. I started to get up, but sat back down and rubbed Gretzky's head. "You know what, boy?" I said to him. "Maybe this was for the best." He put his chin on my lap. "Maybe a phone call would make it too easy."

I convinced the other half of me to stay on the couch and leave the charger in the shop, at least for tonight. Hearing her voice was worth the broken window, but I didn't want another ticket on the merry-go-round. *She'll come to me*, I thought. *If she wants to, she'll come.*

ABOUT A WEEK PASSED AND I DIDN'T HEAR A THING FROM her. I considered calling, but didn't. She never even left a message, so my mind couldn't stop reeling on the reason for her call. Was she lonely or did she miss me? Because there is a difference.

I worked in the shop, catching up on work I missed while playing for Boston. As I finished another stick I thought of Coach J. Nora was worth it, but I still didn't forgive him for what he did. Yeah, she distracted me, but I could've helped them win that last game. Instead, they lost. Maybe he hoped his decision would show everyone how to take it seriously and motivate them to play hard, but I watched the recaps of the game and it was obvious that they all felt defeated before they lost.   I wondered if Coach even cared about their crushed dreams or if he was too preoccupied with his own to tell.

Gretzky barked. I jumped and saw Chris in the doorway. He didn't budge. Gretzky continued barking until I shut him up by releasing him into the grass. Chris kept his arms crossed and his head low.

"Something happen, man?" I said, wiping my hands on my jeans.

He tightened his arms and shook his head.

"Leslie?" I walked back to the stick I finished and set it aside. Chris stayed in the doorway, still shaking his head at the floor. I took a few steps toward him and waited for him to talk.

He reached into his pocket and tossed a coin to the floor. It clinked and rattled, then stopped at my shoe. The diamond lit up. "What happened?" I picked up the ring I saw him buy a few weeks ago. The one she showed off on Facebook with a big grin on her face. Chris sunk his hands into his pockets and leaned into the wall. I set the ring on my workbench and leaned back next to him. "You guys were doing so good."

He moved away from me and still refused to look at my face. I clapped my hands together and whistled. "Wanna get coffee?" I tried. "Starbucks?"

"Sawyer this, Sawyer that," he said. "What the hell is so special about you?"

I squinted and rubbed my hands together. "Nothing?"

"You're a freaking hockey player who always fails, a man who hasn't been laid since he screwed his brother's wife, and you sit here alone in this house with a Maltese of all freaking breeds because you let the perfect girl date some fancy pants just because you didn't like her job." He took a breath and kicked the ground. "But everybody loves you. Every damn person I talk to. Do they ever ask how I'm doing? No. No, they ask how Sawyer is doing. I'm so sick of your name."

"What the hell, Chris?"

"She gave me the..." he pointed to the ring. "She didn't even have the balls to tell me in person."

"Women typically don't have those." I closed my eyes. "Sorry. Why'd she end it?"

He reached into his pocket again and shoved a letter into my chest. I opened and read.

Chris,

I'm so sorry that I have to write this letter, but I've been thinking about what Sawyer said in the hospital and it just keeps coming back. It's not that I want you to be miserable because of me, but ... I've been wondering about it and I feel like your response to him was like a big red flag for me. I want someone who understands why what he's doing is romantic and I feel like you don't get it. You just think he's crazy, but what if one day ten years from now when messes pile up and bills aren't paid ... what if that craziness is something we lack? I'm sorry, Chris. I love you and our time together was fun, but I want someone a little crazy. I guess that's what I'm saying.

I'm sorry,
Leslie

I folded it back up and looked at Chris, but he was already gone. I walked out and saw his car, then spotted him on the ground by the pond.

I went back in and grabbed my phone, then dialed Melody's number. She picked up and I immediately got to the point. "Hey, sorry to call like this, but I need Leslie's number."

"I don't know if I should do that." She paused. "She was pretty adamant about her decision."

"Give me the number," I said.

She didn't respond.

"I guess I could show up at her job and make a scene."

"Okay, okay, but only in return for a kiss."

"I need it now."

"I can come over now."

I imagined some random paparazzi catching the entire thing and making Nora stay with cool guy Dan, then I saw Chris out there skipping rocks on my pond. He was here. Nora wasn't. "Fine," I said.

"And be my boyfriend?"

Okay, that's taking it too far. "Uh ... what?"

She laughed. "I'm kidding, Sawyer. Is this your cell?"

I could breathe again. "Yes."

"I'll text it when we hang up." She laughed again. "Hope it works out."

We hung up and as soon as the number came through I called. She didn't pick up, so I called again. And again. And six more times. Finally she answered.

"Leslie, it's Sawyer," I said. "Don't hang up."

But she already did.

I called again, but her phone was off. I almost left to find her, but she called back.

"Sorry," she said. "I'm driving and lost signal. Look, Sawyer, I think you got the wrong impression."

"I don't think so." I paced through the shop and knocked over a few sticks. Picking them up, I kept going, "I read the letter and I can see your feelings clear as day, but I need to tell you how I feel."

"Sawyer, I know how it seems, but I'm not madly in love with you or anything."

I laughed. "What?"

"I know it's shocking, but not everyone wants Sawyer Reed."

"How flattering," I said, laughing, "but that's not what I meant."

"Oh. Well ... now I feel stupid."

"Don't we all." I tripped over a wire, then decided to sit down. "My best friend is sitting by my pond right now and he looks a lot like Eeyore. Your ring is sitting on my work bench right now looking pretty confused. Look, I know what I said didn't make the most sense to Chris and maybe that worried you. But he's a simple guy. Best guy I've ever known. He'd do anything for you in the drop of a hat. He's just that kinda guy. Willing to play in the shadows when he's the one who really deserves the spotlight. He's a good guy, Leslie. And he loves you."

"But—"

"Don't get into that crazy talk. He is crazy for you. No need for castles and carriages. You may think what I'm doing is romantic, but it's been a living hell."

"Still, though."

"I've got Eeyore here. And a ring. I'm going in my house and hoping you show up soon. If not, then you're not crazy enough for the kind of love you think you want."

I hung up before she had a chance to respond, then yelled out to Chris, "Hey, man. I'm hopping in the shower."

He didn't seem to hear me, but I know he did. I took a longer than usual shower with Gretzky sleeping on the pile of clothes beside the tub. I hoped Leslie would come back. From what I saw they were great for each other and her reasons for leaving weren't even based off of a real point I was trying to make. She completely misconstrued what I was saying.

I finished the shower and got dressed, then checked out the window. Her car was here. Good. I looked around and finally saw their silhouette against the water. Hugging. Good.

If only my own problems were that easy to fix.

Chapter 36
n o r a

It's hard to think when your heart is preoccupied with something. There was an emptiness I felt for the last few days. Like now. I stared at the ceiling from my bed. The slightest hint of hope resided somewhere inside of me, but it was shrouded by this feeling that no matter what I did, no matter which choices I made, some kind of calamity would strike. Something would go wrong.

I got dressed in disguise and went to Central Park to watch random people enjoy their lives. Or not enjoy them, depending on the person. With each passing stranger I sunk into the bench more and more. What had I done with my life? Even the movies I made weren't incredible pieces of art. They were simple romances with maybe a tiny bit of depth. I thought I was living from a place of passion, but now I wasn't so sure I knew what real passion was. That Sawyer made me question so many things about myself that never crossed my mind before. I was still trying to figure out if that was a good thing or not.

I pulled a pocket-sized notebook from my purse and a pen. Starting at the beginning, I wrote down notes about my relationships up until now. Whatever came to mind first.

Boy from picture – idealistic romance, Gavin and Ella-ish, emotional, unbelievable, fairy tale

Peter – 3rd grade crush, didn't know I existed. Wrote letters to him and buried them in my backyard when he moved away that summer. Nothing ever happened after that, but it sticks with me for some reason...

Jayden - 7th grade. Most popular kid. Finally wanted to date me. Got my first kiss out of me and broke up with me for a cheerleader who was prettier. Retreated into acting and didn't date for a while. Don't even remember having any crushes until....

Greyson - 11th grade. High school sweetheart. Perfect until he cheated when he went away to college. Came back and ended up in a class with me at my college. Fell in love again, he was sad and needed someone when his sister died. I was there. I thought we'd get married, but he moved away again. I waited a few years for him and continued pursuing acting to focus on something. He never came back and it was hard to get over him, but I did... somehow....

Spencer - first guy I dated since Greyson. Surreal type of gorgeous face and body... and fun. Helped me with my first film experience. Made kissing scenes real and honest. Made my heart skip. Everything felt like a dream, a good one. Then saw him kissing another girl on set at his trailer. Decided not to date him, but agent said it would be good exposure. I didn't want to date him, but I didn't want to mess up my career. So if he called, I answered. If he kissed, I kissed. Yadda Yadda ... ended up cheating on me with said agent. All done. No tears. Just done.

Sawyer - not my typical type of guy. I like

blondes. He isn't. I like outgoing ... He's kind of a hermit. So on and so on. Something drew me to him though. And I gave him my number. Didn't expect the recluse to call, but then I never wanted him to stop. We had so much in common it's kinda scary. But then we hit the things we didn't have in common and he couldn't let it go. He wanted me to change, but not himself. Maybe I was selfish and I see that now ... But he was too, right? There's no ending yet. I hope there never is. I still love him.

Dan - just like Spencer he said and did all the right things. Unlike Spencer, he was smart and made me think. He hugged me when Sawyer hurt me and kissed me when I felt alone. I guess I just fell into his trap without realizing it. Haven't caught him cheating that I know of, but I'm suspicious. He has trust issues and I'm beginning to wonder if it's because he knows he's not trustworthy. I could be reading into things, but London's right whether I want to admit it or not. She thinks I've jumped from guy to guy throughout my life, with no breaks, but that's not true. It's just that acting became "my guy" when there was no guy there to hold. What she is right about though ... is Dan. I don't not love him, but I'm not sad when he's gone. I just think of Sawyer. Always.

I reread the list a few times and saw a few patterns. I pulled out my trusty iPad and googled a few things, then finally came up with a conclusion.

None of those guys were ever the problem. The problem was me.

And I was done being the problem.

LONDON COULDN'T HELP BECAUSE OF AN IMPORTANT CASE at work and I didn't trust anyone else, so I packed up whatever fit into my car and showed up at Ella's house. When I pulled up I noticed quite a few cars outside and decided to call instead of surprising her, but she didn't pick up. I turned the car off and walked up to the door. Lots of movement inside. I knocked. No one answered. Louder. No one answered. I turned the knob and peeked inside.

"Nora!" Ella ran over to me with a baby wrapped to her chest. "What a lovely surprise!"

The room silenced and everyone stared at me. I waved awkwardly and hugged Ella, then Gavin as he came up to me. Ella turned so I could see the baby's face. "This is Gavin Junior," she said.

"Not my idea." Gavin laughed. "How've you been?"

I looked at everyone sitting on the couches, still staring at me. "I'm good," I said without thinking. "Actually, no. I'm not good, but I'm okay." I smiled at Heidi and Patrick across the room. "I'm ready to make some changes and part of it is to make time for new friends."

Ella smiled and a little one tugged on her shirt. "Mama." She lifted her hands up.

"Love," Ella said to Gavin. "Could you pick her up? She's probably tired."

"Wow," I said. "Is this Adelaide? She's gotten so big since last year."

"Yeah," Gavin said, lifting her into his arms. "And now we have another one on the way."

"What?" I looked to Ella. "You guys are pregnant again already?"

They nodded.

"Wow. Congratulations you two." I glanced at the others in the room. "Sarah." I walked over to her. She stood and hugged me. "I'm so sorry I missed your wedding. I was filming at the time ... or maybe in the hospital. I can't remember."

The man beside her pulled her into himself and shook my hand. "I'm

Vasili." He held her hand and looked into her eyes. They seemed lost in each other for a few seconds, then he turned back to me. "It's nice to finally meet you."

"Yeah, I'm so sorry. I wish I had met you sooner. How was the wedding?"

Sarah grinned. "It was perfect. Simple and beautiful. Nothing too fancy." She looked gorgeous, even amidst the burn scars from her accident. And she looked happy. Really happy. "And," she said, patting her stomach, "we're expecting a little one this winter."

"That's so wonderful." I gave her another hug. "Wow. Everyone's moving on with weddings and babies so fast." I moved on to Heidi and Patrick. "Don't tell me you guys are pregnant too?"

Heidi tried to smile. "Not yet."

"We're trying," Pat said. "Haven't been so lucky."

"Oh, guys. I'm sorry."

"It'll happen if and when it's supposed to."

Heidi nodded.

"Where's Matt and Lydia?" I said. Ella looked down. So did everyone else. I didn't know them well at all, but suddenly found myself concerned. "Everything okay?"

"How are things with you?" Sarah said. "Movies good? I heard you were nominated for an award. And you're married now?"

"I'm hoping I'm not actually married because I have no recollection of it and I'm not the type to get drunk and forget things."

"What?" Ella said. "Didn't you want to marry Stan?"

"It's Dan." I sighed, sitting down. "I'm sorry I haven't been in touch."

Ella sat beside me and put her arm around me. She could win an award for compassion and love. I leaned my head on her shoulder and stared at the baby. "I don't want to ruin your party," I said. "I didn't realize ... I thought I'd surprise you and I really didn't want to come here all bummed out tonight."

"Don't worry about it," she said. "It wasn't really a party. Just a little get together. I'll go get your room set up so you can stay a few days."

"Thanks, Ella."

She disappeared up the steps with the baby and Gavin followed with

Adelaide. Heidi stood and touched Pat's arm, then nodded to the door. "We should get going," he said, then hugged Vasili and Sarah, but not me. Heidi waited at the door with her daughter. I kissed Pat once before they were officially together and it meant nothing. His heart was always set on her, but she never liked me. At least it felt that way.

I walked to the door and hugged her anyway, but she pulled away fast and walked out the door. Pat quickly followed, nodding my way as he left. Maybe she believed I was a cheater like the rest of the world.

I closed the door and sat back down across from Vasili and Sarah.

"So what's your next movie?" Sarah asked.

"Oh, um...." I shifted my position and looked down. "I don't know if I'm going to keep doing this."

"Really?" Vasili said, exuding peace like no one I'd ever known. "Why not?"

"I'm kinda processing it all still. One thing is for sure though ... I'm not staying with Dan."

"I understand," Sarah said. "I was engaged before Vasili to a guy I felt obligated to marry. He was really nice on the surface, but I think everyone closest to me knew I wasn't happy. I guess I just wanted to save him from his depression, but it was killing me. I wasn't strong enough to be a savior or a martyr and it was painful to realize that. I had to come to a place where I realized how weak I was. How much I needed love too. I was being emptied and never filled up. People don't realize it, but selflessness can kill you in all the wrong ways if you're doing it for validation and not out of your own strength of love. I didn't have that strength so all of my so-called altruism was ruining me. But ... then, in my weakness, I found something amazing. The love Vasili and I had from the start was so real and honest and I think the best part about it is that it's the one romantic relationship I've had that has challenged me and he helps me become a better person." She stopped suddenly and looked at him. "Sorry. I got carried away. Did you want to say something?"

"Well," he said. "I agree with that all the way through. I think the best thing about what we have isn't that we can laugh and talk for hours like best friends." He put her hair behind her ear and smiled. "Any marriage can have a good friendship, but what makes it special to me is that we never stay the same. We don't make each other worse, we make each other better. It's beyond commitment too. It's ... I can't explain it," he said. "But I love it."

I smiled. "You guys are gonna make me cry. And now I gotta spend a few days with the King and Queen of romance." Ella and Gavin walked downstairs. "I'm not sure whether I should be inspired or depressed."

Everyone laughed. I smiled.

"You'll find the right one," Sarah said, then raised her eyebrows. "Oh, no. I sound like Ella."

Ella smiled and rolled her eyes. "It feels good though, doesn't it?"

"To sound like you?" Sarah laughed.

"To believe in something that seems impossible."

"And," Vasili said, "to realize that it's the people crazy enough to believe that make impossible things possible."

"I believe," I said, nearly jumping out of my seat. "I believe and I have found true love and guys ... I'm ready to wrap my hands around what seems ... well, I'm ready." I stood and flushed with warmth. "I'm the one stupid enough to find the best fish in the world and then throw it back to the sea, but ... I know what I need to do now."

I thanked everyone, especially Ella and Gavin for their hospitality, then retreated upstairs to the guest room where I smiled at the ceiling knowing I'd never be able to fall asleep.

THE NEXT AFTERNOON GAVIN AND ELLA SHOWED ME AROUND Lancaster. Compared to New York it had such a quaint and delicate feel. They took me to the town square which was nothing like Times Square, and we got lunch and snacks at the local downtown market. A lot of Amish people passed us on scooters and even some horse and buggies could be found up and down the city streets. A city is a city, no matter how small it is, but this particular city had charm and peacefulness, even amidst the busy nature typical to a city. I loved it and didn't want to go back to the house, but they needed to get the kids down for a nap and I guess after all the traveling I needed a little rest too. So we went back and everyone napped for a little. I woke up an hour later and stared at the beautiful golden, auburn, and burnt orange leaves dangling to their branches, desperately holding on to those last few days of life.

I thought of Dan and everything he'd done for me. He wouldn't understand my decision to go back to Sawyer. I'm not sure many people would. Only those who knew Sawyer like I did. Knew his heart and the way he never gave up, no matter how hard some things got for him. Dan loved me though and I really cared about him, but looking into his eyes was nothing like looking into Sawyer's. Like Dan said, sometimes it takes the wrong path to help us see what's so special about the right one.

I bet he thought he was the right one.

The award's show was only six nights from now. I already had a dress picked out and a hairstyle planned. I figured everyone would think I lost my mind, but I couldn't wait to show them that I actually found it.

Some kind of loud noise disrupted my thoughts. I cracked open the door to my room and listened. Down the hall it sounded like Ella and Gavin were fighting, but that seemed impossible. I held my breath and listened again.

"I'm doing everything I can," Gavin said. "There's just nothing left. You have to stop spending on other people so much. This family comes first."

"Gavin, I don't spend that much."

"I don't know what to do."

"Is it that bad? How could you let it get that bad?"

"It just did. I don't know. We have five days to pay or we'll lose everything."

I closed the door and sat on the bed. Gavin and Ella arguing sounded nothing like a typical fight, but it definitely made me uncomfortable.

Someone tapped on my door.

"Come in," I said, sitting up on the bed.

Ella walked in, smiling. "Are you enjoying your stay?"

"I always do. You guys have a way of making people feel like your home really is their home. I love it here."

"I'm so glad." She set a stack of fresh towels on the dresser across from me. "You know, this was Gavin's room when he grew up. I knew right away I wanted it as a guest room because it's one of the brightest rooms in the house and I love the window seat here." She sat down and peered through the sheer curtains. "Sometimes I sit here and imagine him as a teenager, writing songs or reading his huge stack of books, and I wish that I could've been with him all of those years. Life is so short." She sighed and turned back to me. "I hope I get more years with him in my life than I had without him."

"You most likely will," I said. "You two are such an inspiration to me."

She smiled and closed her eyes as though she were imagining his hand in hers.

"Are you guys the types to miss each other when you're in separate rooms?" I laughed. "Oh, no, my husband is in the backyard and I'm here cooking without him. I miss him so much."

"Pretty much." She laughed. "So what are you planning to do about Dan and Sawyer? Seems like a tough position you're in."

"It is and it isn't." I took a deep breath and pictured both of their faces. "Dan is special and it's going to hurt when I tell him the truth, but I think he's always known. Besides, as much as it's going to hurt him, it'll help him in the long run. I'm not the right one for him. He deserves to find that person."

"And you think for sure that Sawyer is that person for you?"

"That's just the thing," I said. "I've been trying not to think it. I've tried to avoid it. My mind would just create these weird reasons and excuses about why it wouldn't work or why it wasn't right, but no matter how much I try to think that it's not right, everything else inside me points to him. You know how Sarah was saying that Vasili makes her a better person? Well, Dan is amazing, but he spoils me. He never disagrees with me or challenges me. He lets me do whatever I want constantly and I'm sure some people would love that in a spouse, but I've realized that I'm not going anywhere like that. I'm not changing or growing. It's like being a caterpillar stuck in the metamorphous stage. My wings are growing, but I feel like I'll be stuck in this cocoon until I die." I imagined the many disagreements Sawyer and I had over the course of our relationship. "Sawyer challenges me to become better. Even if it feels intolerable sometimes, everything about him pushes me to be better and stronger and he's not afraid of my wings. He wants me to grow beautiful wings and fly about as I wish." I paused. "I love him, Ella. I don't just love him for what he does for me. I love everything about him.

Good, bad, in between—I really, really love him."

She nodded her head with a slight smirk on her face. Cupid at her best. I often wondered if she'd ever get tired of seeing other people fall in love. Same story over and over again with different settings and characters. Girl meets boy, some obstacles keep them apart, then they end up together. Seems so trivial, but it's so much deeper than that and although I could relate to the smirk on Ella's face and the beauty of finding love as she did with Gavin, it was different for me. It's different for all of us and I think that's what makes it never get old.

"So, what will you do?" she said.

"I'm going to tell Dan when I get to New York. He's meeting me at our house. I mean, his house, a few days before the award's. I'll tell him then," I said. "As for Sawyer, I have a cute little idea that I hope he loves as much as I do."

She stood. I did too. She hugged me tight and touched the stack of towels she brought in. "Inside these towels," she said. "Is something special for you." She walked back out and closed the door. I shook my head and laughed, wondering if it was possible for her to be rude.

I looked inside the towels and pulled out a picture frame of Sawyer and me on the bridge, kissing. My red scarf around his neck was the only thing in color. A small quote on the bottom read:

Love is composed of a single soul inhabiting two bodies.
Aristotle

Nothing could be more true.

MY TRIP TO ELLA'S ENDED WAY SOONER THAN I WANTED IT to. After checking with my financial advisor, I wrote a check for fifty thousand and left it on the pillow with a little note that said, "You give so much. Please let me give too." I smiled as I left the room and couldn't wait to surprise Sawyer. But the thought of breaking up with Dan rattled my insides. Growing up, I broke up with people over the phone. Yes, I was one of those. I couldn't confront them face-to-face because I hated hurting their feelings. Probably didn't help that I was broken up most of the time by a text message, no matter how deep I felt the relationship had grown.

"Okay," I said to myself as I parked in Dan's driveway and thankfully avoided paparazzi most of the trip. "You can do this."

I responded to Dan's text when I got out of the car, telling him I'd be inside in a few minutes. *Can't wait*, he typed back, making my stomach flip a few times. Apparently, some butterflies in the stomach can make you want to spit them out.

I walked slow, very slow, then finally stood in front of the door. The doorknob intimidated me. It's shiny brass metal waiting to be touched and turned, leading the way to a moment I wished I could fast forward through and get to the good parts. I touched it gently and held my hand there for a minute. Sweat formed between my palm and the metal. I twisted, pushed, and opened the door to a million rose petals all over the hallway. Vases of red and white roses lined the walls, forging a bath to the living room where candles flickered. My record player hummed a sweet blue's tune from the 60's by Otis Redding called *The Glory of Love*. One of my favorites. It never sounded so bad before. Every note of his soulful voice made me want to run back to my car.

Decorated in a suit and tie, Dan took a few steps into my view. He smiled, his winsome eyes dimmed by the soft glow of the room. I stood with my hands at my sides, looking at his gorgeous face in the perfect atmosphere for a proposal. Otis Redding sang, "That's the glory of love. Cry just a little bit, yeah. Sigh just a little. And let that old wind cast blow right on by a little, yeah. That's the story of … good ole glory of love."

Dan stepped toward me and held out his hands. I took them as water formed in the corners of my eyes. He pulled me into him, caressing my back as he led me in a slow dance. Otis continued to belt out a beautiful melody, "When this whole world gets through with us, we'll have each other's arms. Cry just a little…."

My forehead fell to his shoulder and a tear dropped to my eyelashes. He stopped dancing and held my face in his hands, then knelt down before me. I tried to pull him back up, but he held my hand and said, "Nora, my dear Nora. I know you've been hurt a lot in the past. I know this is soon and maybe unexpected," he said, tripping over his words. "But every second I spend without you is a second I don't want to be alive. I love you, Nora, and not because I need you. I need you because I love you." He pulled out a tiny box and opened it, revealing a diamond ring the size of my head. "Will you be mine for the rest of our lives? Will you let me love you until we're old and tired?"

I trembled and rubbed the wrinkles in my forehead as the song ended and left us alone with a silence that screeched louder than a broken record. "Dan … I …" My heart broke for him. "I can't."

He looked at the ring, then back to me. I knelt in front of him and closed the box. "I'm sorry." I pushed it back toward his chest. "I'm so sorry, Dan, but I'm not good enough for you."

He held the box against his tie, staring down at our chests expanding. I fought tears and tried to look as serious as I could. He nodded, understanding why I was doing it, but not wanting to speak it into the air. Not wanting to say the name that haunted our relationship from the beginning.

"So, this is it?" He looked at my lips. The pain in his eyes was unbearable. "Is this the end?"

I closed my eyes and nodded, hoping he'd be gone when I opened them, but he still knelt before me, looking into my eyes. I wanted to tell him that he was amazing and special, that someone else would be thankful to accept his ring one day, that I wasn't rejecting him because of him. I was letting him go because I loved him, because it wasn't right and because the other one still had his face painted on my heart.

I stood. After a few seconds, he did too. I hugged him tightly, then walked to the door as rose petals scattered beneath our shoes. Head down, he opened the door. The record player popped and hummed throughout the room. I tried to speak, but gave up. I walked outside without looking back, wanting to smile and cry at the same time.

The Otis Redding song I loved since a child would never sound the same. I'd probably never be able to listen to it again.

A new beginning, I thought. And perhaps music was exactly what I needed in order to show Sawyer how I felt. I was finally ready to empty every last piece of me into him.

When the City Sleeps

Here we go....

Chapter 37
s a w y e r

Chris and Leslie came over to visit. I had a rough few days thinking about Nora. She never called again since that one time. Her big award's show was coming up so at least I knew I'd get to see her face on my television screen tomorrow night. I tried to get over it and think about other things, but every single second of the day held some temptation to pick up my phone and call her. Chris told me not to give in, to keep my cool and wait for her to choose me, if she ever did, but when they came over to keep me company he seemed different.

"Why are you looking at me like that?" I said as they both stared at me, their faces more brilliant than a Christmas tree. "You guys have something to share?"

Chris shook his head without wiping the smile off of his face. Leslie sat on his lap, kissed his cheek, then continued to flash her pearly whites in my direction.

"Okay ... can I have some of the happy pills you took?" I walked over to my record player, once again a reminder of her, and put on an old Beatles album, once again ... a reminder of her. When I looked at them again, they were smiling even more. "Well." I clapped my hands and rubbed them together. "Want to go get lunch?"

They stood up and walked to the door, looking back at me as I followed. Weirdos, is all I could think, hoping they weren't about to tell me they got married already or were expecting a child. I wanted them to be happy, but man....

We picked up a few sandwiches at a local deli, then went to a park and spread out a blanket. Felt strange to be smashed between two cheery faces disrupted by love, but I tried to ignore their giddiness and enjoy the afternoon. Gretzky chased balls and frisbees as I ate my sandwich, stopping to throw it back into the grass for him. Finally, I couldn't take it anymore. "What is going on with you two?" I said. "Starting to freak me out with this incessant smiling. A little Tim Burton-like, if you ask me."

Chris laughed. "I can't tell you."

Leslie shook her head. "We've been sworn to secrecy."

"I swear, if you guys are fixing me up with Melody again I'm going to be pissed."

"Nope," Chris said. "This one's even better than Melody."

"I think you'll really like her," Leslie said. "She's, well, she's a lot like Nora."

"No. No. No." I waved my hands like a referee. "Absolutely not going to happen, guys. I don't want someone *like* her. That's not the point."

"Eh, trust me on this one." Chris slapped my hands down. "You're gonna flip when you open this."

"I thought you were sworn to secrecy?"

"Messing with ya." He shoved the large envelope into my hand. "Open."

"Why?" I handed it back. "Is this a folder of a bunch of people I'm supposed to choose from?"

"Open the damn envelope and stop asking so many questions." Chris laughed and handed it to me again.

I felt around to see if I could figure out what was inside.

"Open."

"Fine, fine." I opened it and peered inside. It was just a CD staring back at me in a paper sleeve. I pulled it out and looked at the cover. It was a picture of our bridge, Bow Bridge, and the title of the CD was "When the City Sleeps."

I looked at Chris, who was smiling like a child, and Leslie, who was tearing up and holding her hand over her mouth while squeezing the life out of Chris' hand.

"What's this?" I said, looking at the back and inside. "From Nora?"

"The only thing we can tell you," Chris said, "is that you need leave tomorrow morning to get to Bow Bridge by midnight. You're supposed to listen to this CD on the drive. No plane. Specific orders."

"Is this … is she …" I rubbed my face. "She's…."

232

Chris laughed. "Hang in there, buddy. It's gonna be a fun ride."

Chapter 38

n o r a

My driver pulled up to the red carpet and my ears rang as my pulse played an upbeat rhythm, which I could feel all the way to my toes. Cameras and fans and reporters lined the carpet, while beautiful people donned in fancy evening wear graced the walkway with their smiles and confident poses. I don't belong here, I thought as I pulled the lever on the door handle and stared at my reflection in the tinted window. My dress was sure to shock the masses and a few pangs of fear shot through my chest. Fear of their reactions. I pushed the door open and set one foot on the ground. Cameras already pointed toward me, ready for action. I shoved the door a little more and stood, turning back to the car and waving to Phillip, the driver who cared enough to keep me company during the trip. I shut the door and faced the million and three flashes, attempted a confident smile, and began walking along the glamorous strip.

My black and yellow dress, representing The Bruins colors, grazed the floor, hiding my feet as I stepped up a few stairs. The number 23 was custom embroidered on a black strip of satin that stretched across my chest, creating an empire waistline. I waved to the cameras and smiling faces, trying my best to be graceful and not fall. I didn't stop to talk to reporters this time and barely stopped for pictures and posing. I got inside as fast as possible, avoiding anyone who knew me and found my seat at a beautiful table in the middle toward the left. I sat down, overwhelmed with gratitude, but shaking so bad I wasn't even about to attempt to pick up the wine glass in front of me.

Never in a million years did I think I'd be nominated for an award so soon. I didn't really care if I won, but I hoped so because I had a speech written on my heart that I really wanted to share with the world. My table soon filled with other supporting actors and crew members from the film I did with Spencer, but thankfully they seated him a few tables to the right. A new girl was wrapped around his shoulders like a scarf. I shook my head and made small talk with the people at my table. A few of them eyed the empty seat next to me and the 23 on my dress, but no one said a word. I liked speaking without words. I liked not caring what people thought of me.

The show finally started after an eternity of meaningless conversation. Spencer lost the Best Actor award to Brad Pitt. I smiled inside, but tried not to have a reaction as a cameraman focused on me from only two feet away. A few awards later there was a brief break for music. I nearly jumped out of my seat when Jack White took the stage. He tipped his hat as he approached the mic and played his heart out. I stood the entire time, clapping, dancing, and singing along to "I'm Shakin'" without caring about the cameras on me and the other people still in their seats, who were most likely staring at me. I thought of Sawyer on the road and wondered if he put the CD in yet. Jack finished his song with imperfect precision as usual. I applauded him as a few others gave him a standing ovation. He had yet to win his own award, that I knew of, which only proved that they meant nothing. Best musician of our time without a trophy on his mantle and the greatest thing about him was that he could care less.

I sat down as he exited the stage, then waited knowing that my nominated category would be next. Julia, one of my favorite actresses, came out with an envelope in her hand, wearing a beautiful classy black dress that fell to the floor and highlighted her curves. She announced the nominees and my name sounded like a whisper among thunderclaps. Did I really get nominated with women I admired for years? I watched Julia and the screen and waited for the envelope to open, for my name not to be pronounced. She slipped her finger along the edge with a huge smile on her face, opened the card, and said, "And the winner for Best Supporting Actress is ... Nora Maddison." The crowd didn't erupt in applause, but my ears nearly drowned in the lack of noise. My name? She just said my name? Someone tapped my shoulder and urged me to stand. I did, but couldn't force my feet to move.

Looking around, I held my hands to my chest to slow the excessive thumping. "Go on, Nora," someone said. "You deserve it."

I walked forward, still in complete shock, and lifted my dress to make my way up the stairs. Julia greeted me with a comforting hug and ushered me toward the microphone while handing me a trophy I absolutely did not deserve to have. "Wow, um..." I looked around the packed room at all of the faces I grew up watching in my favorite movies. Tom Hanks, Angelina Jolie, Leonardo DiCaprio, Kate Winslet, Orlando Bloom, Johnny Depp. "I ... I don't know what to say. I mean, I really don't deserve to be up here. I'm so new and inexperienced compared to so many of you." I turned back to Julia, then faced the crowd again. "I want to say first of all, thank you to Jack White for showing me that this trophy isn't as important as the desire to produce good art . And ... I want to use this as an opportunity to say that I am in love with a man who has given his life for me in so many ways. It's time for me to do the same. So ... I guess what I'm saying is ... thank you for this award"—I held it up—"but it will be my first and only. I've realized that love is a simple thing, you know. We make it complicated, but it's so simple. I want to spend the rest of my life with my best friend, the one who makes me experience life with a deeper appreciation for beauty and art. I want a simple life. So ... thank you. Thank you everyone, but this is my goodbye." A shaky smile stretched across my face as I linked my arm with Julia's and walked off the stage.

"That was beautiful," she said as a camera snapped pictures beside us. "Thank you for that."

I smiled. "Thank you. I was so nervous up there. Really didn't expect to win."

"Sometimes it's the ones who don't expect to win who deserve it the most." She hugged me. "I hope you come back one day and we can work together. It would be an honor."

"It would be amazing to work with you, but I don't know if I'll be back." I looked at the clock on the wall. "I gotta go. There's something I need to do."

"Good luck," she said.

We said our goodbyes and I ran out of there, my dress flowing behind me. Phillip was outside exactly where I asked him to be. A few rows of fans remained near the car behind a rope. I handed one of them my award and hopped into the car. "Let's go," I said to Phillip.

"I thought you wanted to meet on Bow Bridge at midnight?" He looked at me through the rearview mirror. "It's only 10."

"I can't wait that long, Phillip." I leaned forward and smiled. "He's probably on his way. I'm going to text his friend and try to surprise him on the way. Head toward Jersey. That's the way he's coming."

"Yes, ma'am." He pulled away and I texted Chris to ask if he could figure out where Sawyer was.

He responded a few minutes later: *Maryland.*

K thanks. Tell him to put the CD in now. I'm gonna try to meet him halfway from here and there. I'll text you again in an hour to see how close he is.

Sounds good.

"Hey, Phillip," I said. "Let's head toward Delaware area. When we get closer I'll see where he is."

Chapter 39
sawyer

hris sent me a text and told me that I should put in the CD Nora gave me. The only thing I knew at this point was that I needed to be at Bow Bridge by midnight. So far, it looked like I'd be a little early, maybe not. I wasn't the best with time. Chris used to say I had horrible depth perception with time. Not sure if he knew what he meant, but I got the point. I could be certain that I'd show up early and end up an hour late.

I popped the CD into my player, which had been unused for as long as I could remember. If I listened to music in my car it was mainly through my phone or iPod. Gotta love Apple. Sometimes I felt like a walking advertisement for their company. Probably exactly what they wanted.

The CD had a few seconds of silence, then Nora's voice swept across my car and gave me chills. Last time that happened I was standing on NHL ice for the first time.

"Okay, Sawyer, so you should be about halfway to the bridge by now. Maybe it's about 10pm or so. I'm going to be your DJ for the next hour and a half or so, then leave some time for you to think before you get to me. You have realized that you're going to get to me, right?" She laughed a little. Felt so good to hear her voice ... and to hear her voice saying my name. "I'm going to take you on a little journey and it starts here. See if you can guess what significance this song has."

The song played about halfway through and I couldn't figure out what it was, much less the significance. A woman's voice. Lyrics that seemed to make sense for what we went through together, but I still couldn't figure it out. The song ended and Nora came back. "Chances are," she said, "you didn't get that one. I didn't expect you to. It was the song playing at the restaurant when I first saw your face. I guess it's fitting. I guess you know by now that we'll meet again somehow." I could hear the smile in her voice. "Okay. Next song. You'll know the rest, I think."

Michael Jackson sang *Tabloid Junkie*. The song I always referred to about the media and its lies. Then it went right into Coldplay's *Fix You*, which I played for Nora one night on the phone when I was in a funk about Quin. She started talking again after it ended. "When you played that song for me," she said, "I felt like I was falling into you. Maybe it sounds cheesy, but I felt like I was beginning to melt into you. Do you know what I mean?" She paused and sighed. "You were opening up to me and because of that I wanted to know you more. I wanted you to know me. I wanted to love you."

Another song began to play. Jack White, of course. *Hip (Eponymous) Poor Boy*. Nora's favorite song. At least for now. Her favorite song had the ability to change weekly, but she loved Jack White like no other. I did too, but maybe not quite as much as she did. After that, the acoustic version of Ed Sheeran's *I'm a Mess* played, then *Hallelujah* by Rufus Wainwright. That one surprised me. I didn't remember telling her that it was one of my favorites, but somehow she knew. She came back on after that one. "You may not remember, but one time your phone rang when we were together. It was so brief because you turned it off, but this was the song playing. You never mentioned it before, but I figured it has to be one of your favorites and it happened the night we were on the bridge. I don't know why, it just sticks with me." She paused, leaving the car in an awkward silence, then continued, "You'll know this next song. And the one after that made me cry when we stopped talking."

The Taylor Swift *Everything Has Changed* song played and I hate to admit, it almost made me choke up thinking about her, picturing her face, and knowing I was about to see her again—hold her, touch her, kiss her. The next song was a little depressing and I wanted to skip through to hear Nora again, but I let it play. Don't tell her, but I turned it down a little. Another Taylor Swift song, something about keeping a scarf and knowing all too well. After the first song I wanted to stay on the happy note. Next she played Jack White again. This time it was *Would You Fight for My Love?* And after that John Lennon's *Instant Karma* came on. I wasn't exactly sure why she played that one, but hoped her voice would come back next. It didn't. Grass Roots did, with their song *Let's Live for Today*. When that came to a close, she said, "So, the Jack White song is obvious and yes, Sawyer Reed, I want to fight for you like you've fought for me. The Lennon song meant a lot to me during a tough night. So did the Grass Roots. They got me off my feet after surgery, after that time you kissed me in the hospital. It helped me tell Dan the truth. It helped me feel alive again for the first time in a while. I think it was a step in the right direction. In the direction that leads to you." She paused again, then said, "This next one, my Sawyer, is for you."

I sang along. "Oh, my love, my darling, I've hungered for your touch...." Then it hit me. She must've heard me sing it while in a coma. I leaned into the steering wheel and kept singing, my heart feeling like a puck flying across the ice, hoping this time ... that the net wouldn't catch me.

Halfway through, my phone beeped.

A text from Chris. *Where are you?*

Got a detour and just got on the Ben Franklin Bridge. Traffic is nuts though. Haven't moved for 10mins.

It was an unusually warm Fall night, but cool enough to warrant a window being down. I cracked mine and waited for Chris to respond. A few minutes of no beeps or texts, then: *She's on the other side of the bridge.*

I tossed my phone on the passenger's seat, flung the door open, and ran full speed. The lights from the bridge glowed on the river below. Everything blurred by, like it only served as a backdrop to the beautiful picture waiting for me on the other side. Why didn't she wait at Bow Bridge? I wondered, still sprinting at full speed. I passed dozens of cars. Each of them playing music from their own cracked windows. Then I saw her. Probably about a hockey rink away, running to me in a full length gown the color of my Bruins jersey. My smile became a laugh as my sprint slowed down. Out of breath, I still ran as fast as I could. As I got closer I noticed the number 23 repeated on part of her dress and laughed again, an excited type of laugh that starts in your fingers and vibrates all the way up to your lips.

There she was. Stopped about ten feet away from me, catching her breath with her hands still swinging by her sides. I slowed to a walk and heard *At Last*, by Etta James playing from someone's car window. I couldn't have picked a better song for the end of the CD she made. My heart quite possibly may had been left in my car, because as fast as I'm sure it had to be thumping, I couldn't feel a thing. All I felt was the beauty of her face in front of me, grinning at me like she loved me, like she wanted me after everything we'd been through.

Like we'd get through it all, at last.

I stood in front of her and grabbed her hands. Etta James sang in the background. People beeped from their cars, yelling things I couldn't hear. The only thing I let my ears attach to was the sound of her breath, right there against my lips. I touched her cheek with one hand and wiped a tear away, then put my other hand on her hip and pulled her toward me. She fell into me, her cheek pressed against my neck, her hair falling around my shoulder. I wanted to kiss her, but I let her stay like that for a few seconds. It felt so good to hold her, to feel her chest against mine. To gather the back of her dress in my hands. Then Etta sang, "And here we are in heaven." I pried the beautiful woman from my shoulder and looked into her eyes, far into them, as far as I possibly could. I didn't need to say, "I love you." She knew. And as Etta sang, "For you are mine ... At last," I kissed the life right out of me and into her. I kissed her with every feeling I'd ever felt in my life and I didn't want to stop. I started with her lips, moved along her jaw, kissed her ear, her neck, her collarbone, then made my way back up to her lips. She sighed, her eyes closed in content passion, and I stopped, looked around, and realized everyone was clapping. Some people were standing beside their cars, hollering and waving. Nora opened her eyes and looked around too. We laughed, then she took my hand and jumped into my arms, her gown dangling all around us. She titled her head back, giggling like a little girl. Happy. I wanted to see her happy for the rest of her life. I kissed her neck as she leaned back, then she moved her face back up toward me, looked into my eyes, and whispered, "Sawyer."

I smiled. Nothing sounded so perfect.

Nothing ever would.

Epilogue

nora

A few weeks after our magical moment on the Ben Franklin Bridge, I visited Sawyer in Virginia to try to find an apartment near his house. He tried to convince me to marry him and move in with him right away, but I wanted to have a real wedding and enjoy the anticipation of waiting to be his wife. I wanted it to be different than the experience I had with every other guy I'd ever been with.

We spent the morning in his house, listening to records and drinking hot chocolate while cuddling on the couch, as Sawyer ranted about how amazing rich black coffee is compared to milk-diluted sugar coffee. I brought Niles with me and Gretzky bonded with him immediately. It felt so … right.

After talking for hours and snuggling under the blankets, the fire began to crackle less and less. Sawyer played with my hair, running his fingers up and down my arm in silence, then finally said, "Want to ice skate on the pond?"

I kissed his hand. "Love to."

He gave me a pair of ice skates, just my size and brand new. I laughed and took off my shoes, then laced the skates as he slapped his on lightening fast.

"I'm not the best at this," I said. "Kinda clumsy and never really mixed well with ice."

"You'll be fine," he said. "I won't mind if we end up on the ground."

I grinned at him, shaking my head. We got our coats, scarves, and hats on, then I followed him out into the snow. We trudged through a few inches that had accumulated since I arrived, making footprints so close to each other's that you could barely see that it was two people walking beside each other. It looked like one.

I liked that.

We finally got to the pond. He helped me onto the ice, then held my hand as we started off slow. I laughed, telling him to go ahead and show me his stuff, but he insisted that we skate together. I loved that about him.

We danced in the snowflakes and it reminded me of the snow globe dream I had in the hospital, but it felt so much more beautiful and comforting. The difference between the ocean at night and the ocean during the day. We held each other, danced, skated, fell a lot of times, kissed a lot of times, and finally went back inside and warmed by the fire. He threw another log in and set another record in the player. We fell asleep in each other's arms and woke up around 11p.m. He kissed my forehead and said, "Come on," as he got up from the couch. "I want to show you something."

"Now?" I said, yawning. "Can't we sleep here in this cozy loveliness?"

"We can," he said, "but I don't want to."

"What is it?"

He picked up my coat. "I'll show you when we get there."

"Get there?" I yawned again. "You mean, get in the car in the freezing cold winter night?"

"Yes. That's exactly what I mean." He laughed. "Don't worry, princess, I have four wheel drive."

I shook my head. "Oh, stop. I'm not a princess."

"Yeah. And I'm no prince."

WE PULLED UP IN FRONT OF AN OLD ABANDONED HOUSE. I looked around, a little afraid of doing something illegal. He tapped my shoulder and I jumped. "Don't worry," he said. "This is where I grew up. The county owns the house now because it's historic, but they haven't done anything with it. I've tried to buy it back, but I can't. It's just sitting here."

I exhaled in relief as he turned off the car and walked over to open my door for me. He always opened my door. I wondered if he always would even if we had three kids to get out of the back seat. He took my hand and led me around the house, our footprints melting into each other's again.

Then he stopped and stood in front of a tree.

"Hm," he said. "Wasn't what I imagined."

"What?" I said, staring at the bare branches covered in snow. "It's a tree."

"It's ... dead." He touched the bark as though it could speak to him, then pulled me toward it. "We've spent so many nights talking when the rest of the world sleeps. I feel like the most meaningful times we've had have been around midnight." He touched the tree again. "This is something I wanted to share with you." He turned to me and held my hands. "At midnight."

I watched the moonlight glisten in his eyes as I waited for him to continue, but he just stared at me. The magnetic feeling came over me again, pushing me toward him, making my lips touch his. We kissed for a minute, or two, or three. Time didn't exist with him. Only when it needed to.

He looked toward the top of the tree. "Weird that it's dead," he said, then turned back to me. "This tree is where I learned the most valuable lesson I've ever learned in my life." He pulled me into him as we stared at the tree together. "This is where my mother taught me that there is only one goal that I need to worry about in life. She said, 'If you're going to fall in love, fall in love. If you're going to play hockey, play hockey. If you're going to be a doctor, be a doctor. If you're going to climb a tree, climb a tree. But whatever it is ... that doesn't matter ... all that matters is no matter what ... you never give up when you fall or make mistakes. Never give up for any reason, because the second you give up you'll prove that you never really wanted it in the first place. And the biggest mistake you can make in your life is to live without desire.'" He pulled me into his chest. "When I finally got to the top of this tree I thought it was the biggest accomplishment of my little kid life. Maybe it was," he said. "But now the biggest thing, the most important thing I've ever done ... it's you, Nora. Loving you." He kissed me, soft and quick, then continued, "I'll never give up. I hope I never reach the top, because I don't want this to end, but I'll never give up, okay? You ... are my desire."

I reached into my purse and pulled out my keychain. "I want to show you something." Leaning my back into his chest, he wrapped his arms around the front of me and took the keys from my hand. "See this." I

pointed to the paper that said: *Our soulmate is the one who makes life come to life.*
"When I was a little girl I met this boy in preschool and we had this picture
taken. When he told me he was moving away during a school field trip I
took a picture of us and ripped it in half, then gave him the half of me.
We played on the playground for a little and I kept that picture of him for
years. I kept it until recently." I titled my head back and looked up at Sawyer.
"I always dreamed that I'd find the man who had that picture and we'd live
happily ever after."

"Well," he said, "I have something to show you."

I spun around and searched his eyes. Could it be? Could it really be
him?

He reached into his wallet and showed me two pictures beside his
credit cards. One of us on the bridge and the other … the other half of
the picture. The picture. The one I gave to the little boy on the playground.
The one I'd been waiting for my entire life. My eyes darted back and forth,
waiting for Sawyer to explain, to tell me that he was waiting for me all of
those years too. "You?" I said. "It was you?"

He smiled, pulled out the picture of me as a little girl, and closed the
wallet. "When you were in the hospital recovering from the kidney transplant, your dad walked me outside and we talked for a little bit. Later, I
realized somehow he must've snuck this picture into my shirt pocket." He
handed me the picture. "Flip it over and read it."

I turned it over, slowly, and read the back.

*June 6ᵗʰ, last day of preschool. She gave this
picture to a boy today, but he dropped it by the
sandbox. I couldn't let it get lost. It always
was my favorite picture of her. My little girl.*

I looked up at Sawyer, confused.

"Your dad found the picture. He kept it in his wallet all of those years."
He held the back of my head, letting his fingers get caught in my hair. "I
called him and asked if he meant to give it to me and he said, 'Yes, son. It's
my favorite picture and I think you are the one who should have it now.'"

"It's like …" I stopped, kissed him, then stood on my tippy toes and hugged him as tight as possible. "It's like he was the man who stole my heart when I was little girl, and now he's giving me to you."

Sawyer lifted me up. I pushed off of his shoulders and stared down at his gorgeous face. He slowly let me fall toward him, into him. It was in that moment, enjoying the depth of his eyes and the way he looked at me, when I realized that climbing to the top of the tree didn't matter. And neither did staying at the bottom. What matters most is finding someone to sit at the bottom beside you or climb to the top without rushing ahead of you. Someone, anyone—a friend, a parent, a lover—to experience the lowest and highest times of life alongside. To realize that being together, living life with others, is hard work but it's what makes life worth living. It's what makes life come to life.

Acting, dreams, passions, goals ... they were nothing compared to this. They were nothing compared to simple, real ... love.

The End
is only the beginning

a starless
MIDNIGHT

Marilyn Grey

book 7 of the unspoken series

A decade after eighth grader Asylia Kenneth's father, Mwenye, arrived in America from a brutal journey that began in his homeland, he is found guilty of a horrendous school shooting that killed dozens of autistic students and injured many more. While the general public and family members of lost children root for the death penalty, Mwenye s lips remain silent and the only person aware of his secrets is the one person who refuses to tell.

Asylia and her mother, Tylissa, flee to another state to try to avoid the controversy involved with the case, but Asylia's days at school are filled with bullies. As Asylia unravels her father's secrets, she is determined to stand up to the racist kids at her school and show them that it's not the color of the skin that makes a person, it's the color of their life.

Inspired by past hero's and her current hero her father she embarks on a journey that will change her life and those around her forever.

Coming Fall 2014

A Starless Midnight
chapter one - asylia

When I cry it's not like these big huge sobs that can be heard across the room. They are mostly little cries inside my head, except for today. Today I took a bathroom pass from Mr. McShae and walked as fast as possible I the nearest empty stairwell. My school was huge and I knew all of the places to hide.

I ran down the stairs and sat on the floor at the bottom. Knees to my chest, I buried my face in my jeans and cried. I don't think I made a sound, but when I finished my hair was wet. That's okay though, my hair always kinda looked wet.

No one knew the stairwell. At least I never saw anyone use it. So I felt like it was my home in a way. My place to run to when they said too much. Or did too much.

Ten minutes went by. I stood, brushed my pants off, and fixed my hair. When I got back to class a few kids snickered.

"That's enough," Mr. McShae said. "Work quietly or go to the office. Your choice." He looked around the room, glancing through me as though I didn't exist. No one knew how to look at me, but that didn't stop Jason and Sean from glaring at me with red eyes, like some kind of poisonous snakes hissing across the room. Mom told me not to hate anyone, no matter how much they hated me. I stared back at them, then looked down at my worksheet.

The clock ticked. And ticked. And ticked. They made sounds over there non-stop, then passed a note to me. The girl next to me, I think her name was Caroline, handed me the folded paper. I shoved it off my desk.

Mr. McShae looked up, then at the note. Jason and Sean pretended to work on their classwork while Mr. McShae walked to the note, picked it up, and waved it in the air. "Anyone care to tell me who wrote this?"

No one looked at him. No one except me.

He unfolded the note, crumpled his eyebrows together, then looked at me, but only for a half of a second. After that he looked above my head, staring at something that seemed like nothing, and walked back to his desk, tore the note up, and put his nose in a book.

Jason and Sean hissed. I looked their way. Sean held up a paper with big dark letters.

What do niggers and apples have in common? They both look good hanging from a tree.

They high-five'd each other under their desks. I looked around the room at the others who didn't seem to notice. Jamall, the one other black kid in class, never talked to anyone and I hoped he'd talk to me, but we were three weeks into freshmen year and he didn't seem interested in talking to anyone except teachers when they asked him for an answer.

I tried to finish my worksheet, but ended up drawing pictures of rain clouds and tornadoes. Something comforting about twirling my pen into all of those circles until they formed that funnel shape.

The bell rang. I grabbed my stuff and got out of class before anyone else, hoping to make it to my Algebra class before anyone jabbed my head with sharp objects.

"Asylia."

I turned back toward the classroom. Mr. McShae waved me back. I clutched my notebook to my chest and looked down as Sean and Jason passed me.

"Yes, sir?" I said, still looking at the scuff marks on the white and grey speckled tiles.

"Why did your..." He pushed his glasses back toward his eyes. "Just try to pay more attention in class."

"Yes, sir." I turned around and followed the lines in the floor, hoping to avoid the red and white sneakers to my right.

"Hey, little nigger," Jason said as I walked by.

I moved faster into the crowd of people. They caught up and stepped on the back of my shoes. One of them pressed his hand under my butt and squeezed. They laughed. I walked faster.

"Got any friends? Want to make an Oreo?" Sean whispered in my ear as I pushed through the crowded hallway. "Oreo's suck without cream, you know."

Something jabbed into the back of my head and stung. I didn't rub my head even though I wanted to.

"Your dad dead yet?" Jason laughed.

I pushed through a bunch of people, getting all kinds of nasty comments, but none as bad as Jason and Sean. Thankfully I lost them and made it to Algebra before anyone else.

I sat down in my assigned seat at the back of the class, a row where no one else happened to sit. Mrs. Paley was black like me, but more white. She didn't like me though. I don't know why. She was my only teacher with somewhat brown skin, and she avoided me like everyone else.

I opened my notebook and pretended to do the drill on the board, but instead I wrote this:

> It's hard being a freshman in a new town and a new school, but it's even harder when you are black and most kids are white, and even harder when your dad is on death row and everyone knows him as the guy who murdered a bunch of kids. Never mind that he's innocent, or at least Mom says so. But why does Dad say he's guilty? Mom said he's doing something admirable. But did he think of me before he did this? Did he think maybe it could also be admirable to stay home and love me?

I put my pencil down and waited for class to start, knowing that it didn't matter. I was forgotten, alone in the back, like nothing more than a black shadow behind all the white people.

Your Questions Answered

Q: Do you really write all of your novels on your iPhone?
A: Yes, actually I do. Where Love Finds You was written on the computer, but now I write on the go. I think I have written around 225,000 words on my phone so far. I know it sounds crazy, but it works. The only negative to if is there are more autocorrect typo issues, but we do our best to catch as many as possible during the editing. I'm sure my editor hates that part about it. :)

Q: I read the sneak peek to A Starless Midnight and it seems pretty heavy. Will this one still have romance like the other stories?
A: It will have some aspects of a romance, but I definitely don't consider any of my books romance books, although I know they are classified as romance pretty often. I consider them "life laced with romance." Maybe it's just me, but I think they're about more than just "boy meets girl and happily every after." I hope they are, at least! So for Starless it is probably going to seem a little heavier and darker than the others because of the absue and racism issues going on there, but you'll still feel like it's part of the series.

Q: I wanted to see Sarah's wedding! And Miranda and Derek ... will we get to see those too?
A: I have a special little booklet coming out between When the City Sleeps and A Starless Midnight. I don't consider it an actual book within the series. More like a bonus book that includes little glimpses of what's going on in all of your favorite character's lives. Since Star-

less jumps ahead almost a decade and is told from Mwenye's daughter's perspective, I figured I'd give some special little bonus chapters in a small booklet sometime this Fall. Keep an eye out for it. Join my newsletter for info!

Q: What's the benefit to joining your street team?
A: You get special gifts and packages with each release. Every book in the series is on your doorstep for free and I like to make the packages extra special for each of my street team members. I have been crazy busy lately, but I have some other little surprises in store for them too!

Q: So the series will end with Ella and Gavin?
A: Yes, kinda. It will be told from Adelaide's perspective. :) I'm excited for that one.

Q: Any movies?? I want to see these turn into movies!
A: Take that up with Dreamworks! I haven't been offered any movie deals lately, but I would love to see these books on the screen as well!

Thank you to all of my readers for your support and love. The best thing about you is that you get my stories. I love that we can relate and understand each other in that way. If you love these books, we'd be amazing friends. Shoot me an email sometime! I love hearing about your experiences with The Unspoken Series!

Love,
Marilyn

If you have any questions you'd like to see answered in the next book, please email them to Marilyn at marilyn@marilyn-grey.com and we'll select some to answer. You will also receive an answer from her via email. She adores her fans and responds to every email she receives.

Do you love The Unspoken Series?

Don't forget to connect with Marilyn on
Facebook, Twitter, and GoodReads. She is so excited
to hear from fans and talk about the characters
in *The Unspoken Series* with everyone!

www.ingramcontent.com/pod-product-compliance
Lightning Source LLC
Chambersburg PA
CBHW020556180626
46810CB00007B/2534